HEART OF SHATTERED GLASS

J. DARLENE EVERLY

Copyright © 2022 J. Darlene Everly

To request use of the copyrighted material, please contact the author at jdarleneeverly.com
Hardcover: ISBN 978-1-954719-27-9
Paperback: ISBN 978-1-954719-26-2
Ebook: ISBN 978-1-954719-25-5
First paperback edition January 2022.
Edited by Jupiter Alley.
Cover art by Miblart.
Layout by Wishing Well Books.

J. DARLENE EVERLY

HEART OF SHATTERED GLASS

CINDERS IN MIDNIGHT GLASS 2

For the ones who think they have to save everyone, save yourself first

INTRODUCTION

Heart of Shattered Glass is just the second book of the Cinders in Midnight Glass series, the first book, Heart of Cinders is out now. And the third book, Heart of Midnight is coming soon! If you would like to be the first to hear about the next book in the series titled Heart of Midnight, get an exclusive prequel to this story and more free books, as well as see what else the author has written, please go to jdarleneeverly.com and sign up for her newsletter.

CHAPTER 1

NOW

"I must implore my councilors, for the safety of all involved, to end the hunt for a potential queen, and send all the participants home."

All? Did he mean me? I wanted him to send me home all this time. Now that I no longer wanted to go, was he actually doing it?

Jacquetta grabbed my hand on one side, a strange high-pitched sound coming from her.

Gus grabbed my other hand and squeezed. A little bounce made me pull my gaze from Tristan. She was smiling.

None of the other potentials had smiles on their faces. They looked crestfallen or downright hostile.

My Ladies in Waiting thought this was some big announcement of a proposal, but Tristan wouldn't ask anyone to marry him in front of the whole palace, let alone in front of some who may be hurt by it.

But...

I swallowed, far from feeling like I should smile as he looked out on the crowd, and waited for everyone to focus again.

A chill rode by on the wind, making me regret this dress again.

"This idea to find a queen was not a flippant one. I want to assure you all that it has been an honor to have you here, but I cannot in good conscience put you all at further risk." He turned without looking at me, and walked back into the palace with a stiff spine.

"What?" Gus whispered, all the joy disappearing from her face.

"He's not proposing?" Jacquetta mumbled, like she was as lost as I was.

Chamberlain Rezan, followed by a herd of other advisors, hustled after Tristan, calling his name.

General Pace sighed and turned to me, "Stay. Don't leave yet. I'll get him to change his mind."

She climbed the stairs after all of them, and I was left to pretend I was fine. That the smug looks on the faces of some of the other Ladies in Waiting—as if him calling it all off was some kind of personal failure on my part—didn't leave me even more confused.

And as if some part of me that I didn't understand wasn't in agony.

I shoved all of it away, and pulled Jacquetta and Gus forward toward our apartment.

"Let's go pack. We need to be ready to go. I'll take you both back to Madam's, and then I'll have to order a carriage to take me home."

They shook their heads, but didn't argue. Nor did they try to stall and keep us in the courtyard. For which I was grateful.

At the top of the stairs leading to the royal wing, a gaggle of advisors were yelling and gesturing. I didn't want to be Tristan at the center of all their ire, but it let me breathe a little easier that their volume and wild hand waving rendered it impossible to see him or hear his voice.

I wanted to be sent home. I did. It was all I wanted for so much of the time I was here, but now…

Shaking my head, I focused on what I had to do next.

First, pack. Then, go to Madam's.

Beyond that…

Going home—the thought of it, as much as I usually wanted to, now made all the past aches, pains, bruises, and breaks flare so intensely in my mind that I missed a step.

Ash would be furious.

The other potentials seemed to think their sneers were some kind of condemnation of me and my failings that led to this. But none of them knew what condemning failure really looked like.

Opening the door to our suite of rooms sent a pang through my heart.

How was it that this space—this apartment of oversized rooms in the home of the King I was supposed to kill and hated for seven years—somehow made its way into my heart? It was stamped there alongside Gus's laugh, Jacquetta's smile, and heat on my cheek as I slept.

Jacquetta and Gus looked at me, then at each other, and went toward their rooms while I went into mine, shutting the door behind me.

My beautiful, gem-encrusted dress was like wearing a joke now. The dragon down my back was pushing me out, and the flames on the bottom the color of hellfire water were an ominous warning about returning to Lehar ground.

But I didn't bother to try and take it off on my own. Somehow, I had to try and resell the dresses made for me. I didn't have reason for them as Ash's sword arm, and my people could always use the money.

Mostly, though, I didn't want to try to do too much while still in the palace. It was already more than I was ready to process.

I dragged in a shuddering breath as I started to pack the

trunks with my discarded nightgown and other random things scattered through the room.

Worrying about what Ash would do to me was stupid. This whole thing was an exercise in the ridiculous and a waste of resources. I needed to think about my people. They needed the money far more than my wardrobe did. And they needed me to think about them.

So, no matter how hard it would be, or what kind of danger it would put me in, I was going home.

All I had to do was talk my brother into accepting Tristan as King for the good of the people of Lehar and the good of Onyx itself.

Yeah. That was all.

No matter how improbable success was, if another war was coming—this time with Corvid and their very real magic—he needed to ready Lehar. And we needed to support Tristan.

Mom and Dad were right about that.

Tears, ones I wasn't expecting and couldn't deal with, dripped off my chin and onto my mother's shoes as I put them back in the trunk.

I swiped them away, and took a moment, eyes shut, to banish all threat of more before I opened my bedroom door again.

Gus and Jacquetta were already in their cloaks, and quietly directing servants to their trunks.

"You're fast," I said, biting my lip, and begging them silently not to talk about what just happened, to just focus on the work for now.

"Well, there's no reason to delay." Gus smiled and followed them into one of the other bedrooms.

"And Mom's is just across the bridge." Jacquetta patted me on the arm, and went into my room, leaving me alone in the parlor with nothing to do.

After so many years of doing everything myself, I almost

laughed at the thought that these women so often left me with nothing to do.

But, soon enough, I had to leave them behind, too.

I went to the window, watching as guards went about their duties, a stable boy led a horse through the courtyard, and a regular-sized bird flew overhead.

Looking at it all now, no one would see the blood-soaked cobblestones of only days before.

Going home could help stop that from ever happening again. That made it worth it. Even if...well...I didn't want to think about the 'if.'

As I watched, one hand to the cold pane of glass, Tristan stormed out of the front doors and down the steps, his advisors at his heels.

CHAPTER 2

READY

My breath caught in my throat, and my hands balled into fists.

He was still in heated discussion with his advisors. With every second that they pursued him and he resisted, it became clearer and clearer to me that this was more than just his concern about the coming war.

Tristan really did want us all gone from the palace. He really did want *me* gone.

I should have known. I did know, really.

Sword arms and weapons were tools, not friends.

And I was a weapon.

"Cinder," Jacquetta said behind me, "one of the guards is getting someone to bring a carriage around for us."

"Good," I said over my shoulder, not tearing my eyes away from the gathering in the courtyard.

Jacquetta sighed and put a hand on my arm before she walked away.

The sounds of the room seemed far away, but it was clear our trunks and things were being carried out. I spent the entire time staring at Tristan as I hardened my heart to everyone.

My list of people to protect was intact, but I could do that from a personal distance. And that was best.

Finally, as a carriage rode in through the gate, Tristan shook his head and looked down at the ground. The gathered advisors slowly walked away, one by one.

When they were all gone, he looked up and turned toward my window.

I turned my back to the view as it no longer held anything for me, and found Gus and Jacquetta standing not far from me, my red cloak in Gus's hands, their eyes on the floor, and their mouths in matching thin lines.

"Thank you," I said, taking the cloak and putting it on. "Are we ready to go?"

"Yes, we're just waiting on the carriage," Gus said, her voice flat and not sounding like her at all.

"No need. It just pulled up." I gestured toward the door, and followed them out, not looking back at the rooms we shared for a while.

Making our way through the hallways, there were still the guards posted at regular intervals, but they didn't bow, and they didn't salute. They nodded, one by one, as we passed.

Somehow, I had to find a way back to the woman who came to Madam's house the first time. I had to put away the assassin who managed to be saluted by the guard. That was a different life now. One that didn't really belong to me.

If war came, I was going to do what I knew how to do best.

Once upon a time, I wanted to be in charge of the guard in Lehar, to train all the people in it, and to lead them in battle.

Now, all I was going to do in this conflict was protect my friends, my brother, and the King. By striking each head off the snake, no matter how large or small, and no matter how many times it regrew.

Corvids had to come down from the sky to sleep sometime.

The best part of being so good at killing one person at a time as silently as possible: all I had to do was find the right people and do what I did best.

Simple.

And yet...

We walked out the front doors of the palace, the cold wind in the air stabbing against my cheeks. The wind brought winter with it. Even in the time since we were last outside, the world itself had grown colder.

At the top of another set of stairs, on the other side of the courtyard, the Chamberlain looked from me to the carriage and back before turning away and walking in the other direction.

I clenched my jaw, clutched the cloak tighter around me, and climbed into my ride away from here.

Once we were all inside, and the wheels started to turn, bumping us over the cobblestones, I bit down on my lip. Hard.

Somehow, I needed to find a way to convince Ash not to kill me, and let me return to fight Onyx's enemies.

But as we rode in silence through the darkness of the tunnel, my mind was just as devoid of light.

Of all the things I was sure of, that Ash would punish me for not killing Tristan was clearer than anything.

The only question was, how badly did he want to hurt me?

Did he want me dead? My life in exchange for the one I didn't take?

We came out of the other side of the tunnel, the too-blue light of the oncoming chilly weather pouring in through the windows.

Last time, Jacquetta and Gus thrilled to watch the palace come into view. This time, there was no joy as we left it behind. They sat in their seats, their faces drawn, and stared straight ahead without seeing what was in front of them.

All their hopes and their work were always going to come to this, and I should have been brave enough to warn them. I should have made arrangements for them with one of the other potentials like I planned.

But how could I have when I didn't even heed my own warnings, and allowed myself to grow close to them and Tristan knowing it was a terrible idea that could only end like this?

Questions. That's all my time at the palace earned me. Questions and whatever pain Ash wanted me to experience.

"Did either of you leave a note saying goodbye to General Pace?" I asked, breaking through the block on my words, and finally thinking about how the General said we should wait for her to try and change Tristan's mind. Which I knew would be a futile prospect from the exchange in the courtyard.

"Yes," Jacquetta said, not elaborating on what she wrote. Not that it mattered. As long as she knew we appreciated her time with us.

The likelihood I would ever see the General or Tristan again was small.

Well, I would see them from a distance as I watched out for them. But they wouldn't see me. It was better that way.

Maybe one day, Tristan would think of me and wonder if I was real again. Because Lady Cinder Ahmya of Lehar was going to disappear, and the only thing left behind would be a string of corpses.

The carriage pulled to a stop. As Jaquetta and Gus climbed out, I wasn't sure I could bring myself to face Madam Valentin.

But there wasn't much choice left to me. This was the palace's carriage. I couldn't take it all the way home.

I took a deep breath and shoved everything else away. No matter how many times I had to do it to make it stick, I wasn't going to stop trying.

Stepping out of the carriage, Madam stood at the top of the steps, directing servants where to take the trunks, not looking at us for a moment.

Jacquetta stood tall, although her light was dimmed.

Gus stared straight ahead, every bit of the person she allowed out while we were in the palace retreating to hide behind the mask she wore as a maid again.

After everything, it was never real.

Not when it just led us all back here to exactly where we started.

"Lady Cinder, Jacquetta, Augustina, we are all very proud of you, and blessed to welcome you back," Madam said with a tilt of her head before she stepped back and gestured for us to walk inside.

Well, something had changed then. This time she didn't try and hide my presence from the neighbors.

I nodded back to Madam as I walked in the door, and then froze, unsure where to go next.

"Forgive me, Madam Valentin," I said, "But I must change into my traveling clothes, and beg your assistance to call a carriage to take me back to Lehar as soon as possible."

Gus and Jacquetta both turned toward me, their mouths opening as if they were going to say something, but Madam spoke before they managed.

"You are not staying on with us for a time?" she asked, her mouth pressing into that line I tried to avoid at all costs when she was preparing me for the palace. Now, it made me miss her already.

"No. I am sorry, but I think it is for the best."

Jacquetta lifted her nose in the air, and looked so much like her mother it almost coaxed a smile from me.

Madam only nodded and patted my shoulder before she walked away.

But Gus...Gus' face fell, and a tear started to trickle down her cheek.

I looked away, up the stairs, not sure where to go to find my clothes, or what there was possibly left for me to do after I made one of my best friends cry.

"Lady Cinder," Madam said, returning to us with servants in tow, "your trunks are in your old room if you wish to change, and I have called for a carriage for you. It should not take long."

"Thank you." I nodded, and headed up the stairs, holding myself back from sprinting.

Sure, killing people was no problem. Running headlong into a battle with magical giant birds I did without a thought. But facing the disappointment of my friends was so much harder, and took a kind of courage I didn't think I would ever possess.

My trunks waited for me just as Madam said.

Focusing on them, on digging through the beautiful gowns and things from my pretend life at the palace was at least useful for ignoring the room I was in and the memories in the walls.

Taking out the things I needed to keep was easy. There wasn't much, but looking down at my mother's shoes, my heart turned to ashes in my chest.

How could I take these back to Lehar with me when I wasn't sure Ash would let me keep them?

As much as they seemed to belong in the duchy, in the lands where my parents lived, loved, and died, I didn't want to think about what would happen to them if my brother's rage burned as bright as I feared it might.

I took off the red cloak—there was no way I could wear it home—and placed the shoes inside, wrapping them up together.

Getting out of my dress was impossible by myself, but only if I wanted to keep it in one piece.

Madam would probably be angry because it would fetch a slightly lower price, but I gripped the scoop neckline in both hands and tore, scattering gems across the floor and tinkling into my open trunk.

Finally, I tossed the destroyed dress on top of the other gowns, put on the clothes I arrived in the first time I came to Madam's, tucked the Breakwater sigil ring into the hidden pocket at the top of the lining of my boot, and strapped all my weapons on.

Shaking out my shoulders, refusing to let them curl forward in that small way that I used to live with, I walked out of the room, not looking back.

No matter how ready I was or wasn't to face Ash and his wrath, it was time to go home.

CHAPTER 3

FRAGILE

Madam, Jacquetta, and Gus were all gathered in the parlor in hushed conversation when I walked down the stairs.

"I hate to ask anything more of you, but I must." I held out the bundle of the cloak and my mother's shoes in their direction, waiting until they recovered enough from my appearance for Jacquetta to take it from my hands.

"What is this?" Jacquetta asked.

How was I going to explain this?

"The red cloak cannot come with me, and neither can my mother's shoes. I am sorry I am unable to explain more, but if it is not too much, can you hold onto them for me?" My heart thundered in my chest sending pieces of it flaking off.

If Ash killed me, this was the only thing that would be left of me.

Finally, Madam nodded, taking the bundle from Jacquetta as tenderly as if it were a child.

"Of course, I will take care of this," Madam said.

I nodded and tried to smile, although it felt hollow.

"Well," I said, taking a deep breath, "then I will leave my

trunks here. You can sell them and either keep the funds as payment for all your well-done work, or send it to the people of Lehar or the Shield Home here in Bridgeton."

Madam blinked, her brows raised.

Gus gave a tiny shake of her head, and looked to the others as if they might hold the answer to the question she didn't say out loud.

Jacquetta's breath caught, and the corners of her mouth twitched down as if she was going to cry.

"So, is the carriage here?" I looked toward the window, not able to handle their reactions much longer.

"Yes. It should be now," Madam said, her voice strong, as if the faces on the people around her didn't affect her at all.

"Thank you," I said, balling my hands into fists so I could hold it all in as I looked at each of them, committing their faces to memory. Just in case.

Madam smiled, her eyes softer than usual, and I held my fists tighter.

Gus nodded, biting her lip with watery eyes, and I nodded back to her, pressing my fists into my sides.

Jacquetta's chest heaved in frantic bursts of air, but it wasn't enough to stop the tears from leaking out of the corners of her eyes and trickling down her dark skin. I dug my fingernails into my palms.

"I could not have done all of this without you all," I said, my voice thin, tears threatening the back of my eyes, and my jaw clenched. "I love you."

Turning on my heel, I fled from the house into the back of a waiting carriage, not even seeing the other people who might have been around.

"We're going to Lehar," I yelled to the driver as I shut the door and laid down on the bench, finally letting the tears flow as the carriage started to roll through Bridgeton on the way back toward a home that didn't want me.

. . .

AFTER DAYS OF TRAVEL, I DIDN'T BOTHER TO HAVE THE DRIVER leave me at the edge of the duchy, or even the edge of the manor's grounds. I let him take me all the way to what was left of the courtyard of the manor itself.

Home.

No matter how many years went by, no matter what I thought I might face when I got there, I could still see past all the damage from the fire to what it was before.

The layers of ashes, soot, and rubble peeled back in my mind, and showed me the manor as it was when Mom and Dad were alive. When roses climbed along the walls because Mom loved them, and Dad loved her. Although he hated the thorns.

Being able to see the manor for what it once was made it easier to get out of the carriage, and step into the drifts of ashes as more fell from the sky and landed on the black of my cloak, dulling the rich brown of my hair.

My memories made it easier to believe my brother would spare me even as the muscles in my body tightened and my shoulders curled just enough to protect me without him being able to see it.

While my body prepared, my mind held on to the hope that was as fragile as the roses were after the fire, when they were reduced to flower-shaped ash sculptures, scratched away by a breath.

Every step closer to the entryway sent tingles running down my arms and legs, the nerve endings screaming to turn around and go back to Bridgeton.

But this was my home.

And I needed to see it through.

Jocelyn, my trainer and a fighter who appeared during the last war, stepped out to the top of the stairs, her face unreadable.

It didn't matter that I spent more hours with her, devoted more time to master skills she laid out for me, and hung on her every piece of wisdom for the last seven years. Especially after Sandan, her partner, died from the lung problems the ashes caused in so many. No, I still couldn't see through to her thoughts when she put on that mask.

Her ability to block me from guessing what she was thinking when she wanted me to remain in the dark made her an ideal trainer and sparring partner. And a damn irritant when I needed a hint.

"Where's my brother?" I asked, my voice hollow and thin, the sound of it almost choked out by the ashes falling around us.

"Duke Ash will come out to meet you," Brix said, walking out to stand next to Jocelyn, his grin cruelly edged. "When he's ready."

She didn't hide what she thought of Brix standing next to her. She stepped down from the stairs, and moved three strides to the side.

It wasn't lost on me that her move brought her closer to the weapons sheds.

Ash, what were you doing?

Behind me, the muffled sound of many feet made me turn just enough to keep Jocelyn and Brix in my peripheral vision while I watched a whole regimen of Lehar guard pour into the courtyard and fan out behind me.

They had me surrounded.

In my worst expectations and most out-of-control worries for what would greet me when I got home, I didn't think Ash would use my own people against me.

Once, these same people looked to me when we were under siege. When we manned the ramparts that now lay in piles of scorched rubble where they fell when the blast hit, these same people hailed me as a hero.

Not Ash.

Me.

But now? Now they stood around me, not to ask for direction or encouragement in a battle. Now I was the battle.

My hands were ready to reach for my few weapons if any of them even breathed wrong, but I couldn't be the first to move. Not against them. And Ash knew it. He coordinated this on purpose.

He stepped out onto the top stair, his nose high, and his lips pursed, looking down at me as if I were a noxious weed.

"Lady Cinder," he said, his voice caustic enough to make me wince, "you shouldn't be here."

CHAPTER 4

THE TIME

My heart fell into my toes, making me drop from the balls of my feet to land flat in the ashes.

"Am I not welcome at home, Duke Ash?" I asked, my voice flat, unable to imbue it with anything, even the begging he no doubt wanted.

His mouth twitched at the corner, and my lungs ached in my chest, no longer used to the air. But I couldn't cough. Not now.

"You have a job to do." He walked down the stairs, his gait even and deliberate, even as hands clenched on weapons all around the courtyard.

"There was no way to do the job," I said, coughing on the last word, unable to hold it back.

It was the opening they were waiting for.

Behind me the guards moved in, but I crouched down, pulling both my spikes—the new, thin one, and the old, thick one—in position as I turned on them.

One of the guards was faster and more foolish than the others. He got to me first with a wild swing of his short sword.

I stabbed my thin spike into his hamstring, grabbing his

sword with my now empty hand as I stood up and kicked him away while he wailed.

Coughing again, the swift intake of breath from the move making it worse, another guard came at me with a spear while the others hesitated.

Shaking my head, I blocked his spear with my stolen short sword, pushing the spear shaft straight up, locking us up at the hands. At the same time, I lifted my thin spike right under the guard's chin.

I didn't want to kill these people. They were my people. From my lands. I trained with them, sparred with them, taught them.

"Drop it," I yelled in his face, lifting the point of the spike enough to force him to tilt his head back.

He let go, hands raised, and stepped back while I pushed the sword forward just enough for the spear to slide down, the bottom hitting the courtyard. It sent up a tuft of ashes, and the rest of it leaned against my shoulder.

Behind the disarmed guard, the rest of the guards lowered their weapons, and darted looks between me and my brother.

Ash clapped behind me, laughing his fake chuckle that bunched up all my muscles, preparing for a blow.

"Well," he said, and I turned to bring as many in the court-yard into view as possible, straining to hear if the one I couldn't see moved, "now that is the Cinder I know."

My brother moved closer to me. The only move the others made was to step further back.

Holding myself still, the spear leaned against my shoulder, the short sword ready in my hand, and my spike aloft in the other, I barely allowed myself to breathe. But I didn't break my stance, even though I knew he wanted me to. Expected me to.

One of the other guards helped the man I stabbed hobble away to have his wound seen to, leaving behind my spike and a patch of blood, turning blacker by the second as it soaked into the ashes.

"You see," Ash said, coming to stand just in front of the blade of my sword and stare into my eyes, cocking his head to the side, "dear sister," his fist struck me in my stomach, making me cough, "after your failure, I thought perhaps you had changed."

He kept striking, shoving my arms wide to get better access to my mid-section.

With each blow he listed the ways I was a failure, a disappointment, and a traitor.

Finally, I couldn't breathe. I doubled over, dropping all the weapons to scatter around me, coughing until blood sprayed the ashes at my feet.

"You," he punched me in the back, right in the kidney, "should," another blow to the other kidney, "have," another, "killed," he reared back and kicked me in the face, knocking me off my feet to fall across the blackened blood in the ashes, mine and the pool of my opponent's, "him."

"No," I yelled, surging to my feet and throwing ashes at him, every part of me screaming from his battering.

"What?" he asked, his voice ice and his eyes on fire.

"Corvid magic is real," I said, forcing down the cough clenching my chest, making my oncoming bruises louder. "I had to fight giant crows. And they'll be back. War with Corvid is coming, and the only thing staying their hand is the *possibility* of the Dragon King. He's the last of the line. We need to be at his back when the war comes."

"At his *back?*" His voice was an unhinged scream, his fists clenching and unclenching. "You suggest we, who already suffered enough in the last war, fight this one, too?"

I stood up straight, putting on every bit of Lady Cinder, no matter how much my body fought the movement.

"Of course not, brother."

He sneered.

"Good. For a moment I thought you left your brain in the Obsidian Palace."

"No, I would never suggest you would fight any battle."

Red took over Ash's face, while his knuckles turned white.

"Jocelyn," Ash yelled, looking behind me toward the fighter, "take care of Cinder for me. No foils."

No foils? My breathing sped up. So, this was how I would die, at the hands of the one who trained me.

He wanted Jocelyn and I to fight with full blades, which would only mean a fight to the end.

My end.

I didn't move.

"This is not in the prophecy, Duke Ash," Jocelyn said, her voice from far enough behind me that I knew she had not moved either.

"You and your fucking prophecy. Fine," he said, turning to one of the guards, grabbing the short sword from her, and turning back toward me. "I'll do it myself."

Ash held the sword up with both hands, his grip as abysmal as ever.

But he didn't need a good grip.

Not for this.

I wasn't going to gut my brother.

I was right. This is how it would end.

Looking past Ash's shoulder, into the grayed-out lands of what was left of Lehar, I closed my eyes and imagined the world as it had been. Lush and green. A world where I was loved. By my mother, my father, and my brother.

A tear trickled down my cheek as I heard his heavy steps toward me, muffled by the ashes, pick up speed.

CHAPTER 5

REMEMBER

The sound of hooves thundering through the ashes and into the courtyard drowned out my brother's advance. I snapped my eyes open as I jumped back.

Ash's wild, wobbling swing passed narrowly in front of my face toward the ground as he dropped his arms, and turned to look at the black carriage rolling in with palace guards sitting three across the driver's seat and three across the footman's.

His eyes were huge, his mouth working around unsaid words, and he looked as if he wanted to kill whoever interrupted him.

I took a deep breath, the places where his blows landed making it hitch and stutter, and I bent over to rest my hands on my knees.

"Lady Cinder," General Pace called, and I lifted my eyes back to the open door of the carriage where she stood with her hand on the sword at her side.

"This is my house," Ash yelled, his voice cracking as he walked toward her, his movements disjointed jerks. "How dare you come here and address her."

"General," I yelled, freezing Ash mid-step. He didn't know

who she was, or if he did then his fury overrode common sense. But he needed to tread carefully with her. "What are you doing here?"

My question was lighter than the barked address in part because I had to stand up straight in front of her, and pain shot through me like lightning. I hoped no one realized that.

"You're needed at the palace," she said. Ash looked back and forth from me to her. I understood even less than he did.

I shook my head, not trusting my lungs not to cough, and my pain not to spike so much I might cry out in the process.

"All the potentials still wanting to be part of the search for a bride are needed," the General said, her smile smug. And only then did she turn to my brother, the smile falling from her face as she looked him up and down with a withering stare.

Did I want to still be a part of the search?

If I went back, I would live for a little while longer at least, but Ash would still expect me to kill Tristan. And now I knew what he would do to me if I didn't.

"Go, Cinder," Ash said, holding the sword at his side as it if it was no more than a walking stick rather than the method he was going to use to kill me just a moment before. "This time though, dear sister, please don't forget your promises to Lehar."

Right. The ones he thought I would still follow.

"My Lady," General Pace said, her voice a question even as she kept her words just an address.

Lehar needed me.

Not in the way my brother believed it did, but in the way I knew the kingdom did. To fight in this war. To back the kingdom. To stand behind the King.

Ash wanted me to go, but he couldn't be allowed to think I was his sword arm for one more day.

Finding the words behind the pain lancing through my brain was impossible. I couldn't think of a way not to scream at him that I wouldn't kill the King.

Tristan didn't want me anymore. He made that clear. And I wasn't the right person to be the Queen. I should bow out and try to repair my relationship with Ash.

But if I did that right now, I knew what he would do.

And all the ways in which I could fulfill my promises to Lehar, and to Onyx, would be reduced to the empty words of an unmourned corpse.

I made my way to the General slowly and deliberately so no one saw how bad my injuries were, but she narrowed her eyes just the same.

No matter how well I managed to walk, the speed absent in those movements compared to normal was obvious to her.

"Lady Cinder," Jocelyn called behind me, running up with my two spikes she recovered from where they had fallen, "don't forget these."

"Thank you, Jocelyn." I took them from her, and returned them to their places along my thighs. I took a moment to look at the fighter as if I could finally get an answer to the questions that she made roll around through my brain since she and Sandan first arrived—and even more since they first mentioned the prophecy.

But, as ever, she was inscrutable, and returned to her place by the weapons.

"Sister," Ash said, but I didn't look at him. I couldn't. My brother was going to kill me. After everything, every excuse I made for him all these years, he was actually going to do it. With his own hands. "Cinder, please."

His "please" snagged on the jagged place in my heart where my love for him was. I looked, unable to hold back the pain for a moment in the process.

Ash looked lost with the sword trailing out of his limp hand, his mouth searching for words, and his eyes roving my face like the place he was trying to find was somewhere on it.

"No, brother," I said, my voice hushed, and swallowed up by

the drifts of burnt things around us as if it were snow. "My promise to Lehar is to do what's best for her people. Always."

Every shred of remorse, humility, even humanity fell from him, and he gripped the sword in his hand, his knuckles turning white.

In a daze, I turned away from him, and finished making my way to the carriage.

The General held out a hand to help me up, but I didn't take it.

My body might have wanted to fall to the ground and wail before it ever wanted to climb up into the carriage, but my mind didn't want any of them to know how hurt I was. And it wanted so desperately to avoid thinking about the real implications and meanings of what happened here today, that I forced myself not to scream and got inside.

With gritted teeth, I held my breath, got into the carriage, sat down on the bench, and squeezed my eyes shut.

Today, for this moment, I chose life over death.

Even if this small, temporary life killed me a little more each day with the look on Ash's face seared into my mind.

General Pace followed me inside and shut the door. The second she did we started to move.

She looked to me and opened her mouth, but I shut my eyes and dropped my head back against the cushion behind me, trying to escape her questions and the view of Lehar passing outside the windows.

"Cinder," she said, her voice soft, "what happened?"

Opening my eyes again, I found only one did as I asked. The other was swollen shut.

Maybe Tristan would send me home when I came to the palace looking this way. Maybe he really did just want the gaudy decoration of potentials vying for his attention to distract himself and everyone else from the looming threat.

But it didn't matter.

He was the King. The hope of his power was enough to bring the country together under his banner and win the war.

And we couldn't fall to Corvid.

The best way for me to protect him was from a place beside him.

Still, I couldn't tell General Pace what my brother did. Or attempted to do. And especially not what I was going to let him do.

"Nothing."

Everything.

CHAPTER 6

RETURNS AND REASONS

We rode non-stop. Only pausing for bathroom breaks at roadside inns where we took food to eat in the carriage. Even when we slept, we did it while riding.

The guards riding with us slept in shifts of two at a time inside the carriage. The General took her turn outside on one of the seats.

I was the only one who didn't take my shift outside with them.

Although, in my state, I wouldn't have been a lot of help.

Everything hurt. My eye was still swollen shut. That entire side of my face was so bad I couldn't eat on that side of my mouth. And I peed blood.

"You left Madam Valentin's so fast that you were already gone by the time I talked the King into keeping everything going," General Pace said when she explained her rush across the country to get me back before one of the other potentials could worm their way into Tristan's good graces.

"Why is he continuing with it? He's not wrong. We're under threat. Having everyone at the palace only increases the risk to them, and makes them a target." If I were in charge of Corvid, I would send someone like me to attack the palace.

"Because he knows what the old stories say."

If it wouldn't have made my brain explode in pain, I would have rolled my eyes. We were back to magic.

"The idea of finding a queen distracts some of the people in Onyx from the worst of the threat."

Some of the people in the country were distracted by it, some remained on high alert, and still some more were lulled into a false sense of security thinking that it would only continue if everything was fine. Whether that was a good enough reason to keep going or not, I couldn't say.

"And, most of all, he found someone he doesn't want to leave."

General Pace looked at me, and I turned to the window.

No matter how much she might have thought it was a good idea to tell me that obvious lie, it only made me angrier.

It didn't matter enough to him to talk it over with me, to even warn me before he just made the announcement. It couldn't have been that important to him.

While I was busy making out our friendship as something that mattered in my mind, he was busy just having fun with an odd woman who taught him how to throw knives.

After that, all the time he spent in my apartment was just because of the way the guard decided I mattered.

Tristan wasn't stupid.

Being saluted by the guard like only the King would be after the battle with the Corvids meant he had to keep me close and care about what happened to me. But public sentiment didn't make a queen.

Part of me expected the General to order a stop at Madam's house, to drop me off to be treated with all the flower baths and tinctures for my injuries.

Instead, we rolled right onto the bridge, to the island the

palace was on, and into the dark of the tunnel.

No matter how much I didn't want to be at home facing Ash —or dead—coming back here, made me go cold.

The first time I came to the palace, I was covered in a layer of beauty and a veneer of the best version of myself according to court society.

But now, I was covered in a layer of ashes and road grime, blood and pain, with a veneer of the battle-hardened assassin I really was.

If they wanted the potentials to be a beautiful distraction, I could only offer a distraction.

After battling the birds, exhaustion was my biggest injury. That, and shock from the fact that Corvid magic was real and terrible.

Now, though, anyone who saw me would know that the person they proclaimed a hero was fallible and beatable.

They didn't know, couldn't know, that I *let* Ash do this to me. Or why.

But they would all see my obvious injuries.

What would that do to morale? If they thought I didn't have magic that made me invulnerable, would they discount the advantage they believed in because I was on their side?

It didn't matter if this was a strategic error. It was too late now.

The light returned through the windows as the carriage pulled into the courtyard of the palace, and all the reasons for me to run away from this place flooded back with it.

After the carriage came to a stop, the General pushed open the door and climbed out, not saying anything further to me, and probably expecting me to follow on her heels.

But I stayed in my seat, the war already going on inside my mind while my body screamed for a bath, a bed, and time to heal.

Someone shoved their hand into the open door of the

carriage, palm up, as if they were offering me something to hold onto as I climbed out.

I closed my eyes and ignored it as I levered my way up and stepped down the little wooden, portable stairs into the court-yard. My eyes were trained on the careful placement of my feet so that the awkward way I had to step to avoid shooting pains in my abdomen didn't force me to fall.

"Cinder," Tristan said, sucking in a breath and reaching for my face.

Pulling away from his hand, I bumped into the carriage behind me, and gritted my teeth to hold in the groan from hitting my sore back.

When did he start greeting random carriages? He couldn't have known when we would arrive, and this was just another palace carriage from the outside.

His hand hung in the air between us for a moment, close enough that I felt the heat pouring off it, before he dropped it back down to his side.

"One of the physicks will meet you at your apartment," he said, his voice hard as if he was going to fight off these injuries.

"No. The only person I need is Jacquetta. She can treat me," I said, trying and failing to lessen the anger in my voice.

Tristan blinked. All the fury from a moment ago disap-peared, replaced by a furrowed brow and wide eyes.

Did he really think his choice was just going to be no big deal? That I wouldn't have thoughts and opinions about what he did?

"But I…" He looked over my shoulder at General Pace and wilted, "Can I help you to your rooms?"

"I've managed to do this much on my own," I said, not both-ering to wait for his response, or even to finish the sentence before I moved off toward the towering main stairs to the palace.

No matter what he thought, and no matter how much it was

going to hurt, I was going to climb this set of stairs and the next one without assistance from anyone.

The muscles in my stomach and my back screamed at me. It was everything I could do to keep my head up and my back straight as I took the stairs one deliberate step at a time.

Finally, long after it would normally take me even in a gown, I made it to the hallway where my rooms were.

When I first got to the palace, there were signs depicting the sigils from so many places along the walls next to the doors it was like one of the massive charts of royalty Mom made me study.

But now, the hall looked empty with only a few doors marked at odd intervals. It felt as if no life went on in this entire wing.

Maybe someone wanted to move all our rooms closer together as there were less of us taking up space here, but I was glad they didn't and I got to return to the familiar door with the sigil of Lehar on the wall.

I put my hand to the green flame and closed my eyes, wondering if I would ever see my home again. Would I become someone *from* Lehar, not *of* it?

However long it took me, I was going to win this war, and make it safe for my people.

And then, whether Ash wanted me to or not, I would return.

There was no way to know if I would return alive or in a box, but I would get back there one day because Lehar was home no matter how comfortable I got in these rooms and in this place.

Somehow, in all this, I needed to find a chance to get to Breakwater and find out what Inara could do to help Lehar's air recover.

Even if my brother killed me when I got back with it, if it made things better for my people, that was worth all this.

I opened the door.

CHAPTER 7

BARBED

Jacquetta and Gus ran from their rooms as I stepped inside, pulling up short on their way to me.

Jacquetta's eyes filled with tears, and her shoulders slumped.

Gus covered her mouth with her hands, her face twisted into a wince that didn't fall away.

"Hi," I said, not sure what else there was to say.

"Oh, Cinder," Jacquetta said, "I'll get the bath ready, and we'll get all that healed up." She darted away, squeezing one of my hands on her way by.

"Who?" Gus asked, her voice low and humming with a contained rage that sounded large enough to rattle the world.

"It doesn't matter," I said, patting her hands where she gripped them together in front of her like she was strangling them with each other.

"Yes, it does, damn it. I want to know who did this, and why the fuck you let them," she said, her voice was a low, ominous rumble but no less a demand than if she had shouted.

"How do you know I let them?"

"Because your knuckles aren't damaged, and your clothes

don't show enough blood. No one died for doing this to you, so you had to let someone do this. And I want to know who."

Gus was smarter than anyone gave her credit for. I knew that, and I still underestimated her all the time. None of that changed the facts.

"I can't tell you," I said.

"Stop it. Yes, you can. We know who you are. Don't tell me I'm not allowed to know, and don't tell me I'm not allowed to want them dead."

There weren't words left in me to explain, to try and make her understand.

My brother taught me lessons. Pain was his tool for teaching. I accepted it a long time ago. This lesson—the most important he ever taught me as far as he was concerned—was not to defy him.

And no matter how much I would have wanted revenge on anyone who did the same to Gus or Jacquetta, this was different.

My friends and my brother weren't going to kill each other over me. Not if I could help it.

"Don't worry. Just a training accident." My lie was paltry. Based on the way she crossed her arms over her chest, narrowed her eyes, and pressed her lips into a thin line, she didn't believe me. But I didn't have a better explanation, and I didn't have the energy to come up with one.

I made my way into my bathroom, hunched over, trying to keep my upper body as still as possible.

Jacquetta was already bustling around, dumping fragrant flowers and powders into the steaming bath as it filled with water.

The heat wafting off it floated through the room, and made my taught, swollen skin relax a fraction.

Dropping my cloak was the easiest part of getting undressed. Even shrugging my shoulders back to do that flared the bruises on my stomach and I sucked in a breath.

"Let me help," Gus said, touching my arm, her voice and her face returning to softness and care from the flames of before.

I nodded and let her unstrap my spikes, setting them aside with more ease in her movements than I would have expected with her and weapons.

But she was the same person who attacked a giant bird with Jacquetta and the help of a short sword she didn't actually know how to wield. Her ability to handle my spikes just to set them aside shouldn't have been a surprise.

She pulled my shirt off over my head while I held my breath and tried not to yell.

The worst, though, was not running from the room, no matter the pain, when she and Jacquetta saw my body after she exposed it to the light.

All across my abdomen and my lower back, lurid black and purple bruises bloomed on lumpy, swollen skin.

My face, with one side of it so swollen I still couldn't see out of the eye, and purple and red bruises spidering out from the lump until they turned into sickly yellow and green splotches, was the most obvious of my injuries. But it wasn't the worst.

Ash might have been shit with a sword, but no one threw a better punch that could do more damage.

"Cinder," Gus said, her teeth gritted and clutching the shirt in her arms as if holding it tight enough would undo what was done.

"Oh, no," Jacquetta said, biting a quivering lip to stop the shaking words. She darted back to the containers splayed open on the counter and grabbed wildly at all manner of things stored there.

Gus nodded, looking at Jacquetta, and helped me out of my boots and pants, a process that took long enough for the bath to need to be shut off before it overfilled.

Finally, I hunched naked before them, every piece of my body, the scarred, the battered, the bleeding, and divine on display whether I wanted them to be or not. And whether they wanted to witness it or not.

Sitting on the edge of the tub was the only way I could swing my legs over, one by one, to get in.

Even in that, Gus and Jacquetta helped, bracing me so my core muscles didn't have to, and lifting my legs so my body didn't have to do that work, either.

Once I was submerged, the heat of the water and the stinging of the things Jacquetta added to it allowed some of the torn and damaged tissue to relax fully for the first time since Ash hit me.

"Cinder," Jacquetta said, looking at me as if my face caused her pain, "I think you need to put your eye in the water, too."

I nodded. That made sense.

"And keep it there for as long as you can stand to," Gus said, fury still thick in her voice so that it sounded like she wanted me to drown, when I knew what she meant. And, in theory, it made sense, although how she expected me to hold my breath long enough for it to work as well as it always did on my body, I couldn't guess.

But the second I put my face to the water, the stinging it usually caused turned into a sharp burn.

I snapped my head back, spraying water all over the room, and screamed while I clutched at my eye.

"What happened?"

"You must have done it wrong!"

"Cinder," Tristan yelled, slamming through the bathroom door.

Gus flung a bath sheet into the water and herself over me, in some attempt to cover me, but I couldn't stop screaming and writhing as barbs of pain lashed themselves through my brain, digging in.

"Go get my mother," Jacquetta yelled, letting go of me to shove at him.

"How did she get so hurt?" He held Jacquetta by her upper arms, keeping her from pushing him out the door.

"You need to get my mother. She can help her eye." Jacquetta's voice was like a whip, lashing out at anything that moved.

Every word they said reverberated through the taught cords of agony in my head, making me flail worse, splashing water everywhere.

"General, get Madam Velentin," Tristan yelled out the door before setting Jacquetta aside like she was a doll, and kneeling beside the head of the tub where I turned and wailed, my vision blurring in my good eye.

"Cinder, please," he said, putting his hand to the side of my head, with even more heat emanating from it than before. "Please get better."

My world went dark.

CHAPTER 8

DECIDE

I woke up in the bed in my room. Something that was growing to be all too familiar for me since coming to the palace the first time.

This time, though, there was no heat running along my hairline, and no voices in the doorway.

No, this time my hair was still wet, there was a bath sheet draped across my chest, another across my lower half, and someone was sobbing.

"She rode all the way back here like this?" Tristan asked, his voice hollow. "Why didn't you stop and get her treated, General? You could have sent word."

Hearing Tristan slip from his formal speech in front of other people made me pay closer attention.

"Lady Cinder didn't say anything about needing to get help, and I thought the worst of her injuries was to her face," General Pace said.

"None of that matters right now," Madam Valentin said, and a cool wash of something that smelled vaguely of milk and fresh honey suckle poured over my face.

The second it dropped into my eye, the barbs in my brain started to loosen their hold, and the sobbing stopped.

It was me. I was the one sobbing.

After every injury I had endured, and after all the travel with these new ones, it was a bath that made me sob so hard I didn't recognize myself.

"See? Good. That is better." Madam Valentin patted my hand, and she spoke in hushed tones to Jacquetta about the way she made the concoction she poured over my face, and what had gone wrong with the bath.

Apparently, it was just a case of her wanting to help too much, and those levels of ingredients not being good for my eye.

Whatever it was, I was just happy it was over.

Except…

"How did you all get me out of the tub and to the bed like this?" I asked, not opening my eyes.

I didn't really want to know what they all thought about the very naked me.

Footsteps, shuffled and not, left the room, and I sighed before I opened my eyes.

The only person still in the room with me was Tristan, standing near the head of the bed, staring down at his hands wringing together.

"Cinder, I'm sorry. You didn't even give me permission to be in there, but I wanted to talk to you…and when I heard you screaming from your parlor…"

"What does that have to do with why I'm now here in the bed?" I asked, my voice flat, and my hands balling into fists as I anticipated what he was going to say.

"I carried you to the bed, but I was respectful. And Augustina and Jacquetta took care of everything else." He peeked up at me, looking as scared as the children at the Shield Home did.

"Please get out of my room," I said, no longer willing to look at him and accept that this person who seemed so meek and caring, wasn't and didn't. Because I knew he didn't. I knew he didn't want me here.

"Sure, yeah, I'm sorry." He turned around, shaking his head.

"And Tristan," I said, waiting until he looked at me again, "You don't have to pretend. Just send me home any time you want to."

He sucked in a breath, and I turned my face away, closing my eyes again.

It would have been best if he sent me away right then. I wouldn't go home. I learned that lesson.

But then I could just heal somewhere, and camp out in Bridgeton waiting for my chance to help in the war.

At least I wouldn't have to look at him every day, at his mercurial eyes I wanted to see every color of, and the lips that looked as if they might be soft, and know that it was all a lie.

"Cinder," he said, coming back to the bed and sitting on the edge of it.

His movement sent a jolt up my side when I automatically tried to hold myself still.

I sucked in a breath and held a hand to one of the lumpy bruises on my abdomen.

"Shit," he said, "I'm sorry. I'll…talk to you later."

He got up from the bed, slowly and carefully, managing not to jostle me the same way, and I didn't stop him as he walked out.

Once he was gone from the room, a shiver ran through me as the chill in the air settled on my still-damp skin and deep into my wet hair, leaving me cold down to the bone.

The shivering drew a whimper from me no matter how hard I tried to clench my teeth tight together and stop any noise from slipping out.

Jacquetta and Gus slammed into the room and pulled blankets over me, trapping what little heat I still had in my body inside the bed with me.

"We need to get some warm food into her," Gus said, draping my head in another blanket so my wet hair was covered but my face still poked out.

"Yes, but I don't want her moving too much," Jacquetta said.

"I'm right here. You can both talk to me instead of talking about me," I said, my voice thin and worn, but I felt better than I had since I left Lehar. Considering my reaction to the bath, it surprised me.

"Do you want me to get some food?" Jacquetta asked, finally looking at me.

"Soup." I couldn't imagine trying to eat richer foods. Eating while we were traveling was bad enough, but now I was out of the energy to even try. Sleep dragged at the edges of my vision.

"What did the King say?" Gus asked as Jacquetta got up and moved toward the door where she paused and looked back as if she was waiting to hear my answer.

"I told him to stop pretending, and send me home."

They both dropped their mouths open, and then their faces morphed into fury.

"After everything that's happened?" Jacquetta asked, flinging her hands out before bringing them back to rest on her hips.

"Have you lost your mind?" Gus asked too loudly. Her words rattled inside my head, forcing my eyes closed.

"No. I haven't. He sent me home before, and now I'm just supposed to forget that?" I opened my eyes to watch as they spluttered, unable to find the words they were looking for.

"Listen. I'm staying because it's the best way to help with the threat of Corvid and protect him, which is what's best for Onyx. But I don't want him in here and acting like he gives a shit." It hurt too much.

Even looking at him hurt as much as the barbs that had wrapped around my brain, but if they kept letting him into my rooms to try and talk to me, I was going to walk out of the palace no matter how much easier it was to do what I needed to from here.

"So…do you want him to send you home, or not?" Jacquetta asked, sounding genuinely confused.

"I…" Fuck. I groaned and squeezed my eyes shut for a long beat. "I want to eat something, and get some sleep."

Gus and Jacquetta looked at each other, nodded to me, and left the room.

They left me to figure it out, and I didn't understand why I couldn't. It should have been easy. Did I want to protect him from inside the walls or outside?

Home wasn't an option.

And I was needed here.

But was I needed in dresses and meetings with Tristan where everything hurt, and my mind was distracted by him? Or was I needed outside the walls, unsure of what exactly was happening inside until it was already going on?

I didn't know yet. But it felt like I was on borrowed time to decide.

TOASTS

The next day, after another bath, and more dousing of my eyes, I still looked terrible, and felt worse, but at least I could see out of my eye. Even if my vision was blurry and the world was tinged red.

But I needed to go to brunch with all the potentials, if only because Marquessa Ziya, who just wouldn't go away, was going to be there. And that snake needed to know that I was back.

"Are you sure I shouldn't just embrace the whole thing and wear an eyepatch?" I asked, turning to look at the work Gus and Jacquetta did for my face.

"Very funny," Jacquetta said and shook her head while Gus grinned.

It was a minor miracle that I looked bruised and battered, but not scary like I was about to lose an eye.

Plus, the dress—loose and billowy with a wrap around my middle that managed to support all my healing abdominal muscles without hurting them more—hid the fact that my stomach and back still looked like a child went crazy on me with paints. The color though...

"And are we sure that this green doesn't make me look ill

right now?" As much as I normally loved the bright green of hellfire water, any color near my bruises was questionable to me.

"Yes. When we tried the red, you looked like someone stabbed you in the eye," Gus said and shrugged.

"Great. Maybe we should go with red then, and see if it scares the snake away."

"Not funny." Jacquetta's voice was a sing song, the same tactic she had been using on me all day, and it made me want to throw something across the room.

"Is all of this really necessary? I should be talking to the guard and to General Pace about what updates we have."

"Cinder," Gus said, rolling her eyes because she was more than a little tired of me saying the same things.

"Please stop," Jacquetta said, although the way she crossed her arms and stared me down made me think the 'please' was just a formality. "Unless the next alternative to going to brunch with these women is you spending one-on-one time with the King, I don't care what you say."

Now it was my turn to cross my arms.

They knew full well why I didn't want to spend any time with him. They knew full well that I hadn't even made up my mind yet about whether I wanted to stay or to go. And being around him made it much more difficult.

"You two are a problem," I said, pointing back and forth between them. Their double dose of taking care of me was wonderful, but when they doubled up against me, I wanted to take out my aggression on some poor sap in a sparring session.

"A wonderful problem," Jacquetta said, sticking her nose in the air.

"The best kind of problem," Gus said, grinning. "And you would be lost without us."

I laughed, and put a hand to my stomach as I winced. Laughing was a bad idea.

"We should go," General Pace said from the door.

"General," I turned toward her and made my way out of the room, her presence making me look forward to learning something, "has there been any news?"

"No. There was a skirmish at sea, but Breakwater is well defended. It amounted to little."

Breakwater was well defended. At least that much was accomplished from all this mess. My friend, Duchess Inara, got her worries heard.

"I am glad to hear it was not a large problem, but there has been nothing of size since the attack on the palace. Does that seem odd?"

We kept our conversation to a low volume as we made our way down the hall and to the stairs. The baths and Madam's help with Jacquetta's ministrations had already made a marked difference in the way I moved as we went.

"Everything about war is odd," General Pace said, slowing as we started down the stairs, as if she were making sure I could keep up with her, "and war with Corvid, after what we know, is even harder to predict."

There was no arguing with that.

How would a people who could attack from the sky in the form of giant birds conduct a war?

Where would they strike? Would they attack on the ground and in the air at the same time like they did at the palace since that seemed to work so well for them?

Or would they rely on their bird form more than their ground troops for ease of moving through the country and attacking wherever they wanted to with little warning?

And were we sure that their ground troops weren't slaves led to slaughter by those feathered assholes?

I chewed on my bottom lip as we neared the doors to the grand ballroom.

"So, everyone is still dining in here?" I asked, my voice a whisper.

"For today," the General said, pulling open the door and leaving me confused.

Why would today have been different?

Maybe it wasn't, but the way she said it sounded like on other days we were going to be dining elsewhere, which didn't make a lot of sense because there wasn't much that could change with only four of us left here.

But I was wrong.

Walking into the grand ballroom, I spotted what would probably be different right away.

Tristan stood at the head of the table, his eyes on me.

All the other potentials were standing behind their seats, my arrival as late as ever because of the extra work Jacquetta and Gus put into attempting to make my eye look less awful.

But the other potentials still saw it and recoiled. It seemed as if the sight of me made them wonder if the same would happen to them.

I smiled and curtsied to the King, trying to remember how to play the part of Lady Cinder who wasn't bothered by the way the other potentials reacted to me.

Tristan's answering smile was soft. He moved from behind his chair to my side, holding out his arm for me to take.

Part of me wanted to push it away. Part of me wanted to leave the room entirely and head back to my apartment.

But the stormy look on Ziya's face that matched the darker strands of purple in her hair reminded me of why I still needed to be a potential: so I could ruin Ziya's chances.

No Amethystian snake was going to be queen of Onyx if I had anything to say about it.

I put my hand, my touch as light as the dawn, on Tristan's arm, and his answering smile was as brilliant as midday sun.

While I blinked to recover, he led me to my seat, one that was further away from him than the others.

But it didn't matter the distance.

Not when he reached out a hand, and, with just the tiniest of touches as if he were waiting for me to stop him, ran a finger of warmth along my jaw on the injured side of my face.

The heat that always came from him soothed my eye and the throbbing still there in the swollen lump. I shut my eyes for a second longer than necessary and smiled.

Marquessa Ziya sucked in a breath, the sound almost like a hiss, proving she really was a snake.

While Tristan released me and made his way back to his seat, I looked at Ziya, and turned my smile into the kind of grin that had a threat riding in it.

Like I was a wolf baring my teeth, warning this bitch.

If she only knew.

After I made sure we won against the Corvids and their damn birds, it would be nice to make a clean sweep and rid Onyx of the Amethystian venom too.

Tristan turned to all of us, picking up a glass from the table and holding it aloft.

"Here is to returns, and to being safe, together," he said, looking right at me the whole time.

Being safe, together.

I tilted my head to him, and took a drink.

My decision was made.

No matter how hard it was, I was going to stay in the palace and keep Tristan and the country safe from in here. I wasn't going anywhere.

All I had to do was get better, and hope the Corvids didn't attack in the meantime.

CHAPTER 10

WRONG

"Lady Cinder," Marquessa Ziya said a few minutes later, waiting until I had just put food in my mouth to interrupt, of course.

I looked up at her, not bothering to speak, and choked on my piece of soft bread in the process as I used only half my mouth.

"Forgive me, but what happened? That looks dreadful."

She didn't say it looked like it *felt* dreadful. No, of course not.

"Training accident," I said, after I swallowed my bite. Tristan and General Pace were the only ones at the table who knew it was a lie. Everyone else bought the explanation. And Tristan didn't know exactly what had happened, although I suspected the General had some thoughts.

"You see," I said, placing my hands gently in my lap in an exaggerated, slow movement, "after what happened with the birds, I doubled my efforts to make sure that no one is a threat to me or the people I care about. Ever again."

Ziya opened her mouth like she wanted to argue with me and take offense, but the other people in the room nodded approvingly. I smiled.

The smile probably made my cheek and eye look even worse, but I didn't care. I made my point to the one person in here who needed to understand it.

All of them knew what I did when the Corvids came. All of them knew that my knife thrown at the raven bitch was more than an idle threat. Now, Ziya knew I was making the same kind of warning to her.

If she wanted to side with Corvid in the coming conflict, I would make sure that she saw one of my blades. Up close.

"Well, maybe we can take it easy on the training until you are fully recovered," Tristan said, still looking worried.

There was no point in arguing with him, even while Ziya tried to bring him into a conversation in her whispered tones to block us all out.

He turned further toward her, and an odd panic ran through me.

Was she the reason he asked us all to leave?

Was she the one he wanted to stay?

Was he going to marry the Amethyst snake?

My breathing was too fast and too hard. It sent pain flaring up in my abdomen until I closed my eyes, and I focused long enough to stop the fear coursing through me.

Somehow, I needed to find a way to stop them, to stop her from pulling him in, from convincing him to give Onyx a purple-haired, slave-trading queen, and to stop him from falling in love with a snake.

But...how did anyone stop someone from falling in love?

I looked around as I ate, trying to tell if I was the only one concerned by what was happening at the head of the table.

None of the others seemed to pay much attention to it.

To the flirting and the shameless, false coquettishness.

My food, the bite in my mouth, turned from fluffy, sweet bread to thick, dry paste as I watched them.

Ziya reached out her dainty hand again to touch Tristan on

the arm, but he moved. It was a swift and seamless movement covered by an adjustment to the napkin in his lap while leaning back in his seat.

When he looked up, his eyes found mine already on him, and his smile softened into something that looked more real.

But it was all a lie. And I needed to remember that it was, no matter how much the thought of it being real made my breath come easier, and the flavor return to my food.

Tristan cleared his throat and put his napkin on the table, a movement that signaled what he was about to do.

It gave me enough time to do the same and prepare to stand, which I still wasn't as swift at as before.

Once we were all on our feet, Tristan tipped his head to us.

"Excuse me, and please, enjoy the rest of your meal. I hope that soon I will see you again between all my duties." He smiled and looked around at us, lingering on me for an extra moment before he turned and walked out.

As soon as he was gone, the door shut behind him, I tipped my head to the others, and left the room via the main doorway.

General Pace followed in my wake, not bothering to hurry as she caught up to me easily on the stairs.

I needed to finish my meal, but I didn't want to do it in front of the snake without Tristan as a buffer between us forcing me not to kill her and forcing her not to say anything too likely to make me. Even in my current state, I could still kill, and would have if she said the wrong thing. A fork was an easy and efficient way to open a jugular.

"Do we have to keep going to those damn brunches?" I asked, my voice thin as I took the last step up into the hallway, the muscles in my stomach aching.

"Unfortunately, even as a queen, you won't be able to get away from all the people you don't like," General Pace said, and I laughed the half laugh I limited myself to since a full one hurt too much.

"And that is one more reason," I said, although I left out the 'I would make a shit queen' part of the sentence.

"Wrong." General Pace shook her head.

"Not wrong. We should have all picked a different Onyxian potential to back. Including me."

"Listen, Lady Cinder," the General said, grabbing my arm to force me to stop and turn toward her, her voice low and dangerous, "King Tristan makes the choice. And you're the right one. I don't want to hear this from you anymore."

I nodded and she let me go.

We walked the rest of the way to my rooms, and I didn't say anything else.

My nod wasn't because I agreed with her. I still knew she was wrong. My nod was because I understood that I needed to keep it to myself.

Once I was inside my apartment with the General on the other side of the door, I was able to slump, which was still more comfortable.

Gus and Jacquetta were nowhere to be found. Maybe they had another brunch with the Ladies in Waiting.

At least it gave me time to set it all aside—the hopes that I would be able to get them all to agree with me, and help me come up with a plan. They weren't going to do that. None of them were.

In this, the attempt to save the kingdom from me as queen, and from a snake with power, I was on my own.

Not exactly a foreign concept in my life.

I filled out my order for food to be brought up. Sending it off, a yawn cracked my jaw, leaving me whimpering and bent against the table.

Behind me, the door opened, and footsteps thundered across the room to me, wrapping me in arms of heat and tenderness.

"Shhh," Tristan mumbled. "It's okay, Cinder. Let me help. Anything. Was brunch too much?"

"No, no, I'm fine," I said, my voice sharp, but it didn't matter how much I wanted to push him away, I clung to him instead, leaning my damaged eye against his chest.

The heat of him, that strange artifact of his heritage everyone had wrong and probably led to the Dragon King legend, eased the ache in my face that reached so deep into my mind.

"Eventually, I'm going to get you to tell me how this happened."

"I already did."

But as he ran a hand along my back, and kissed the top of my head, he made a noise that told me he knew I lied. And he wasn't going to push.

"Do you want to go back and lay down?"

My small laugh left me groaning, and pulling him tighter against me.

"What's funny?"

"Say that again inside your head, and tell me what innuendo you hear?"

"Oh."

His small sound of surprise left me laughing more and taking my hand from him to press against my stomach.

"We have to stop talking. It's hurting you."

"I just need to wait for my food to come."

"You did it again?" He pulled back to look at me, his eyebrows raised and amusement on his face. "You left as soon as I did even though you weren't done eating?"

"There's no reason to stay, especially when I don't have to pretend that I'm using both sides of my mouth to eat when I do it here."

His brow furrowed, and he touched that light and gentle finger to my jaw.

"But why are you pretending? There is no shame in pain."

"You're right. But it isn't shame. It's that some people see someone in pain as someone weak. And I refuse to let anyone see me as weak." I left out that I didn't want them to think it was a good idea to take the opportunity to stick a knife in my back.

"Pain isn't weakness. Especially when the pain comes from being too damn strong for your own good."

I gave him a small smile, the only kind I could manage at the moment.

"No one is ever too strong."

His face fell, a sadness washing over him as he looked away from me to where my hand still gripped the front of his shirt, right over his heart.

"Sometimes, though, they can be."

CHAPTER 11

GOOD SURPRISES

My food came and Tristan helped me bring it into my room where he set me up in my bed with pillows piled at my back.

"Are you really only eating soup and bread?" he asked, scooting the tray closer to me and handing me a spoon.

"Trust me, I wish I was better already, too." I scooped up some of the soup with my spoon, and sipped at it before I dropped one of the rolls into the bowl to soak up some of it.

"We have to be able to find something else you can eat. Something we haven't thought of yet. This isn't good enough." He shook his head, looking down at the meager spread.

He went out to the parlor and came back in moments while I focused carefully on eating.

"It's okay," I said, when he returned. "It's only temporary." I shoved the roll soaked in broth into my mouth, and scooped up some of the bits within the soup.

Of all the food I normally ate, none of it was as soft as this. It got old fast. I wanted to be able to chew again, but I wasn't lying. This would be a short irritation.

"Yes, but...I'll find you something."

I smiled with half my mouth around the bite.

He smiled back, leaning on one arm as he watched me.

"Why can't it always be like this?" he asked.

I looked around the room, trying to figure out what in the hellfire he was talking about.

"Do you mean, why can't I always be wounded and trying to heal? Because that's pretty terrible."

"No." He shook his head, laughing and sitting up to lean closer to me. "I wish we could just be able to talk openly about things, joke about things, instead of dealing with other people and all the things that go along with..." he waved a hand in the air like he was including the entire palace.

And maybe he was. Maybe he was talking about being royal.

"Most of my life I thought the same thing," I said, looking off into the distance. "My mother used to tutor me in all the houses, all the lands and their people, their trade and their connections. I tried to ignore most of it, tried to read anything else, tried to return to the training grounds, or get back to my horse. But now," I looked up and around me at the walls and then at him, the King. "Now I wish I paid more attention. Maybe I wouldn't feel like I don't belong here."

'Please send me away,' I begged him in my mind.

If he did it, if it was his choice, then I wouldn't be stuck trying to find my way through all of this. I wouldn't have to feel like I needed to make sense out of it.

"Cinder, I know that it's hard to feel like you belong in this mess. I think I don't belong, and lament my place by the accident if my birth every day with every new decision I have to make. But you..." he bit his lip and breath heaved in his chest as he leaned toward me, his eyes intent on mine and his fingers threading through my own while I stiffened, "You belong..."

His voice trailed off, his fingers grew warmer still, and the door to the apartment slammed open, making him jerk back.

Tristan cleared his throat and smiled at me.

"I should go and let you get some rest. I'll see you soon." He kissed the top of my head, and squeezed my hand before he got up from the bed and left.

"King Tristan," Gus and Jacquetta said from the parlor as he passed.

"Ladies, make sure she gets some sleep, okay? Thank you."

He left the apartment, the door latching behind him. Gus and Jacquetta poured into my room seconds later.

"What was he doing in here?" Gus asked, her voice less asking and more insinuating.

"Very funny. He was helping me." I took another bite of my food, thinking that, yes, he was trying to, at least. Even if he wasn't actually able to do much to change the circumstances around us. He was trying.

Damn it. I shook my head, and ate another bite. This was exactly what I didn't want to happen. I didn't want him to make me think he wanted me here. I didn't want any of this to make its way into my heart again.

Every bite I took, while Gus and Jacquetta told me all about their brunch, I stoked a fire around my heart, to burn away all the parts of him that made their way there, and protect myself from more.

"So, did he tell all of you?" Gus asked, and I tried to run through the words she said right before that sentence to see what I missed.

"Did he give you all a schedule with ideas?" Jacquetta asked.

"No, we don't have a schedule, and we didn't get any ideas." That I could say with certainty, although I still couldn't remember what they meant when they referred to ideas.

"He didn't even bring it up, did he?" Gus asked, flinging her arms.

"Tristan didn't bring up anything like it." Since I didn't know what 'it' we were talking about, I thought that was a safe thing to say.

"Well, we were told that he has a plan to spend a meal every day with one of the potentials at a time. It's all the Ladies in Waiting can talk about," Jacquetta said.

I wanted to laugh, thinking about Tristan actually having the time to devote to a whole formal meal with one person.

Although...he did spend almost a whole meal with me already today after the brunch. How did he find the time away from his duties for that as often as he managed? Especially now? Was he an absentee king?

"Look, she just figured out that he's going to be spending time with the others, too," Gus said, leaning over to Jacquetta and fake whispering.

More food in my mouth let me keep it shut as they made fun of me, missing the point entirely, and, yet, making me think.

Of all the ways I could protect the King, it wasn't while he was spending time alone with the other potentials.

If he was going to do it, going to set out on such a terrible idea, then I was going to have to find a way to save him from himself.

How I was going to do that, I didn't have a clue.

"Jacquetta, is there any way to get me better faster?" I asked, breaking into their conversation.

"I'll ask Mother. She'll know." Jacquetta jumped up and ran into the parlor. Gus stole a piece of bread from my tray, and I slapped at her hand.

"You get enough food. This is mine." And it was all I was able to eat.

"Cinder," Jacquetta called from the other room as she came into the bedroom, her eyes wide, followed by a series of servers with carts piled with food.

"What is this?" I asked, leaning forward and almost spilling my soup all over the bed.

"King Tristan ordered the kitchen to send up all the things

that someone could eat if they had difficulty chewing," Jacquetta said, reading from a card before she handed it over to me.

His seal was on the bottom of it.

The food was far too much, but it all looked delicious. The servers explained to Gus and Jacquetta what each of the dishes were while I carefully climbed from the bed and looked over my gift.

Because this *was* a gift.

More than any stupid amount of money spent on something would have been, this would help me get better. And I wanted that more than anything else at that moment.

Although I knew it was a short piece of time before all my worries would flood back soon, the relief of real food almost made me cry.

CHAPTER 12

THROW THINGS

"It's been three days and I'm fine," I said, pacing back and forth in front of my open window, staring down at the maneuvers going on in the courtyard.

"You're not fine," Jacquetta said, hands on her hips.

"And your bruises prove it," Gus said, shaking her head.

True, the bruises weren't completely healed, but I felt much better. Not good enough to try and sneak out via my balcony like I had before, but they didn't need to know that.

"Come on. If I stay in here for much longer, I'll start using the furniture for target practice." Especially since they stayed with me every second of the day as if they knew I was formulating plans to get out to the training grounds.

"But if we take you down there, you won't be able to help yourself," Jacquetta said.

"I...I'll be fine." Because, no, I wouldn't be able to stop myself from training, but that wasn't a bad thing.

"What if you make it worse, and then you'll be stuck up here longer?" Gus asked, but there was an edge to her voice, like it was an accusation.

"Please, I need to go down there and see what they're doing. Even if I don't get involved at all. I need to."

How did they not understand that this wasn't because I was bored? The only way I knew how to heal, the only thing I knew to do when my mind was full, was train. This, being part of the preparation for the war, was good for my new mission protecting Tristan and Onyx. But it was more than that. It was a need.

Jacquetta and Gus looked at each other, having some kind of conversation with their eyes I wasn't privy to.

But when Gus lifted a brow and pursed her lips, and Jacquetta sighed, dropping her hands to her sides, I knew.

"Thank you," I said, running out of my room as they laughed behind me.

I didn't change out of the dress they had me in for brunch. Instead, I grabbed my red cloak, and threw it on as I darted out the door.

At least my dress today was warm because the weather had turned completely. By the iron gray of the sky that I watched all day through my window, I guessed it was going to snow.

Down the stairs and through the grand foyer, I didn't see a single person who wasn't a guard or a servant.

Besides brunch, the advisors weren't spending any time with any of us potentials, and Tristan hadn't made another appearance since the first day. Preparation for the war was far more important to everyone than this stupid bride hunt. Which made continuing the whole thing make even less sense.

Stepping outside, the chill of the air seared into my lungs, making the twinge of ache around my middle worse for a second. But it was worth it.

The sounds of an entire regiment being put through their paces rang out across the courtyard, bouncing off the obsidian walls of the palace.

I shut my eyes and listened to the synchronized shuffle of

feet, the way they all moved at the same time. Heavy steps, light, careful, sure, and some just off the count of the others, all came together to make the sounds that brought me back to hours in the courtyard of the manor.

But why were they training with maces?

Scanning the courtyard, I tried to spot General Pace, Tristan, anyone that could explain to me what they were thinking when the weapons they should have been working with were ones that could do what we needed against the opponents we knew we were going to face.

Each of the trainees should have been working with arrows and throwing knives, or at the least a spear. They should have been training with something swift and light for the closer men on the ground. Not a mace.

None of the Corvids we fought wore heavy armor. They didn't even wear plate or chain, just leather.

Hand each of the trainees a good short sword, teach them to use a long-range weapon, too, and we were doing okay. This strategy, instead, made no sense.

Finally, I found General Pace over by the range, looking on while she waved her hands and talked with some very large people in a strange version of the guard uniform.

Making my way to them meant skirting the entire edge of the massive courtyard, avoiding the people that seemed to be running in all directions with missions.

The number of messages and things being coordinated would probably make my head spin, but dodging them was a pain in the ass and slowed me down.

Reaching the place that the General had been, I tried to find her again, looking around and even behind a pillar.

I spotted her as she pointed a finger at the large people and turned away from them.

"General Pace," I yelled, waving a hand over my head and darting toward her.

Some of the people around us looked my way. Most stayed focused, which I took as a good sign, while she stopped and raised a brow at me.

"Lady Cinder, what are you doing here?" she asked, her voice sounding amused instead of surprised.

"What I wanted to do was maybe train a little with everyone else, but this," I waved a hand at the people in the courtyard, "isn't what they should be training with."

The General grinned, her smile without humor, as she looked past me to the large people from before.

I turned and made eye contact with the biggest of them. Bald, thick brow, but no eyebrows, guard uniform, but with some kind of long jacket overtop that I didn't recognize. Part of me wasn't convinced he was human.

"Handler Silas, Lady Cinder has some concerns about the training program," General Pace said, and Silas got larger.

Nostrils flaring, he grew and expanded while red tinged the pasty pale skin of his nose and bald head.

"What, Lady, could you possibly have to say?" he asked, but his voice was a thick rumble that still made me wonder where the hell this guy came from.

"How about this? I fought the Corvids," I said, not about to let some asshole think that being big and looming while trying to use the fact I was a noble girl as some fucked up version of an insult was going to work.

That heavy brow moved, and a line appeared in the middle.

"What you have them doing—and I don't give a shit if it's the way you always do it or whatever—isn't going to help. Our enemy will be in leather, no armor, and they have giant, magic birds that attack from the sky at the same time their ground troops hit you."

Silas looked at me for a whole minute without speaking, and without changing his expression.

"Listen," I said, stepping up to him until I was right in front of him, my head tilted back to maintain eye contact, "if you needed a light and fast weapon for the troops on the ground, and something to go long-range to fight things in the air at the same time with, what would you use?"

He blinked, his face clearing, and he surveyed the yard.

"But this is how we train. They need to know this to move on," he said, and turned and walked away.

"Do I need to fight him?" I asked the General, seriously considering killing the giant man just to get him the hell out of the way.

She laughed.

"No, he's good. We need him. He's just old and stuck in his ways at this point."

Right. And that meant he was in the way of my mission for the country.

"Where's King Tristan?" I asked, finally pulling my eyes away from the retreating form of Silas.

"Probably in another meeting with the Chamberlain." She shook her head, and her eyes went dark, making me wonder exactly what kind of meetings he had with Chamberlain Rezan.

"So…I should find a way to change this, and maybe keep King Tristan out of some of these meetings?" I raised my eyebrows and the General laughed, but she nodded and slapped my shoulder, so I took it as a yes.

Now all I had to do was figure out where he was and how to interrupt him.

CHAPTER 13

HER

aking my way into the palace, I realized that my entire plan fell apart in the doorway.

Where would Tristan meet with the Chamberlain?

In this never-ending palace, I didn't know my way around even a quarter of it.

There were whole galleries and libraries people had mentioned—mostly Shield Elio—but did I know where they were? Of course not.

I trained every moment I could, and spent every moment I couldn't tucked away with Jacquetta and Gus. Suddenly, that seemed like a strategic failure on my part.

I sighed. The only place I knew that Tristan would eventually be, was in the private royal wing.

Maybe if wandering aimlessly through the main floor didn't get me anywhere, I could just camp out in his private office.

But wandering without any idea where I was headed landed me in a receiving room.

At the far end a short dais—only a single step—held a lone throne.

The size of it, with its ornate dragons curving up the back and rearing overhead carved out of something so dark I didn't know if it was wood or metal, managed to intimidate even without someone in it.

Along the walls, the black obsidian wasn't obscured or covered, but there were, instead, massive windows of clear glass cut in such a way that prisms of fire and dragons flashed across the space.

Once, before the Corvids, and before the last war, I would have been taught by my mother until I was eighteen, and then brought to this room. I would have been presented at court.

Looking up at the throne, I imagined what it would have looked like when there were two, side by side.

The dragons and flames flashed and shimmered in the glass, lighting the thrones on fire.

It was beautiful and terrifying.

My brother would have loved to hold court here.

But if I had interrupted him in a place like this and not the rubble we had at home...

So many memories told me what his reaction would have been, more than I needed to remember his lesson, and so many old aches flared to life inside me as the images flashed by.

Turning, the lights of mythical glass beasts chasing me, I fled the room.

No matter how badly I needed to learn the layout of the palace, I didn't want to see more today.

I didn't want to see anything more.

Making my way up the stairs from the foyer, I took the side to the royal wing instead of heading back to my rooms.

But a noise behind me in the hallway where the potentials were staying, drew my attention.

For some reason, I didn't just set aside the noise as the usual traffic of guards and servants, and I focused on finding the source down the long hall.

Outside one of the rooms, Chamberlain Rezan stood next to Marquessa Ziya, her purple hair making her easy to identify.

But with them, and the first of the three I recognized, was Tristan.

Someone in the group said something, and Ziya tittered. The kind of ridiculous, false laugh that made it hard not to roll my eyes when we were all gathered together.

I couldn't do it now either because Tristan took her hand in his, and even though I wanted to look away, not to witness this, I was unable to do anything but watch.

He held her hand to his mouth, and kissed the back of it, the noise that alerted me, her high pitched, real giggle, ran down the hallway again.

I turned around to flee, but I was just two steps from the top of the stairs to the royal wing.

Making it down and out into the courtyard before he turned and spotted me was a losing bet, but I might have been able to get into his office.

First, I barreled through the door to the short hall of too many doors, and then I ducked inside his private office.

This little space, small in footprint yet towering up inside one of the spires that stabbed the sky outside, didn't feel cozy and comfortable now.

When Tristan brought me here the first time, I thought it was one of my favorite places. But now...the books crammed onto the shelves were too close and too numerous. The ceiling, soaring overhead in an ever-shrinking circle, seemed as if it would crash down on me at any moment. The desk took up too much of the room, and the clutter on it made me dizzy.

Even the fireplace, with its false logs and a hellfire-powered flame crackling inside it, lacked warmth.

I knew this was the way it would be. I always knew this was how it must go.

But her?

The slave-trading snake who disrespected him at the raven bitch's funeral?

My fingers curled into fists at my sides, and I leaned against one of the bookshelves, my stomach knotting and the deep bruises on it that had yet to fade reminding me they were there.

None of it mattered.

I had to keep telling myself that.

Sometimes I forgot. And every time I did, it only made the remembering worse.

But it didn't matter.

Not Tristan's bride game—no matter who was playing—and not my feelings about anything. Or Ash's ways in receiving rooms.

The only thing that mattered was happening in the courtyard.

And in that, I could rely on myself and what I knew. Without worrying it would hit me back.

No, the only thing I could rely on now, just like it always was, had a sharpened edge.

Handlers might have known how to train recruits, but I knew how to fight the Corvid. The next time I saw Tristan, that's all I had to think about.

Behind me, the door to the little office slammed open, and I whirled around, crouching down with my fists up, wishing for my spike.

Tristan was on the other side of the door with two knives in one hand and another in his grip, aimed at me.

CHAPTER 14

CHANGE

"Cinder," he said, dropping his hands and saying my name like a sigh.

I couldn't speak. I couldn't even stand up from my position, and I couldn't drop my hands.

This was my nightmare made manifest in the middle of the day.

Me against Tristan, just as my brother wanted.

"Your cloak," he said, shaking his head and putting his knives away inside his jacket, "I only caught a glimpse, and didn't know who was sneaking into this wing. You scared me."

Scared him.

Like all the people before him who fell to my blade with that look of terror in their eyes right before I shoved my spike into their heart, I scared him.

After all the time I tried not to, after deciding not to kill him, and choosing to believe in him as King, it all still ended in fear. Of me.

I stood up, slowly, my fists shaking as I let them fall to my sides, only holding them balled up to stop the tremors from growing worse.

"Did you just come in here to get away from everything?" He grinned and came into the office, closing the door behind him.

Still, no words managed to form on my tongue. They stayed buried in the deepest places in my soul where the only things I ever said to someone who was afraid of me were curses. I shook my head, trying to suppress the weakness in my knees that threatened to make me fall over.

He grinned and bit his lip, looking down at the floor before he looked back up at me and took a step forward.

With the searing heat that followed him everywhere, he took my hand in one of his, and with the other he ran a thumb over my cheek.

"Does that mean…" he smiled again, it was soft and made me want to scream while I ran from the room, "…did you just come in here to see me?"

"I…" my voice was a thin croak, and I couldn't catch my breath, "I need to go."

Pulling my hand from his, I tried to get past him and out the door.

"Cinder," he said, taking my hand again, a line between his brows, "what's wrong?"

"Nothing." I said it too fast. "Wait…I mean…" I shook my head, and turned to face him as questions raced through his eyes. But I did have a reason to look for him in the first place, and now was my chance to tell him. "The Handler is training the recruits wrong."

He pulled back. Instead of questions on his face, now it was blank.

"Of all the things I thought you would say, none of them were that."

"I just went outside to watch for a while, and only those of us who fought them know how to train for this war." It remained difficult to focus on the war with Corvid when my mind was fighting itself, screaming to run away from him, and yelling that this was important. So I needed to stay.

"Interesting," he said, leaning back against his desk, keeping a hold on my hand, playing with my fingers as he stared down at it.

"But I should let you go back to..." I glanced toward the way out, not wanting to finish that sentence. "You have a lot to do."

Pulling my hand away from him, I turned for the door, wanting the air on the other side of it so badly my lungs ached as if I just returned home with the ashes collecting in them again.

"I should be paying more attention to the training. I wonder..." he said, looking out the window across the river toward Bridgeton.

Whatever he wondered, it wasn't something I could care about. So I kept walking.

"Cinder," he called when my hand reached the doorknob.

Turning to face him again, I held my breath, and tried not to let anything show on my face.

"Do—I mean," he smiled and shook his head before making eye contact again and standing up, his whole body formal and serious, "may I have dinner with you tonight?"

My mouth hung open, and I didn't have the ability to answer.

Was he serious?

After what I witnessed in the hallway, he was acting as if nothing happened. But he had to know I saw him since he spotted me.

He pushed himself off the desk and came toward me, but I still couldn't find the words.

"I know," he said, "that I haven't been around, and there's still so much to say, so much to explain, and there are so many things I can't tell you right now that I want to. But, please, be patient with me while I try to get everything in a place where I can tell you."

Snapping my mouth shut, my hand still on the doorknob, my grip so tight it would probably imprint in the shape of my fingers, I didn't know how to respond. There wasn't one answer in my mind to all the things he said. There were too many. All I had in response were questions, and I didn't deserve to have the answers.

Plus, I wondered how much he was telling Ziya.

"Tristan, we can have dinner whenever you want." My voice was thin and strained, but it was the only thing to say.

My King—the one I needed to remain close enough to for me to protect for the good of the country, and the one my brother wanted me to kill—wanted to have dinner.

No matter how much I hoped he chose anyone other than the snake, this was my duty. This was how I could fulfill my new mission. And make up for my old one.

He took a deep breath, and put a hand to my cheek.

The heat of him, that fevered temperature he carried within him, ran from his fingers all through my body as they brushed my neck and the hair along the back of my head. Like before, my muscles relaxed, and the aches of bruises eased. But unlike all the other times he touched me, tears threatened at the back of my eyes.

"Someday soon, this threat we're all under will be gone. I promise. And so much will change."

I didn't know what that had to do with our dinner, but I hoped he was right, even as he ran his thumb along my cheek and the pressure at the back of my eyes worsened.

"Yes. And I should go so you can work on that," I said, pulling the door open, and fleeing from him before he could say or do anything else.

He knew now. He knew what I wanted to tell him about the

Handler and the training. There was no more reason for me to stay.

But as I fled down the stairs and back up to my own hallway, all I could think about was how much I wanted to still be in that room with him. And how many times Ziya and all the others thought the same.

CHAPTER 15

WRONG DRESS

Standing at the door to my rooms, I fought back all the irrational thoughts running through my head.

If I walked in and tears managed to get past all my attempts to hold them back, Gus and Jacquetta would want to fix it. They would want to know why.

Not only was there no way for them to fix this, trying to explain why would only make it all worse.

Deep breaths helped. Eventually the pressure of unshed tears lessened enough for me to open the door.

But neither of them came running, and there was no noise to alert me of their presence in their rooms either.

Good. Maybe I could avoid spending hours being prepared for a dinner that was probably nothing more than all the times we spent together before.

…all the times we spent together.

Just thinking it sent images flashing through my head. But they meant different things now, and I questioned all my interpretations of them.

I couldn't think about it anymore. It was too much.

Going to the window, I looked down on the training recruits still doing the useless work the Handler set out for them.

But, standing at the top of the main stairs, Tristan watched them.

So, it was worth it.

Going to his office, witnessing him with Ziya, the conversation that made no sense, even the tears that hovered just at the edge of my eyes if I thought about it too much, were all worth it if it meant we would have a better chance at winning the war.

My mission.

It was all worth it for my mission to succeed.

Behind me, the door to the apartment opened, Jacquetta and Gus darting inside laughing and leading a server with a cart full of food.

They thanked the server, and, when the door was shut again, they faced me with all the laughter gone from them.

"What?" I asked, genuinely lost as to what I could have done to upset them when I wasn't even around.

"You weren't going to tell us that you're having dinner with the King?" Jacquetta asked, and I looked behind me to check and see I was still standing up and not asleep in some weird dream.

"How was I supposed to tell you when he only just asked me?"

"But the Marquessa's Ladies in Waiting were complaining about it," Gus said, taking a piece of roll from the cart and popping it into her mouth, "because she wanted to have dinner with him, and he made the excuse he was dining with you."

"Then he did it before he asked me." Which didn't matter. He had to know, regardless of how he acted, that I wouldn't tell him no. "Besides, he doesn't seem to be too upset over spending time with her."

"Oh, Cinder, don't believe what the Marquessa or her Ladies say." Jacquetta waved a dismissive hand and sat at the table, taking a plate from the cart with her.

"Should I believe what I saw?" I asked, getting my own plate.

"First of all, eat fast because we need to get you ready," Gus said, pointing at me as she grabbed her food, too. I stuck my tongue out at her because I knew she was going to say that. "Second, what are you talking about 'saw?'"

"Tristan kissed the snake's hand outside her room after spending time with her today when he hasn't been spending time with anyone else." Taking a bite, I watched as Jacquetta and Gus looked at each other, and all their hopes turned to worry.

I shouldn't have said anything.

"We're going to have to get ruthless," Jacquetta said, and Gus nodded.

"Do I want to know what that means?" It was a stupid question since I was sure I did not.

"Just hurry up and eat," Gus said, shoving a massive bite in her mouth which gave me the first reason to smile since I left the courtyard.

They weren't kidding when they told me to hurry up. Before eating as much as I wanted to, they pulled me from the table and into the bathroom.

By the time I expected word on dinner, whether General Pace would be with us, if Tristan would come to my door himself, where we were eating, and exactly how dressed up I really should have been, Gus and Jacquetta were putting the final touches on my hair.

"Are you sure? This is a lot," I said, running a hand down the skirt of my dress.

"Yes." Gus nodded.

"Very sure." Jacquetta grinned.

"What if he just wants to stay here and have dinner in the parlor?" Then I would be the single most overdone person ever to pretend to be comfortable at a meal.

"Not only would he still not mind, but then he'll just really enjoy the view," Gus said with a wicked grin as Jacquetta laughed and I cringed.

"Ew, Gus. That makes me feel about as deep as a tapestry," I said. And it didn't make me feel any better about this whole thing.

But they just shook their heads at me, and stepped back so I could stand from the vanity stool and take it all in.

They were right that the dress was beautiful, but between it and my face, I thought it was probably too much even for a ball.

In fact, I couldn't imagine a place where wearing it would be the right choice. I really couldn't imagine a place where people wouldn't yammer about it for days afterward.

My dress was black lace in a flame pattern with an underlay in strategic places that was the same color as my skin and the occasional red gem glimmering in the lace. The cut was simple, long sleeved, tight fitting, with a slit up one leg that almost reached the waistline.

For my hair, they left most of it down with one side pinned back with red gems.

And it was those, along with which side they pinned back, that I questioned the most. Because the side of my face most on display was the not the fully healed side. So, the red gems picked up on the red-tinged eyelid, and it showed off the pale purple-and-green of the bruise that still ran from my cheekbone up to just above my eyebrow.

"But why can't we move my hair so it can cover this all up?" I asked, gesturing to my battered face.

"Cinder, are you a fighter?" Jacquetta asked.

"Of course." That was a silly question, even if I thought of a fighter as a title for someone like Jocelyn who still had more skill than I did in most things, I knew what Jacquetta meant.

"Right, so why wouldn't you want to show off that side of yourself?" Gus asked.

How did I tell her no, because it wasn't that side that was on display. It was the side of me that never fought back. This bruise was the symbol of the girl who let her untrained brother—who always hid when the fighting started—hurt her.

And it was a symbol of me betraying my brother, my mission, and my parents.

Maybe it wasn't that bad to Jacquetta and Gus, but to me this dress was more than a lot. It was a mark of all the worst things about me.

Knocking on the door interrupted anything else I was planning on saying.

I shook my head and shook my hands out at my sides, trying to reign in the stampeding of my heart.

There was only one way this wouldn't be a disaster, and that was if I could keep any conversation focused on how we could train the recruits the way I thought they needed to be.

Nodding, the feeling of my blood racing in my veins slowing a fraction, I followed after Gus and Jacquetta to answer the door.

CHAPTER 16

WRONG WOMAN

As I walked through the door into the parlor, Jacquetta opened the door to the hallway where General Pace stood waiting.

The General's eyebrows rose when she looked at me, and I didn't think it was a good thing.

"I'll go change," I said, turning to head back into my room.

"No. He's waiting," she said, her face going back to the impassive mask she usually wore. "I'm just surprised at some of the gowns Madam Valentin has endorsed."

Once again, her comment made me wonder how well she knew Madam because I suspected they were very close. It also made me wonder if the General could explain to me how Madam knew Ash.

Ash sent me to her. I assumed it was just a business relationship, but after Madam seemed to choose me over my brother, I wasn't sure anymore.

Just business wouldn't have been worth bothering to take a side, but Jacquetta had, and Madam through her. Jacquetta wouldn't do anything her mother didn't approve of.

Well...other than wielding short swords to hack a Corvid to

death. But even she had to admit that under the circumstances it was more than fine.

"You should take a cloak, though," the General said, and I nodded, realizing I was just standing in the doorway to my room being confused.

Why I needed my cloak, I had no idea, but at least it gave me something to do with my hands.

I picked up the red cloak, and followed her out into the hallway.

"General, do you know what King Tristan is planning tonight?" I asked, fighting the urge to curl my shoulders in, and turn away to hide my face.

No matter what Gus and Jacquetta said about it, I didn't think it was going to be a good thing to remind Tristan I was able to get hurt.

"The King has not informed me of his plans," she said, and I turned toward her confused.

"But you had me get a cloak. You must know something."

"All I know is that the King has his own cloak on, and has been wandering back and forth in the grand foyer for half an hour waiting for the time he told you dinner was going to be."

"Half an hour? Then why didn't he come get me?" None of this made any sense.

"My understanding is that he wanted to avoid anyone else seeing him in the hall and causing a delay."

Oh. He didn't want the Marquessa, and her snakiness, to see me with him any more than he wanted to admit to me what he did when he was with her.

"You should tell King Tristan some time that snakes are cold-blooded," I said. And Ziya would steal all his heat from him without giving anything back.

"What?" she asked, but I didn't have time to answer because we were at the top of the stairs, and Tristan stood below looking up at me.

His face went from clouded like the sky before a storm, to clear as a summer day.

"Cinder," he said, my name a soft benediction I didn't hear but felt as his mouth formed the word.

I walked down the stairs, holding onto the cloak tightly with one hand and the General's arm with the other, thankful I had the cloak to grip with the same ferocity I wanted to snap a certain neck with.

Tristan wore a cloak and a formal suit, but not the court finery with the ruffles and the lace. I was starting to wonder if I would ever get to see him in the truly fine attire I had heard so much about growing up. Somewhere in my chest, a flare of panic rose even though I didn't understand what caused it.

Maybe it was just being faced with him, knowing what I did about him, the snake, and what I assumed about this dinner. Or maybe it was because I knew what was true about me being here, what had always been true. And now all I wanted was to go back in time and pretend I didn't, just so I could enjoy the way he looked at me.

"Sometimes," Tristan said as I stood in front of him for a long moment before either of us spoke, "I think you can see into my mind."

I laughed long and loud. My laugh just burst out of me until I weaved forward, and Tristan caught me, a confused smile on his face.

"I'm sorry," I said, while trying to get myself under control, "but if you only knew how little I can see into what you think, you would understand why that was the funniest thing you've ever said."

"Little you can see?" he asked, taking my cloak and laying it over my shoulders, "Does that mean you wonder about it? What I think, I mean?"

"Of course I do." He was acting coy, but he had to know that was silly. "You're King. I'm pretty sure every Onyxian wishes they knew what you're thinking sometimes."

The bright smile on his face faltered for a moment, but whatever he was thinking about now to make his light dim, he got back on track as we stepped out into the frigid wind and the dark of the night.

With the cold slicing through the scant fabric of my dress, I hugged myself tighter to his side, the heat of him acting as a better protective layer than the cloak on my shoulders.

"Don't worry," he said into my hair as a carriage pulled up, "I'll make sure you stay warm."

A shiver ran through me, but not because I was cold.

"We're leaving the palace?" I asked as we made our way down the stairs to climb into the carriage.

"Yes," he said, climbing in behind me. He sat next to me, wrapping his arm around me and settling me into his side. "But we'll come back here for dinner. I just want to show you something."

"More Shield Houses?" I smiled at that. It was my favorite part of Bridgeton. And I was pretty sure it would stay that way, even though I hadn't spent much time at all in the city. A few of my kills happened here. But sneaking in, killing someone, and sneaking back out again didn't allow for tourism.

He smiled, too, looking at me. His kaleidoscope hazel eyes looked a deep, rich brown.

"One day soon we should visit again."

"I would love to see the children again, maybe spend more time with them than last time."

Tristan nodded, rubbing a hand down my arm, his smile softening and turning to the kind that made me watch his mouth and my stomach flop over.

Darkness from the tunnel to the bridge, absolute and blinding, descended over us.

Using the distraction, I adjusted my place on the seat and hoped I put my face a bit further from his.

"Maybe this time you'll let me bring you in a carriage back and forth?"

His voice was disconnected from him in the dark, and although I laughed and said, "Yes, of course," what I meant was, 'We should stay like this.'

Somehow, in the deep black of the tunnel, I was allowed to bask in the warmth of him next to me and the soothing rumble of his voice without the weight of Onyx on our every interaction.

But a moment later, the barely-there light from the moon came in through the windows again, plunging us back into the icy waters of the political currents around us. Even when I crossed the bridge in a carriage instead of swimming across the river, it still left me with goosebumps running up my arms.

"Are you going to tell me where we're going?" I asked him to get back to what we were doing and to stop thinking about all the other things hanging over us.

"Yes." He sat up a little straighter and turned his body so I had less of him as a king-shaped personal furnace, and he could look me in the eye, his face setting into the same look of seriousness as when he tried to send us all home.

CHAPTER 17

SHARP EDGE

Every muscle in my body tensed, sending pain shooting through the last of the bruises in my abdomen which were already better than they had been in the morning. It was the only reason I was able to stifle the sucked in breath that followed seeing that look on his face.

"The Handler has full purview over training systems at the palace," Tristan said.

"What?" Of all the things I was bracing myself for, that wasn't on the list. While it didn't cause me to be any more panicked than before, my taught muscles didn't relent either.

"I know." He shook his head, seeming to miss entirely how still I sat next to him. "I can't do anything to change how the recruits will be trained at the palace."

The carriage slowed to a stop and Tristan smiled before he scooted closer to the door, pulling me after him.

"But I can do this," he said, as one of the footmen opened the door.

While Tristan climbed out, I made my way to the door, and took the hand he offered me as I stepped out myself.

Here the air was even more chilled than at the palace,

carried on a steady breeze that smelled of fresh water. But we were in a massive field surrounded by stone ramparts with the flags of the Dragon Kings flying at regular intervals.

"I don't understand," I said, pulling my cloak tighter around me.

"This is the old tournament grounds," he said, turning to take it all in.

"But there haven't been tournaments in years."

"No, I've preferred to spend the money on things that actually benefit the people of Onyx. Food distribution and what not. Of course, that's caused a lot of the royals to be angry with me more than once."

He laughed, the sound swallowed in part by the wind as if this place disapproved of its disuse.

"So, are we going to have a tournament? Because that seems like it would only be good for a distraction."

"A tournament would make a good distraction." He let go of my hand to step away from me, leaving me with my teeth chattering, while he turned in a slow circle, an odd concentration on his face.

"Tristan?"

"I'm sorry," he shook his head and stepped back to me, wrapping an arm around my shoulders, and rubbing his hand along my arm, stalling the chattering of my teeth. "Actually, instead of a tournament, I was thinking about relocating all the training here so the guard could all be trained as you suggested."

"Really?" I smiled, looking around at the space, imagining the way I would lay it all out if I was in charge of everything.

"Of course. It was a very good idea."

But how would they make that work while keeping the palace safe and Tristan protected?

"Are they all going to travel from the barracks and back every day?" I tried to imagine how they would do that. The logistics of that many people going through the city at once would be a nightmare.

"No. They're all coming to stay here while they train. Except for the smaller force of guards who already fought the Corvids, are already trained, and have a better idea of how they would fight them again."

"You need to stay here then," I said, the idea of him at the palace with a smaller force made my throat go dry.

"What? Why would I stay here? The palace is safer." He looked up at the night sky and back at the carriage. "Speaking of which, we should get back."

I didn't argue with him about leaving, just turned and climbed into the carriage, thinking about how we could make this place work better.

Tristan sat down beside me with a smile and tucked me back into his side again.

"You should move out here," I said, "Where you'll be surrounded by more troops. At the palace, the Corvids could dive bomb you before a smaller number of guards even spotted them in the sky. But here, you could have a canopy erected over you at all times, and be surrounded by fighters. If you need to go to the palace, it would be easier for just you to make the trip than a whole bunch of guards."

"Cinder," he said, his voice soft and sweet like a caress.

As much as it wasn't smart when he spoke that way, I couldn't stop myself from turning toward him, from looking into his eyes. Like a flower turning toward the sun, that kindness fed me in a way I didn't know I needed, and didn't know how much I missed from when my parents were alive.

"For some reason, when I brought you here, I thought you would regale me with a detailed outline of how I should implement the training they'll do here."

"Oh, that's coming," I said, and he grinned.

"But first you were worried about me." He lifted his free

hand and carefully, a tiny bit at a time, he ran his fingers along my cheek right under my remaining bruise, his gaze intent on me as if he was checking to see he didn't hurt me.

He was so far away from hurting me, his touch lessened the worst of the remaining ache in the space right by my eye.

"Yes," I said, and his breathing hitched, "I worry about you."

Moving his hand from my cheek to tangle in my hair at the nape of my neck, Tristan stared into my eyes, his ever-shifting eyes dark and endless.

"And that's why I'm going to train all the recruits," I said, making him freeze in place.

"What?" he asked, hardly even moving his mouth.

"It's the only thing that makes sense. I know how to fight the Corvids, and I know how to teach some of these recruits how to be better than anyone would think them capable of being in a short time."

The ways I was trained weren't the same as the guards. I knew that the minute I saw the guards fight. And after watching for a short time how they were trained under the competent but unimaginative Handler, I wasn't surprised I was more deadly.

"No." He pulled his hand away from my neck and sat back, even his arm around me was stiff.

"You aren't going to tell me why?"

"Listen, I know you're more than capable, and I know you have devoted more time to training than almost anyone I've ever met. But there is no way I can allow you to do this." He shook his head, and I crossed my arms, tilting my head at him.

"No way you can *allow* me?"

"Cinder, please, don't." He squeezed his arm around me and turned to face me again, as if he could go back to that soft place of before.

But now, I wasn't soft. I was as sharp as my blades.

"Don't what? You were more than happy with my ability to plan for your protection, but you don't want me to be a part of it?" That would have made sense when I was planning on killing him, but I had killed *for* him now. He didn't know what my plans were back then, but he had to see the difference in the way I treated him.

"The last thing I want is for you to protect me."

"Oh." I sat forward enough that I pulled away from his arm, but he tugged on my shoulder to pull me back against the seat.

"Please."

"You know what?"

At that second the absolute blackness of the tunnel took over the interior of the carriage and I stopped talking, my entire body taking on the darkness and letting it fill me.

Tristan didn't speak until the moon filtered inside again, saying, "Can we please go to dinner, and not think about this for a while?"

"I am sorry, King Tristan, I am afraid that a proper Lady of the court should not be having dinner alone with you."

Every word out of my mouth, in the stilted, overly formal address we hadn't used with each other unless we were in front of other people since I first came to the palace made him crumple further until he sat in the seat next to me, his arm back at his side and not touching me at all.

Finally, the carriage stopped in front of the grand staircase into the palace, and the footman opened the door.

He climbed out, and I followed, not taking his offered hand to help myself on the way.

When my feet hit the courtyard I kept walking, not looking back, up the stairs and into the palace, leaving the King behind me.

CHAPTER 18

FAILURE

He let me go.

It was all I could think about as I stomped past the General and up the stairs. All the way down the hall to my rooms, I didn't think about the slight, about how he dismissed my work and my expertise so easily. No, I thought about how he didn't try to explain. He didn't take it back. He let me go.

After everything, even the way he looked at me and touched me in the carriage, I was right about it all meaning nothing. There was no point in pretending.

When I opened the door to my apartment and shut it behind me, Jacquetta and Gus looked up from an impressive spread on the table, their mouths full.

"Thank the hellfires you have food," I said, tugging my cloak off and balling it up before throwing it across the room. "Can you please get me out of this stupid dress?"

"Are you okay?" Gus asked around her bite, running toward me, not bothering to put down the piece of food in her hand.

"What happened?" Jacquetta asked, tossing her food down

on her plate and frantically pawing at a napkin to clean her hand before she ran over, too.

"Fine, and nothing, I just want to eat and go to bed."

They didn't argue, but they both paused, their hands stilled on the buttons along my back.

But they got the dress undone, the shoulders of it falling off my own and drooping in the front.

I grabbed onto the dress at the neck, holding it up until I got in my room, and let it fall to the floor before I kicked it away from me.

Maybe it was a cursed dress.

Staring at it in a ball on the floor, I wanted to leave it. The urge to burn it was high. But it was an expensive dress made of expensive fabric and adorned with expensive gems.

Picking it up, I mumbled every swear word I knew, and laid it carefully in my trunk.

Destroying expensive things that could be resold for money for my people was wrong. It was hard enough to ruin all the dresses I did when I climbed down the palace wall, but that had a purpose.

Now, ruining it would only be for my own rage. And that wasn't good enough.

Of course, Tristan thought I wasn't good enough to protect him, so there was a lot of not measuring up floating around.

Finally, in my nightgown, my stomach growling, I walked back into the parlor.

Gus and Jacquetta were back at the table, the smiles gone from their faces, and they were eating again. Although now, instead of leaning forward over the table as if they couldn't get enough of the food in front of them, they slumped back into their chairs and shoveled it in as if it was tasteless.

"You're really not going to tell us anything?" Jacquetta asked, looking at her food instead of at me.

"No, I...just..." I couldn't find the words. The rage was right there, filling my mouth with bitterness, but getting up the courage to explain to them how none of this was going in my favor, or in theirs, was too much.

Too much for tonight.

I shook my head, and shoved more food in my mouth that I didn't taste.

What was I doing here?

My theory before I agreed to come back to the palace was that it afforded me ways to protect Tristan. Not to become queen, because I wasn't the right one for that, but to stop him from picking Ziya the snake as an even worse option than me. And protect him from assassination at the same time.

But now, not even being able to meet Gus and Jacquetta's eyes had me wondering what those few goals left me with.

"At some point," I said, trying to find the words to explain, to allow them time to come to terms with my failure, "You both need to make a connection with one of the other potentials so you can keep working for an Onyx throne."

Jacquetta sighed, the kind that wasn't wistful or full of longing but was instead exasperation in a breath.

"Cinder, what are you talking about?"

"Tonight, he made it clear that I'm not good enough." Another bite shoved in my mouth with my hand clenched around the fork at least shut me up for a while. But I wanted to punch myself and knock myself out. Maybe then I would be able to keep my thoughts to myself.

Gus and Jacquetta both seemed frozen, and I couldn't make sense of their silence, although I didn't understand a lot about people in general and should have expected it. Another failure.

"Bullshit," Gus snapped, freezing me now. "He loves you."

My temporary stillness was gone in a roar of humorless laughter.

"Stop it," Gus said.

"You're being rude," Jacquetta said, narrowing her eyes at me.

"I'm sorry, but it's ridiculous. He doesn't love me. He's playing some stupid game. And it isn't the kind someone like me wins." I stood up and grabbed my plate.

"No, you're not hiding from us in your room like a big, whiny baby," Gus said.

"Exactly," Jacquetta said.

"And you're not going to wallow in this," Gus waved a hand at me with a look on her face like she just drank bad milk, "whatever it is that you do when you get all pathetic and think you're not good enough."

"Tristan said I wasn't good enough, not me." I was screaming now, my voice harsh and shrill.

"What exactly did he say? How did he tell you that you weren't good enough?" Jacquetta asked, her voice cold and low, which only pissed me off more.

I threw my plate full of food back down on the table, sending bits of it flying all over the room.

"He told me he didn't want me to train the recruits even though I fought those fucking birds, and know better than most what they need to do to win."

"There's no way he said that." Gus said, her brows high and her mouth hanging open as she stared at Jacquetta.

"Really? Am I going to train the recruits tomorrow?" I turned and stalked toward my room. No matter how hungry I still was, it wasn't worth looking at all of it in front of them.

"Yes," Jacquetta yelled at my back.

"What?" I whirled around, just in time to catch the roll Gus threw at my head.

"She said you *are* going to train the stupid recruits tomorrow no matter what the King says, you dipshit," Gus yelled.

"And why in all the world would I do that just so I can be

dismissed again?" Part of me wanted to throw the roll at her head, but I just squeezed my other hand into a fist at my side.

"Because," Jacquetta said, "he's not going to dismiss you when you remind him what you can do, and none of the guard are going to let you be dismissed."

"Of course they'll let me. He's their King." What didn't they get about this?

"Yes," Gus said, "but you're their hero. They all want to be able to do what you can. If they think you'll teach them how to do even one of the moves they talk about you doing that day, they'll petition the King en masse."

"Neither of you understand," I said, turning around and shaking my head.

Both of them kept talking, trying to get me to listen again, but I didn't have it in me. My damaged heart was in pieces, and thinking about picking them up was bad enough without risking it shattering further by following their suggestions.

CHAPTER 19

ALL NEW

In the morning, I woke up to Gus and Jacquetta, arms crossed, staring down at me.

"Why are you in here right now?" My voice didn't sound like me. It sounded like a monster pretending to be me.

"You need to get up," Jacquetta said.

"Because you have a job to do today," Gus said.

"I could be sleeping in. There's nothing I want to do more right now than stay in this bed all day." I rolled over and pulled the blankets up over my head, blocking them and the light.

"Nope," Gus said, snatching the covers from me and letting the first air of the morning spread a chill all over my body leaving goosebumps in its wake.

"Cinder," Jacquetta said, that note of exasperation back in her voice, "how is it possible that someone who didn't believe in magic watched a human turn into a giant bird, and barely flinched before doing what needed to be done, then turns into a pile of goo when her feelings get hurt?"

"Maybe if I could stab feelings, I would act more like you want me to," I mumbled into the pillow before I punched it.

"See? There," Jacquetta said.

"Get angry and use it. Stop whining," Gus said.

"Fine." I flipped over and threw the pillow at them in one movement, knocking them both back a step.

"Not at us, ding dong." Jacquetta threw her arms in the air.

"At the Marquessa and whatever stupid worm crawled into the King's head. Fight back. Fight for your place." Gus threw the pillow back at me.

The surprise that she caught it must have registered on my face as I batted it away because she grinned.

"I'm faster than I look," she said.

"One day." I held up one finger and raised a single brow. "I will get out of bed, and do this ridiculous thing, for one day. And if he doesn't relent, then I'm not going to force him to let me train them." Even though I wanted to force him, I didn't think I could. And if he repeated the same concern over my protection again, I would mean that I needed to carry out my new mission from further away than I originally planned.

"Fine," Jacquetta said, walking toward the bathroom.

"Are you going to make me dress up for this?" I asked, sitting up and staring after her.

"We have some new training clothes for you," Gus said, winking and going after Jacquetta.

"You could have led with that." I climbed out of the bed, rubbing my hand over my face.

For a second, I was surprised my eye didn't hurt at all until I looked in the mirror. There was almost no sign of the bruising, swelling, or wounds on my face.

"Jacquetta, at some point your mother should bottle the stuff you used on my face. It's amazing."

"Actually, even with that, I'm surprised you're so much better so fast. You were last night when you got back here, too." She threw her usual petals and things in the bath as it filled. I tried to remember what my face looked like when I left and if I saw it when I got back.

But I didn't think I saw it, so I couldn't argue, even though I doubted it worked on me while I was out. She was probably exaggerating to make me feel better about today.

Steam rolled off the water. The fragrance of the small miracles her mother taught her poured through the bathroom as the tub filled.

While I breathed it in, it helped loosen some of the knots in my chest and steady my stomach even before it helped to heal my body.

Getting in the bath, the heat soaked into me, relaxing me further, fueling me. And I finally accepted that, yes, I was going to try this. Even though I didn't think it would work, and the idea of the end of it made me never want to get out of the bath at all.

"Let us wash your hair," Jacquetta said, her smile matching Gus'.

These friends of mine. So fierce in their own ways.

Hair washed and dried, I walked out with Gus and Jacquetta to my bedroom as the dawn fully crested the edge of the palace. The light outside matched all the light in my room.

Laid out on my bed were not just new clothes like the ones I brought and had been using to train. They were better than those overly stiff things that were too formal for real training. And the new set was far more beautiful than the plain black ones I had back in Lehar. Those were supple and sleek, but they weren't pretty.

But these...

"When did this happen?" I asked, touching a hand to the leather vambrace arm panels sitting on the tunic.

"Gus and I just thought you needed something for training with the King that made sense with the rest of your wardrobe," Jacquetta said, picking up the first layer and holding it out to me.

I smiled, and they helped me don the new clothes, even tying the leather waistband that covered me from the bottom of my breasts to my hips and would have come in handy when Ash beat me.

Nothing about these training clothes would hide me at night, but that wasn't what I needed now at the palace. What they did, though, was make me look the part of someone who should be training the recruits.

"Thank you. This is my favorite of all the outfits so far," I said, staring in the mirror as they grinned.

"How did I know you were going to say that?" Gus asked.

"Because she's predictable," Jacquetta said, "but we need to get her outside to the courtyard before they get too far into their routine. And she still needs to eat."

I did need to eat. Especially because I had no idea how long it was going to take me to make my point.

At some time in the night, while I was sleeping, Gus and Jacquetta had someone come in and straighten my mess from the evening before because the clean table was now covered in an array of breakfast foods.

"Last night, I was terrible, and I apologize for treating you both the way I did," I said, biting my lip and wondering why they put up with me.

"You're right," Jacquetta said, "you were terrible."

"But," Gus said, "At some point we all will be, and the others will forgive us. Because that's what friends do."

I looked back and forth between them, and all the pain of the night before turned into desperate gratitude for them. And for all the things they forced me to do.

CHAPTER 20

LADIES IN TRAINING

In my new training clothes, I walked out into the packed courtyard to watch the training of the guard. Gus and Jacquetta by my side, in their own modified versions of training clothes, fidgeted and seemed less than comfortable in this space. But that was going to change.

Other Ladies in Waiting joined us, and Gus nodded to me, a signal that everyone she expected to be part of this little foray into training was here.

Most of them wore day dresses. Even Jacquetta and Gus weren't in pants, but in split skirts, which limited what I could do with them. But most of them were in families and positions that never allowed them to grow comfortable in pants, and they probably didn't own any. This would have to do.

We moved to the range where not enough guards were practicing, and I positioned them in two lines, only taking over two lanes of targets.

"Alright," I said, stepping into the lane in front of them, and raising my arms to draw their attention from the muttered conversations between them.

One by one, they turned to look at me, women of privilege ready to learn how to take care of themselves.

"I want to thank you for trusting me to teach you, and to tell you all that I'm happy you're going to learn." I smiled and they returned my grin, even if some of them looked unsure.

"Chances are, if you end up needing this information, it won't be in a place where you can easily have a bow and arrow at the ready."

Some chuckles and a lot of nodding.

"The first thing I'm going to teach you is throwing knives." I held one up, letting them see the size of it, and then balanced it on my finger.

"You see, this is easy to hide in your skirts, or wherever you wish. You can have a half dozen of them if you want. Now, I'm going to help each of you with your grip, and then I'm going to show you how to throw it. Only then are we going to work on actually doing it."

More nodding, and some even looked eager. Gus leaned forward and around the woman in front of her, her eyes huge and her smile real.

"After we get some work in with this discipline, we'll commandeer some of the courtyard, I'll teach you some hand-to-hand, and maybe some dagger work if you want."

None of them seemed to know what to do with that, looking at each other and shrugging.

I smiled again and passed out the throwing knives, helping each of them place the blade in the proper position between their fingers.

We went through the motions, me showing them, and then they all took their turns.

For some reason, when I started with this idea, I thought it would be simple. I thought they would all come with some basic understanding, if not some kind of training of their own.

But I was wrong.

A few caught on fast, but none of them were even close to being good enough to protect themselves with the skills they had. This was going to take a long time.

Part way through the day, I was distracted by a change in the guards in the courtyard. They seemed to be forming circles, which looked like an opening for me.

"Ladies, let's take a break," I said, keeping my focus past them to the movement of the guards. "It's a good time for you to go get something to eat, and we can meet back here when you're done."

I started to walk away, patting Jacquetta's arm as I passed her.

"Cinder, where are you going?" Gus asked.

"To spar."

My instincts about their movements proved accurate as the first clashes began.

Circling the different groups, my blood rang with the need to step in, to tell them where they were dropping their guard, leaving themselves open. I wanted to call out so many times and remind them of form, to watch for the small tells of their opponents, to let themselves trust their instincts.

One of the circles of onlookers was deeper than the others and more silent in their attention. It was like they were all holding their breath watching the fight.

Making my way through the throng, trying to get closer, the small hairs on my neck stood on end. Something was happening in this circle that was more than just a sparring session. Something that made me want to jump in, as if my own life was at risk.

Finally, I was inside the group, and what I saw didn't help the panic surging in my veins.

Tristan sparred with a guard.

It took everything in me to shove back my need to protect him from the blade that flashed toward him. But he was good. His moves were smooth and strong, his instincts not hampered by second guessing.

"Careful when you make that turn not to leave yourself open," he called to his opponent. "If you are going to do it, it has to be fast enough not to give them a chance."

He was right, the guard wasn't fast enough for that move. I would have cut him down before he got halfway through it.

Around and around they went, their weapons were metal, but the edges were blunted. Every time they slammed into each other it was clear that they weren't in any real danger from one another. Not unless they decided to bludgeon each other with their sparring weapons.

The crowd remained transfixed by the spectacle, and I wondered if any of them were actually gleaning any information from the pointers Tristan offered as he went.

For some reason, I assumed that he wouldn't be this good. Maybe because he was a king and it seemed like he never had enough time. Maybe because of the way Father used to say that people had to choose what to be best at, what to devote their time to.

But, at least with the bow and now the short sword, Tristan was good enough to give me a workout.

I grinned.

My blood went from coursing with panic-tinged need for action on Tristan's behalf, to wanting to be in the circle with him. Only this time, for the first time in a while, I wanted to be his opponent.

Jocelyn was a great sparring partner when I trained at home, but it had been so long since anyone else gave me much of a challenge.

Looking up at the sky, checking for any signs of birds, small or large, part of me hoped that some Corvid spy looked down on what was happening.

When the Handler was training the guard in things I didn't think would aid us in our efforts against the Corvid, I begged Mother and Father to keep the knowledge of our lacking from the damned slavers.

Now, though, I hoped they saw our King, the leader of our forces, and trembled in their feathers.

Tristan might have been without magic, but he was far from defenseless.

"Dead," Tristan said for what must have been the tenth time, holding his opponent's arm away from his body with one hand, and the point of his sword just under the guard's chin with the other.

His smile as he pulled back and patted the guard on the arm, swinging his sword as if it were just a toy, made me bite my lip and long for the times I thought those smiles my way were real.

"Thank you, King Tristan," the guard said, bowing with a hand over their heart, their breath coming in gasps.

"My turn to spar with the King," I yelled before the guard was done turning away.

All eyes found me in the crowd, and I raised my head while the smile fell from Tristan's face.

He might not have wanted me to protect him or lead the guard, but he was going to learn today that I was more than just a Lady.

I was his best weapon. And he should use me to fight this war.

"Lady Cinder..." Tristan's voice trailed off, and I grinned as someone passed me a sparring sword.

"King Tristan," I said, bowing as the guard had, but not stepping from the line of onlookers. Not yet.

He dropped his sword to his side, his grip barely keeping it from falling to the ground. Almost my cue.

"Maybe we—"

"Should show them a real fight," I said, cutting him off, flying out from the group, and running past him fast enough that with a tiny flick of my sword, I popped a button on his coat.

He smiled and lifted his sword with a shake of his head.

The fight was on.

CHAPTER 21

DEATH COUNT

"For those of you watching," he said, as he dropped into a loose and ready position, "that is one death to Lady Cinder."

His overly formal court language, something that I didn't like under normal circumstances, now sounded ridiculous. I laughed.

"Oh, King Tristan, are you not used to losing when you spar?" I asked, twirling the sword to get used to the feel of it, passing it from one hand to the other in the process.

"No," he said around a huge smile, "I am not."

"Well," I said, darting toward him, ducking beneath his swing, and raising my sword to pop another one of his buttons as I whirled back to standing ready on the other side of the circle, "if you don't stop holding back, I suggest you *get* used to it."

He ran at me, using his size and an outstretched arm to partially block one of the ways I could exit the clash, but I wanted this fight. I wanted it to be as real as possible. He had to learn.

I met his sword with my own, sliding the blunt-edged blade

down to lock hilts as he dragged me toward him so our faces were so close together that I could see that his ever-changing eyes were deep hazel green today.

"Are you sure you want this to be a full fight?" he whispered. "You're still hurt."

"No, I'm not hurt," I said, twisting to wrench our swords apart, but he wrapped an arm around me, holding my back tight against the inferno that was his chest.

Our swords stayed locked together, and he pushed his advantage, pulling the blades closer to me. So I pressed back against him, aware of every part of his heated body touching mine.

"You keep underestimating me," I said, letting go of the sword, dropping down, and kicking my legs out so I fell back toward his legs.

I grabbed one of his legs, and pushed off the ground with my toes. I became a twisting storm turning around him as my center.

Once I was crouched on the other side of him at his back, I jumped up and wrapped my legs around his neck. Leaning forward over his head, I grabbed his sword hand, and brought our locked together blades toward his face just like he had mine.

I pulled the blade of his sword close to his throat, my sword clattering to the ground at his feet, and his other hand tugging my leg where I draped it down his chest.

"Dead again," I whispered, using the blunt edge to tilt his face up toward me.

My heart soared as his jaw dropped and awe flooded his eyes.

"Brace yourself," I said, pulling my legs up and flipping off his back to land behind him again in a crouch, my fingers digging into the dirt scattered on the cobblestones. I shot out my other hand, grabbing my sword from between his legs before jumping back again.

"At some point," he said, turning toward me and raking a hand through his hair, "you are going to have to fight me with a mask so I can focus on the actual fight and not how in the world you move so fast."

I stood up straight, dropping my sword to my side and tilting my head.

"Why would a mask help?" I asked. That made no sense.

He was a blur as he got so close to me his sword was at my side, in the spot that led directly to my heart, and I used for the strikes from my spike. His other hand wrapped around my back, and held me in a gentle grip while his breath, warm and fast, tickled my ear and neck.

"Because when I look at you with a sword in your hand and that wicked grin on your face, my mind doesn't think of fighting."

The hand at my back moved up to cup the back of my neck, his fingers tangling in my hair. I sighed, fighting the thrill ricocheting through my body.

"Making that noise," he whispered, "and wrapping your legs around my neck doesn't help."

I brought my sword up, knocking his from my side, and laughed as I spun out of his loose grip, my hair flying across my face as his fingers brushed through it.

"A death to you, King Tristan," I said, circling him as he did the same, stalking around the perimeter of the crowd.

"Next time we spar," I said, swiping my hair to the side and out of my eyes, "I will wear that mask. Let us see if it matters. But you know that distractions are your own fault."

He threw his head back and laughed, nodding when he was done.

"Why does my very smart Lady Cinder say that distractions are my own fault?" he called out to the crowd, his voice deep and carrying.

The crowd called answers out to us, all of them astute, and

some of them with more than a hint of amusement in their voices.

"Because it's your problem."

"Your opponent in a fight doesn't care if you're distracted. They'll use it."

It was good of Tristan to use this moment to teach the guard some lessons, but the 'my' when he said my name to ask his question made my blood run as hot as his normally was.

Without warning, in mid step, I launched into an attack.

He parried and blocked, trying to get back into a position where he wasn't on the defensive.

But I was relentless, and he was a fraction slower.

Eventually, without resorting to any of my flips and tricks, relying only on my skills with the blade, I tapped into the rhythm of the fight itself. Knowing so many forms and moves gave me notice of what he was going to do without relying on him making a mistake and showing me a tell.

My sword was frozen at his side, where I would have been able to slice through his abdomen and gut him, while his was lifted high to block what he thought was going to be a striking downward blow.

I stepped in close, and lifted onto the tips of my toes making it so he barely had to look down to meet my eyes.

"Dead." I said, my breath heaving in my chest. "Again."

He dropped his arms down, his sword resting at his side, and his other resting on my hand where it gripped my own blade.

Tristan's chest rose and fell in rapid succession, heat pouring from him, his jaw was tight. But his eyes...

Eyes that changed as the light did, eyes that sometimes seemed to see through me, bored into me now.

He swallowed, opened and closed his mouth, his lips flushed and full as he tilted his head toward me.

People around us cheered, their voices breaking the spell between us. When he blinked, the fire in his eyes retreated.

With a smile, he took my sword hand, turned us, and lifted my hand in the air.

The guards roared in response, clapping and shaking their heads.

Looking at Tristan from the corner of my eye, I watched him nod before he stepped back and faced me.

I bowed to him with my hand over my heart, like the guard did, instead of curtseying, and he laughed while he shook his head.

He bowed back, and took my hand as he rose.

"When we go to the field for training, I want you to be in charge of the regimen." His voice was low so only I heard, but I flung my arms around him and hugged him tight.

"Thank you. No one wants you protected more than I do."

Arms locked around me, and head tucked into my neck he said, "I just don't want you to be hurt. That's all I was worried about. Protecting you."

Pulling back, I looked up at him and every piece of the fury and hurt since our dinner fell away.

"You want to protect me?" I asked. No one wanted to protect me. Not even Jacquetta or Gus, who loved me and didn't want to see me hurt, thought I needed it. Not since my mother and my father were alive had anyone thought about me getting hurt.

"Cinder," he said, lifting a hand to my cheek, "if anything happened to you I…"

Guards crowded around us and began to pepper me with questions, Tristan broke our hug and tucked me into his side, his arm around me.

I answered the questions as best I could, although it was hard to explain the training Jocelyn gave me all these years. The entire time we spent talking to the guard, I held my blunted sword at my side.

CHAPTER 22

PRIVATE SPACE

"You're making good progress," I said, walking with Gus and Jacquetta back to our rooms after a week of training the Ladies in Waiting. It was partially true. Some, Gus among them, were doing very well. Others, Jacquetta was one, were much better than they used to be. And some... some I worried would one day be called upon to act, and instead hide under a piece of furniture.

Not everyone was cut out to fight. Some people when faced with a terrifying situation froze. Others ran away. Training was supposed to make it less scary so your natural instinct to either hide or run was pushed aside, and you could do what needed to be done.

But some people remained afraid even in a safe training environment, their nerves wreaking havoc on them the moment a blade was placed in their hands. Those people I wanted to tell to get a club and hope for the best. But I started this little side mission, and I was going to keep trying.

"Ursula is never going to be able to throw a knife properly," Gus said, shaking her head and twisting her mouth.

"Well, she's doing better with the short swords," Jacquetta said, trying to hide her laugh.

"All of you are improving. And I'm proud of both of you." That was true. I wanted to throw Gus and Jacquetta a party because they worked so hard, and kept pushing even when they grew frustrated by their own progress.

My fierce friends smiled and stood taller as we opened the door to our rooms.

"Do you think they'll keep training while we're gone?" Gus asked, and I sighed.

"That, I don't know. None of us will be here to keep helping them. The General said she assigned a few guards to help them as they needed it, but they might just go back to brunches and fancy dresses."

"Brunches and fancy dresses," Jacquetta said, her voice full of longing.

"Do you want me to rub your back again tonight?" Gus asked, smiling at Jacquetta.

"Please?" Jacquetta put her hands together as if praying to Gus, and I laughed.

Gus nodded, but I went to my room and looked at my packed trunks.

It would be a while until they could indulge in all the finery that they both loved…

"Hey, Gus, Jacquetta, I have an idea."

They came into my room, glancing at each other and back at me, bracing themselves.

"Don't worry, I think you'll like this idea." They still didn't relax, but I managed to keep my laughter bottled up. "What if we have a formal dinner tonight with the King?"

"Oh," Jacquetta said, clapping her hands together.

"Will he have time?" Gus asked, but she was already pulling her hair out of the piled high braid thing she put it in when we trained.

"I'm going to him right now to check. Get ready," I said, darting past them.

"But Cinder, we need to get you ready, too," Jacquetta called, leaning around the door frame.

"We'll have time. Let me just tell Tristan. I'll be right back." I hurried out the door and down the hall, back to the staircase in the grand foyer, and up the other side to the royal wing.

The doors were open today, and a steady stream of people flowed in and out. Maybe he wouldn't have time for this dinner.

I bit my lip and made my way to the open door of the public office of the King.

His private office was warm and cozy, like being inside his heart. This place was cold and impersonal, like being inside his crown as it passed from one person to another.

Black obsidian didn't just make up the outside walls. In here, every wall was smooth and black, shining in the hellfire lamp light. A single shelf that looked as if it were made of a solid piece of silver-veined, clear quartz ran along the walls at waist height, becoming the windowsill in places, and acting as a place to hold the occasional book and some things that looked like the kind of stupid statuaries dignitaries gifted.

In the middle of the room, Tristan sat behind a desk of the same clear, silver-lined quartz, making the chair he sat in stand out even more. The chair was black and carved into a dragon, but along all the edges of the scales and all the other points that stood out, a bright green highlighted the shape.

General Pace made notes in a book while two guards spoke to Tristan. In the corner, sitting in a small silver chair, the Chamberlain also made notes, seeming to pay no attention to the other things happening in the room.

Maybe asking Tristan here, in front of the Chamberlain and all the people coming to see him wasn't a great idea. Of all of them, the Chamberlain made me question my decision the most.

But watching Tristan, as he leaned forward and gave complete attention to the people in front of him, made it a lot easier to step further into the room.

Even if he wasn't able to make it to dinner, he would come see me tonight, and be touched by the invitation anyway.

I smiled when he caught sight of me, the corner of his mouth twitching up before he refocused on what he was doing.

Standing there, as if I were just another in a long list of people begging for his time and his attention, gave me pause.

Why wasn't I just another one of them? Why could I call him Tristan? And why was I invited to his private office when all of these people had to meet him here?

He said his private office was a place almost no one ever went, so why did he bring me?

I wasn't special. Not any more special than any of the other potentials, not even more special than the snake. It made me wonder if she ever got to see the over-piled desk and the tower of bookshelves. Maybe she had.

My smile fell from my face. It didn't matter how much I tried to focus on the training and the work of protecting him, it always led me back to the same place: my role as a potential future bride.

It was supposed to be fake. But sometimes it was far too real.

Bowing, the guards finished up and walked away.

After they were gone, I took a step forward as Tristan stood up and made his way around the desk, leaning against it.

"What are you doing here? Do you have everything ready for tomorrow?" he asked, reaching out a hand to take mine.

"Yes, we are ready. But I was thinking, my Ladies have been spending so much time training and will be stuck dealing with me in a very not fancy place for a while."

He nodded with a small smile, looking down at our entwined hands.

It was as if I could read his mind. He had to be thinking

about the war, about what these changes meant the same way I did.

Squeezing his hand drew his eyes back to me and I smiled.

"Because they will not get to for a while, I was thinking it would be nice to have a very fancy, very formal dinner at my table," I said.

"Yes." He lifted my hand toward his mouth. The Chamberlain made a coughing sound, and Tristan turned away from my hand at the last second.

"My King," the Chamberlain said, head tilted, and a tight smile plastered on a face with narrowed eyes, "may I interrupt to say that a formal affair would be an excellent idea for the other potentials as well. Might I suggest that I be put in charge of a ball."

"A ball?" Tristan asked, looking back and forth between me and the Chamberlain. "But there is not enough time to prepare such a big event."

"We can keep it private for the people at the castle," the Chamberlain said, "and if you delay your trip to the training grounds by only one day, I can have it ready by tomorrow night."

"Oh," Tristan said, looking at me and squeezing my hand on an exhale, "well, then, yes. We will delay one day and have a ball."

The Chamberlain's smile changed to something real, and the General pursed her lips as she made another note in her book.

"For now, though, I am going to walk Lady Cinder back to her apartment. Excuse me."

He turned me around, and we walked out of the office without another word.

Passing through the door, Tristan finally kissed my hand and I laughed.

Another guard was in the hall, heading into the office, and stopped mid-step to look at the King and back toward the door as if he wasn't sure whether he should keep going into the office or not.

"Tristan," I whispered, leaning up to be close to his ear, "that guard wants to speak to you. Maybe you should just stay."

"No," he said, before he turned to the guard and said, "Go on in. The General will take your report."

We kept on down the hall, headed toward my room, and I couldn't help smiling. Not only was the Chamberlain angry that I pulled Tristan away, but Gus and Jacquetta would love having another ball.

"Just so you know," he said as we got to my door and I turned to face him, "I'm still coming to dinner tonight if that's okay."

"More than okay."

He lifted a hand and touched my cheek before he turned to go back to the office.

I watched him go, wondering why I meant what I said.

CHAPTER 23

SHINE

Walking in the door, Gus and Jacquetta popped out of their rooms, both wrapped in bath sheets, their hair dripping on the floor.

"Tristan is coming to dinner tonight," I said.

Jacquetta did a little wiggle dance and Gus grinned.

"And tomorrow night we're all going to another ball."

Screams. They screamed and jumped around before both darting back into their rooms.

I shook my head, and made my way to my bathroom. I probably should have waited to tell them to preserve my time before the ball for other things. But...part of me looked forward to spending an entire day with them getting ready for it.

Maybe this time I would be able to enjoy the event more.

Last time, I thought I would get sent home, and at the time the only reason why I wanted to be here was to kill Tristan.

Clenching my fists on the thought of my old mission and my brother, I got undressed and climbed into the filling tub.

Heat soaked into my body, and I relaxed back against the tub wall.

My brother...

Even here, far away from Lehar and healed from what he did, Ash's ghost and the lingering questions of my future with the only member of my family left were better shoved into the back of my mind.

I still couldn't face it.

Somehow, every time I thought of him, I thought about him making me choose. Him or Tristan. My choice still wasn't clear.

No, I wasn't going to kill Tristan. I was going to protect him, and protect the kingdom through him.

But what if, after the Corvid threat was over, Ash still wanted me to kill him? What if Ash punished me even more for not doing it? Would Ash ever forgive me for not giving him revenge?

The water was full enough. I leaned forward and turned it off.

My body was finally clear of all the bruises, and I shoved the wounds in my heart into a box so I could pretend to be rid of them, too, as I sunk below the surface.

After I finished washing up from my bath, Jacquetta and Gus came to my room and we took turns drying each other's hair.

Helping Gus and Jacquetta get ready amounted to me holding things, fetching things, and following all their orders.

By the time they were dressed and ready, beautiful and buzzing with excitement, I was thrilled to sit down and have them get me ready.

Once, a long time ago, my mother wanted me to learn how to do all of this myself, too, but we never got to the lesson. Now, like so much that I missed with her and my father, the ache of what I lost when they were killed grew more acute.

Finally, I stood before the mirror with makeup and hair perfect, and a gorgeous dress on.

"Gus, Jacquetta, are you sure this is the right thing to wear tonight? I mean, the last time I wore a dress with so many gems on it, it didn't go well." I ran my hand down the dress, the shimmers coming off the gems making my hand sparkle in the process like I was a creature made of light instead of a human forged in darkness.

"Yes," Jacquetta said, tilting her head and leaning against Gus.

"It's perfect," Gus said, wrapping her arm around Jacquetta and sighing.

While Jacquetta and Gus both wore the vibrant green of hellfire water, making Jacquetta's dark skin and hair shine and Gus' red hair and pale skin glow, I was in silver.

My dress was slim cut and hugged my body, although the skirt was loose enough that I could move comfortably in it. The neckline was like a basic tank dress with thin straps, but more thin straps covered in gems draped down my arms like stars.

Every part of my dress was covered in tiny gems and made me feel like a constellation or a prism.

"But we're just having dinner here," I said, touching one of the tendrils of hair framing my face that they left out of the complicated updo.

"And?" Jacquetta asked.

I smiled. She was right. As much as I was thrilled to be back in pants every day, there was something that made it all feel important when we dressed up. Not to mention that I got to spend time with the two of them, and help them get ready, too, when I knew they loved the process and the results.

Knocking from the door to the apartment made whatever words I was going to say run from my brain.

Gus and Jacquetta turned and headed for the door before I could even take a whole breath, but I trailed after them trying to get my breathing under control.

"Hello, King Tristan," Gus said, curtseying next to Jacquetta.

I looked to the table and realized he was here before the dinner. Did Gus or Jacquetta order dinner? Was I supposed to do that?

"Good evening, Ladies. I seemed to have found our dinner as I came to your door." He stepped in, followed by two servants with carts full of food.

"Here," he said, taking some of the plates from the cart, "let me help."

Soon, the carts were unloaded, the servants gone, and Tristan looked back and forth between Gus and Jacquetta.

"As much as I am happy to spend time with you, Ladies. Where is Lady Cinder?" he asked.

"Tristan," I said, still standing in the doorway to my room.

He turned and the light sparkling off my dress danced in his eyes.

"Cinder," he said, his voice a prayer and his gaze a caress.

I swallowed and stepped closer, my blood racing in my veins, and my stomach thrumming as if hummingbirds flew within it.

"You look beautiful," he said, reaching out a hand to take mine, and kissing the back of it, the heat from his lips searing my skin and making the fluttering in my stomach frantic.

"Maybe I should have saved this dress for your ball tomorrow." I wasn't even sure what I was saying. He didn't care what dress I wore to what occasion, and he would be polite enough to compliment any dress. Even the ones he hated.

"We can dance tonight. Who needs a ball to dance?" he leaned in and whispered in my ear, "and I would love to see the way the light shines from you when you move to music."

"I would love to dance," I said, my voice managed to sound strong and clear even as the breath remained thin in my chest.

"How about we do that first," Jacquetta said.

Gus hurried across the room, and turned the dial on the hellfire lamps until the light in the room lowered to something closer to the flicker of candles.

Jacquetta was in the other corner, winding the spinner on a small player piano.

I laughed and Tristan grinned while he pulled me close.

"Subtle," he said, which only made me laugh harder.

"They really are amazing," I said, looking at where Gus and Jacquetta were stepping together to dance themselves as the piano started to play a song that I thought was a lullaby and now seemed...something more.

We didn't move in the formal and staid steps of the valz, or any of the other dances I learned at Madam Valentin's.

Instead, Tristan wrapped an arm around my back, holding me tight against him with the other hand folded around mine. I held my free hand against his chest, feeling his heartbeat thump against my palm.

"Seeing you in this light, in this dress, was a very good idea."

His eyes, so green when we sparred, turned dark, and the shine of the gems danced in them. The gems were on my dress, but they made him sparkle.

The song ended and I should have pulled away. Tomorrow, Tristan would hold the other potentials this way. One day soon, I would have to watch as he made someone else queen.

But right now, tonight, I was the only one who could watch stars dance in his eyes. And I didn't want to look anywhere else.

CHAPTER 24

FOR NOW

"**A**re you sure you don't need more help?" Tristan asked Gus and Jacquetta.

"Yes, King Tristan," Jacquetta said, waving him away.

"Go, your majesty," Gus said, grinning and picking up the last of the plates to set on the carts waiting for the remains of our meal.

Tristan shook his head, but when I tugged on his hand, he turned and followed me.

We walked through the parlor and into my room. The balcony doors were closed to the cold, but I opened them and made my way to the railing.

He shut the doors and came up behind me, taking his coat off and draping it over my shoulders.

"You know," I said, taking his arms and wrapping them around me, "when you're close, I don't need the coat as much."

As if it was a trigger to the warmth of him, his chest grew hot under my hands. I leaned in closer.

"Cinder," he said, putting his forehead to mine and closing

his eyes, the smile falling from him. "I wish we didn't have to do this ball tomorrow."

I stiffened and swallowed, wondering if he would have rather we were all going to the training grounds instead of spending more time like this. Together and close.

"Tonight was better than some stupid ball where we have to be proper, and I can't be with you like this," he said and I let out a breath.

"But this is the way it has to be," I said. And even though I didn't like it either, I didn't want it to end. Not yet. No matter how hard it would be when it did.

He pulled his head back and ran a hand through one of the loose tendrils of my hair.

"For now," he said, looking into my eyes, "it has to be this way for now."

I nodded and tried to smile, but it was tremulous and fragile.

"Maybe..." he trailed off and ran his thumb along my cheek. "I want to tell you something, but I don't know if I should."

He shook his head and looked out at the courtyard where guards were wrapping up the last of their preparations for the trip before calling it a night. And still more guards were posted all over the exterior of the palace. Most of the ones on watch looked to the skies, which made me feel better, and allowed me to keep looking at Tristan.

Something ran through his mind, and I had no idea what it was. The joy and the awe that were there most of the night slowly seeped away. In their place, his jaw tightened, and the corners of his mouth turned down. All the lights that shined in his eyes while we danced and laughed with Gus and Jacquetta at dinner dimmed.

Finally, he looked back at me, and his smile was as forced as mine.

"When this war is over," he said, "and I want it to be over soon, I have so much to tell you."

"Are we officially at war?" I asked, my voice a hushed murmur on the winter wind as it moved in with all its chill frosts.

"Yes. There was a skirmish at sea. But Breakwater is okay, and Duchess Inara says her people are ready."

"But there were other, small things, going on before. So this skirmish must have been bigger?" I needed to write a letter to Inara, to check on her.

"Unfortunately, it was a lot bigger. We found out about it today. And at least we know now that they don't use the birds at sea."

"Duchess Inara probably has everything well in hand, but I would like to write her a letter."

His smile at that was real and he nodded.

"Of course. Now, though, we have to worry about when and where they'll march on us."

It was my turn to nod. All of Onyx wondered when and where it was going to come.

"The bigger problem is, we have to worry about Amethyst letting the Corvids use their lands to pass through and attack us."

Right. Why not be a snake allied with Corvid during war when they were snakes allied with Corvid the rest of the time too?

"So," I said, narrowing my eyes and thinking about that scene in the hallway, "you need me to be nice to Marquessa Ziya?"

Is that what that was? Was he just trying to win points to keep her country from attacking us, too, or aiding Corvid as they did?

"Cinder," he took a deep breath and shook his head, "you don't have to do anything. But I need to be nice to the Marquessa, and I need to keep doing these stupid balls."

Laughter burst out of me, and I leaned my head into his chest.

"Tristan, you sound more upset by the ball than you do about the threat of war."

He laughed then, too, but his laugh was low and short.

"You have so much to do right now," I said, pulling back and stepping out of his arms until we were connected only by our hands, the cold of the air rushing into the space he just kept warm. "And I think you need to get some sleep."

"Okay," he said, but he didn't let go of my hands, and he made no move to go inside. He just stared at me, all the sharpness of his face moments before melting into the look he got right before he fell asleep, as if all his muscles started to relax.

"Wait," I said, stepping closer again and putting a hand to his chest, "how tired are you?"

"I'm exhausted," he said with a laugh.

"Do…" I bit my lip and sucked in a sharp breath when he looked at my mouth, "do you want to stay and sleep on the sofa like you did before?"

His arms wrapped around me, and he kissed my forehead, holding me close and taking a deep breath.

"Yes."

We went back inside, past my bed, which would have been more comfortable and was calling my name, but would have ended with me in big trouble with the General and Gus and Jacquetta without explanation. And Madam Valentin would probably kill me with poisonous flowers in my bath.

But when we got to the parlor, Jacquetta and Gus were already behind their own closed doors, and the lights were even lower than they had been before.

He sat down on the sofa and pulled me into him so I was curled up on his chest with his coat still on my shoulders.

"Cinder," he said, running his fingers along my hairline,

"when we get to the training grounds, please come find me if I get too stuck in what I'm doing for too many days."

"Do you want me to make you spend the night in my tent? Because this seems to be the best way for us to get time together."

He kissed the top of my head and sighed.

"One day..." he said, his words ending in a yawn.

I let a small, breath of a laugh out and his hand ran up and down my arm.

"Yes. If I get too caught up, find me," he said, and his voice stopped as his breathing evened out.

Tristan was tired, and I must have been more tired than I realized because I still didn't know what he was going to say after one day. I just knew that it was today. And we were together. For now.

CHAPTER 25

COMMUNICATIONS

Tristan was gone when I woke up, but I wasn't on the couch anymore. I woke up in my bed with the blankets over me in my gem-encrusted dress, and Tristan's coat still around my shoulders.

A note sat on my nightstand.

My Beautiful Cinder,

Last night was a dream and I'm sorry to end it, but I needed to get back to work.

Please don't be upset that I wanted you to sleep soundly once I left, so I carried you to bed. I know it was a breach of your privacy.

Hopefully, leaving my coat with you will mean that I get to see you before the ball tonight. I suspect I will be in my public office all day.

There aren't words enough for me to thank you for last night.

Love, Tristan

Someday, I wanted to leave him a little note while he slept. Maybe at the training grounds I could find a way to make that happen.

It was a silly thing to want to do. But he had done it so many times, and I never got to return the favor.

Climbing from the bed, the gorgeous gown of the night

before seemed rumpled, although I wasn't sure how that happened when it was entirely covered in sparkles.

But at least this gown was easy to take off and lay on the bed. And the red day dress I pulled from the trunk was easy to put on in its place.

What was harder was trying to decide what to do with my hair.

My updo was messier than it had been, but somehow it managed to look deliberate. Like the tendrils were just multiplied.

So I left it, wrote a letter to Inara asking how she was, how Breakwater fared, and if there was anything I could do for her and her people from the palace, and folded Tristan's coat over my arm.

I didn't want to give it back. Not really. I wanted to fold it and put it in my trunk with his letters, and all my clothes, where my mother's shoes once sat.

But he asked for it, and it gave me an excuse to see him again.

Opening my door, I peeked out and tried to spot movement from my friends.

Gus and Jacquetta weren't up yet. I took a minute to order us some breakfast and left them a note that it was on its way before I headed down the hall.

No one else was up yet, either, except guards posted along the hallway.

By the time I got to Tristan's office, I was chewing on my lip and questioning whether he would even be in there.

Voices floated into the hall through the open doorway.

"My King, you need to think this through," the Chamberlain said, sounding exasperated.

"I have thought it through," Tristan said. "Which is the only reason I am waiting." If the Chamberlain was frustrated, Tristan was furious. If I was the Chamberlain, I would have probably shut my mouth.

"But there is an obvious answer here, and you refuse to do it," the Chamberlain said, persisting in what sounded like a suicidal argument.

"Chamberlain," General Pace said, "perhaps you need to explain to King Tristan why only you seem to think the course of action you are suggesting is the best one."

The General was going to kill the Chamberlain, that much was obvious. I didn't want to be around for that, and if I didn't get back soon enough, Gus and Jacquetta would panic on the day of a ball.

I swallowed and knocked on the door as I walked through it and into the office.

"Good morning," I said, smiling all around.

The General looked at Chamberlain Rezan like a smug cat who just stole the milk off the table.

Chamberlain Rezan spluttered as if there were some magic word that was just beyond grasp and it would save the world.

And Tristan...Tristan bit his lip around a smile, walking toward me while a blush spread across his cheeks.

"Lady Cinder, I am happy to see you this morning," he said, coming to take my hand. "I have something for you in my private office. Will you come with me?"

"Of course, King Tristan, I am happy to see you, too."

I turned toward the door and Tristan called over his shoulder, "I will be back in a moment."

We made our way into his office, and he slumped against a bookshelf, keeping hold of my hand and leaving the door open.

"Sorry, Cinder," he whispered, shaking his head with his eyes wide. "How much of that did you hear?"

"Enough to know you're angry with the Chamberlain, but that's all. I wasn't eavesdropping."

Much.

His smile was massive then and he tugged me to him, wrapping his arms around me and tucking his face into my neck.

I could have stayed like that all day, but I had a lot of Gus and Jacquetta time scheduled before the ball that they weren't going to let me forget.

Stepping back, I held out my arm with the coat draped over it and the letter to Inara.

"Your coat, as you requested, and I wrote a letter to the Duchess of Breakwater. Can you see that it gets delivered?" As I asked the question, I realized I was piling more on him at a bad time to do that. "It's okay though. I can get the letter out. Don't worry about it. You're too busy."

"Not for something you need," he said, standing up from the bookshelf and taking both things from me before tugging me back against his chest and holding me with his one free arm.

"Cinder, you ask little of me, and there's little I can give right now. But I'm glad I get to do this."

His eyes met mine. Our bodies close together, and our faces so close I could have bent my head up a fraction and kissed him.

Instead, I took a deep breath, buried my face in his chest and hugged him back.

"Thank you, Tristan." I stepped out of his embrace, letting his hand trail down my arm to lace his fingers with mine. "I'll see you tonight."

"Save a dance for me," he said, and I smiled before I turned to go back to my rooms, wondering what they were arguing about, and how soon it would be that the Chamberlain was reprimanded for it.

Maybe it already happened.

After that thought, my walk back to my room was light, and I was back to being buoyed by the night before.

Now all I had to do was make it through another ball.

CHAPTER 26

NAME CHANGE

"No," I said, looking at the dress they wanted to put me in, my heart twisting and making it difficult to speak.

"What do you mean, no?" Gus asked.

"It's beautiful," Jacquetta said, smiling down at it on the bed.

"Yes," I said, touching the flowing fabric of the sleeve. "But it's not what I want for today."

And I had my doubts I would ever want to see it again.

They looked at each other, sighed, and went back to my trunks to find something else.

On the bed, the dress they picked was pale gray, shining silver in a soft, delicate looking fabric that billowed at the sleeves, and the skirt but was cinched up tight in a corset look for the bodice complete with shaped cups for my breasts.

It looked like a wedding dress.

My heart squeezed looking at it, knowing that it would never be used.

Someone who wasn't me would wear something like it one day to marry Tristan, and if I wore it now, I wouldn't be able to forget that.

As they went through the dresses, one caught my eye.

"How about that one?" I smiled at the gray and silver they held. It was almost perfect.

"But you don't like the off-the-shoulder ones," Jacquetta said, pulling it out anyway.

"You're right." But I liked this one. Even if it wasn't actually practical. Even if I wouldn't be able to have full range of motion of my arms in it. It *looked* like I could kill someone in it. That was good enough.

"Okay, well we don't have time to argue," Gus said, holding it up for me to step into.

They helped me put it on and I was right. There wasn't full range of motion in my arms. But it did look great.

A strap of silvery leather circled my shoulders with the Dragon King sigil embossed on it. From that strap, from my arms around the back, flowed a single layer of organza in white as if it were a cape. The bodice was tight against me in a pale gray with something in the fabric that shimmered when I moved. More of the silvery leather crisscrossed the bodice in a way that made my breasts look far larger than they actually were. And the skirt, in the same shimmering gray, flowed down to the floor but a hand's width of white lace in a dragon pattern stuck out from under the whole back half of the hem and dragged on the floor.

Not only did I look like I could kill someone in this dress, I looked like someone who could do it with a pointed look and a raised brow.

"Perfect," I said, standing in front of the mirror, my hair in an elaborate braid that hung down my back.

Gus and Jacquetta wore the bright yellowish green of hellfire water again, Jacquetta in velvet and Gus in taffeta.

"We look good," Gus said, turning to look at herself in the mirror.

"Now we need to see everyone else." Jacquetta swept her skirt out as she turned to leave the room.

"Yeah," I said, following after her, "what will they wear on the eve of a war?" My voice thick with sarcasm.

Gus and Jacquetta shook their heads, looking at each other.

"Whatever helps them forget," Gus said.

I looked down at the hallway in front of me as we headed toward the ballroom, wondering if she was right.

Maybe my embrace of my position in this war, as someone who was going to fight it, would upset some of the people there.

"Cinder," Jacquetta said, a question in her voice, "why didn't you want to wear the other one?"

"Because it looked too much like a wedding dress to me." There was no point in hiding what I thought about it now. They weren't going to turn me around and make me change. But a twinge still ricocheted through me saying it out loud.

"Wedding dresses are gold," Gus said, as if that was common knowledge.

"Am I supposed to know that?" Because it wasn't like the people of Lehar had big weddings. They came to the manor in their best clothes, which were almost never that great, had Ash perform the ceremony, and left again.

"Have you never been to a court wedding?" Jacquetta asked, her eyes huge.

"No, I haven't." Even when Solaria married Lord Fall, Ash went and I stayed home, training.

General Pace met us at the top of the grand staircase.

"My apologies, I have been working," she said, looking over her shoulder toward the courtyard.

"You have much more important things to do than be at a ball," I said.

She turned back toward me and smiled. "Not if this goes the way I want it to."

I rolled my eyes and stepped past her.

"Tristan isn't going to do anything tonight." He wouldn't want to hurt anyone, least of all at a big ball. And he made it clear, right now, with all the threats in the air, he couldn't afford to send Ziya home and risk angering Amethyst.

"Not anything that would end it all," the General said, walking alongside me.

"Why does it seem like you know something?"

In her answering grin, I saw secrets and tricks waiting for me at this supposed ball. Something was up, for sure.

"Because I know a lot of things," the General said, smiling at me.

Reaching the giant doors of the grand ballroom meant stopping to wait while Jacquetta and Gus situated my skirt so the lace laid just right.

"Are you announcing me again tonight?" I asked General Pace.

She grinned, nodded, and stepped inside.

First, she announced Gus and Jacquetta, who slipped through the doors to leave me standing on my own.

Everything was exactly the same as it had been the last time, until…

"For King Tristan," General Pace's strong voice announced.

Wait, she didn't say that before. The 'for the King' part of her statement wasn't there the first time. My heart hammered in my chest.

"Your Candidate Potential for future Queen of Onyx, Lady Cinder Ahmya of Lehar, friend of Breakwater, hero of the Battle of Obsidian Wings."

I was going to pass out.

Friend of Breakwater? Hero? Battle of Obsidian Wings? Since when was any of that in my announcement?

But I didn't have time to think about it. I didn't even have time to register that there was a name for the fight with the Corvids now.

All I had time to do was shake out my hands, and walk through the doors into the ballroom.

CHAPTER 27

FOCUS

Stepping into the ballroom, every eye in the room turned toward me.

Gus, Jacquetta, and the General stood at my sides, their heads held high.

Jacquetta breathed deeply, her face in a small smile her mother would have been proud of.

Gus was on my other side, beaming with a wicked glint in her eye like she was daring one of the others to top that announcement.

The General waited in her perfect mask, not allowing anything to show.

I swallowed, holding my breath, waiting for…something. For the charge in the air to manifest into something that made sense.

What was that feeling?

But a second later, it happened.

All around the room, the guards saluted and bowed.

Trying to catch my breath, trying not to panic that they were doing it again so publicly, I found Tristan's eyes.

He stood on the dais at the end of the room, smiling that soft smile that made me feel like we were alone.

Then he saluted. And bowed.

My stomach thrummed as if my rampaging heart was centered there instead of my chest.

General Pace held her arm out to me, and I placed my hand on her elbow, my eyes not leaving Tristan's as we walked forward into the crowd of the few who were invited to this shrunken and impromptu ball.

People moved as we drew closer, blocking my view, and it was like a spell was broken.

I took in the looks on all the faces around me.

Chamberlain Rezan's narrowed eyes and pursed lips, the snake's mouth twisted to the side, the tight features of so many others, all of it made me clench my fists at my sides.

Maybe they were angry at my announcement, maybe they were angry at the way the guard responded. But I had to tell myself that the only thing that really mattered was Tristan's reaction.

Finally, we got to a point in the group gathered by the dais where I could see Tristan again.

He smiled as he looked out at us, not the private one that seemed like it held a sweet secret, but the public one of the King.

I took a deep breath as he raised his hands, the movement calling everyone to silence without a word.

"Good evening, everyone. I want to thank Chamberlain Rezan for setting this up on short notice."

Everyone clapped politely, and I pretended I didn't want to kill his chosen potential for a minute. Out of respect. For the Chamberlain's work. Not who the Chamberlain was championing. I had no respect for that. Not unless it was all a ruse and tomorrow the snake was undermined.

"You all know that I wanted to end this attempt to find a queen."

Murmurs and shuffling were all around me, but I froze.

Was he going to do it again? What would that mean for my move to the training grounds? And all my plans to keep him safe?

"But you have also given me support in this difficult time, and I want to thank you for that." He took a deep breath, and I couldn't breathe at all.

"For a while, I will be away from the palace. Unfortunately, I do not know how long I will be away, or how long this threat will plague Onyx. While I am gone, I leave it up to you what you do. You can stay at the palace. It is a safe place. Among the safest there is. Or you can go back to your homes, and wait until we can reconvene this search for a queen. I will promise you that nothing will be done regarding the search until we resume it officially."

Nothing? Nothing would be done? Was he planning on avoiding me the entire time we were at the training grounds? Because I was pretty sure that me having him come into my tent to sleep was something.

Unless it wasn't.

My breathing became my sole focus, something I had to do to avoid punching anyone as he continued to talk. About nothing, about details of the move, and how anyone who wanted to leave would get help and someone would keep in contact with them for when it was time to return.

How many times was I going to be shoved back and forth? How many times was I going to believe something and then have it—

I did it again.

Somehow, I forgot that I had a mission. And it wasn't to be Queen.

Up on the dais, Tristan said, "Thank you," and turned away to come into the crowd.

He was my mission, but not in the way that everyone thought. Not even in the way that I apparently thought.

Making his way through the people assembled around the dais, Tristan neared me, a smile on his face and his eyes on me.

Ziya stepped in front of him, blocking my view of his face until she curtsied.

I tried to smile, hoped it didn't look too constipated, and turned away.

The Amethyst snake was making her case, in whatever way she knew how, and I needed to focus on which of the other potentials still left would be best to steer him toward. That would help me get my own mind out of my way. I hoped it would, anyway.

But the other potentials were closed off, and as I got closer to them, they turned away from me. All of them.

What was going on?

Marquessa Ziya and Tristan were dancing the first dance of the ball, but I already wanted to retreat to my rooms.

Gus and Jacquetta were with a group of people I didn't know, laughing and smiling.

It wouldn't be fair to leave now, no matter how much I wanted to. They loved this. They would miss the palace. They would miss the moments they could chat with others and plot, to say nothing of the finery and luxury.

No, I may not have been someone people wanted to talk with, but I wasn't going to worry about it.

Jacquetta and Gus would know which of the Onyx potentials I should back. I would just leave it to them.

For now, I made my way to the refreshments table and picked up a glass.

Eventually Tristan would find me, or I would feel like I

waited long enough. Whichever came first. And either way, spending time with the food was always a good idea.

"Lady Cinder," Ursula said, and I turned toward her with a smile.

"Hello," I said, nodding when she curtsied. She was a terrible shot with a knife, but she was a nice person.

"I wanted to pass along an apology on behalf of my Lady Tanitha."

"Why would Lady Tanitha need to apologize?" Although I thought her parents should apologize to her for naming her after the former queen and butchering her name in the process.

Ursula stepped closer and turned so I could hear her whispers.

"She wants you to know that she supports an Onyx throne, but with the Amethyst threat, everyone is afraid to show the Marquessa that."

"Did the snake threaten people outright?" I whispered back, turning my gaze to the dance floor where Tristan and Ziya danced as the last notes of the quartanza played.

"No," Ursula said, shaking her head and keeping her voice low, "she is too smart for that."

I nodded. But not smart enough.

"Thank you, Ursula. Please tell Lady Tanitha that I understand, and the only person I am going to hold it against is the snake."

Ursula nodded and grinned, dropping into another curtsy, and behind her, Tristan walked toward me.

Somehow, I needed to keep him away from Ziya.

Maybe we could start with a dance.

CHAPTER 28

DIZZY

Ursula walked away and I waited, not able to stop my traitor heart from speeding up as Tristan came to my side.

"Good evening, Cinder," he said, his voice low and rich.

"Interesting speech," I said, biting my lip so I wouldn't say more.

He took a deep breath and looked over his shoulder at the Chamberlain hovering. "Will you honor me with a dance?"

"The honor is mine."

With my hand in his, he led me out to the dance floor, the people spread out to give us room as a valz started.

"At least with that ridiculous statement the Chamberlain, and everyone else, will just let us be and take care of the war for a while." He shook his head, but kept it contained so it didn't look like he was breaking the careful patterns of the dance.

"Is that why you put it all on pause?" I asked, when what I wanted to ask him was, what about all the time you'll be spending with me? Would that not count?

He smiled and I forced myself to turn away as the dance dictated.

"Not everything will be on pause, I hope," he said, rubbing a thumb along the back of my hand and pulling me closer than the dance said he should.

"No," I said, breathless, "not everything."

My plotting to steer him away from the snake would continue. But I knew what he meant, and his constant heat became indistinguishable to the warmth that spread through me.

"Just so you know, I am going to make this a short visit to the ball and blame the plans of leaving tomorrow."

I nodded. Just enough to let him know I heard, and not enough to make the watchful eyes around us question my dancing ability.

He sighed.

"Our dance in your parlor is my favorite."

"Mine, too." It wasn't a lie, but it was harder to say out loud than any lie I ever had to tell.

With a twirl and a dip, he had me smiling, matching his grin.

"Unfortunately, I have to dance with everyone. But after I dance with you again, I will leave the ball for the evening."

"You don't have to explain. I know you're busy."

"But not so busy that I don't want another favorite dance." His changeable eyes shined in a deep, dark blue like the hidden hollows in the river that teemed with so much life it seemed as if they were magic enough to make sense of the clergy living alongside streams.

"That will be my favorite part of tonight," I said.

He stopped turning me as the last of the notes played, but he didn't let me go when the only music left was the sound of my heart racing.

"Soon," he said, stepping back and kissing my hand, his lips lingering a moment and sending that intense heat ricocheting up my arm before he let me go and walked away.

In the middle of the dance floor, I decided not to watch as he danced with the others, and went back to the refreshments.

But Ziya crowded me, stepping right through my striking distance, and getting far too close to me.

Her purple hair was shot through with a color so dark it was almost black.

"Excuse you," I said. "You are blocking me."

My voice was flat, but the steel in it was so obvious her face fell.

She looked around, as if backup was going to materialize from the floor. But she ground her teeth and stepped away.

"Thank you." I took that last step to the table and picked up a glass.

"Are you having sex with the King?" she asked. "Because that would not garner much trust from the other potentials."

"What?" I asked, because she didn't really ask me that. She couldn't have. It was a ridiculous thing to ask about.

"I asked you if that is the reason he seems so willing to stop the queen contest, because he has a whore instead." She sneered and stuck her nose in the air.

"Listen," I said, leaning in with my voice low and in a sing song while I smiled and showed all my teeth, "you slave trading, worthless sack of skin. What I do, or do not do, is none of your business. And I would think long and hard about calling me names. The last one to do it wound up a little stabbed."

She pulled back, her eyes wide, and the dark in her hair leeched away until it was a pale violet.

"And I would keep this..." I waved a hand in the air like I didn't have the word, even though I did—I just didn't think 'bullshit' was appropriate to use at the moment, "chat to myself if I were you. After all, I am the hero of the Battle of Obsidian Wings."

Finally, she walked away, keeping her eyes on me, her lower lip trembling.

"Holy hellfire," I muttered, taking a big drink of my glass.

This wine I didn't like as much as the other, it tasted as if it came from a bad barrel.

I set it aside and grabbed a fresh one as a server brought out a tray. This one was cold and crisp and so much better. I drank it all down.

Well, at least I wouldn't have to do that again.

How did the snake think that was going to go? And who the hell told her she should try? Like I would…what? Be intimidated?

Laughing a quiet chuckle to myself, shaking my head, I put the empty glass down and wooziness passed through my body.

More than just my stomach, my entire body seemed to float away from me for a moment.

I clamped a hand down on the edge of the table and squeezed my eyes shut.

What was wrong with me? Was I sick? Did I just need to eat something?

On the table all manner of treats were spread on shining trays and towers. I reached out a hand that seemed to multiply as it got further away from me.

This was bad.

Swimming in my head, forcing everything in me to focus, I finally got my hand on one of the little puff pastries and shoved it in my mouth.

I missed biting the pastry properly and instead bit my own finger.

But eating the pastry didn't help.

After I swallowed, I held onto the table harder, focusing on a single point in front of me, praying to Mother and Father that I wouldn't fall down for what seemed to be forever.

"Cinder?" Tristan asked from beside me.

I turned and held onto him, not even bothering to pretend I

was alright. But the second his hand touched mine, heating up my skin, the dizziness started to wear off.

"Woah," I mumbled.

"Are you okay? You look a little green."

"Something hit me wrong. I don't think I should have any more of the wine." My vision cleared and my stomach settled. As fast as it came it left me.

"Maybe we should just get you up to your room then. No more dancing." There was still a line between his brows and his mouth worked like he was chewing on the inside of his cheek.

But his hand moved to my face, and I took a deep breath.

"No, I am fine now. We should dance." I smiled and although he didn't look convinced, he led me to the dance floor.

"If you need to stop the dance at any time, just say the word," Tristan said, turning me into position.

"Just hang on to me. I will be fine." It was true.

We moved through the dance, without the extra dip and twirl, or any additional flourish he usually added, but we did it.

After the music stopped, he leaned down and whispered in my ear, "Do you want one of the guards to lead you to your room?"

"Don't worry, I'll find someone to take me," I whispered back.

"Then I'll see you soon." He smiled at me and walked away.

I turned and didn't bother to check for anyone. None of the odd feelings came back. But I did avoid any of the food and drinks offered to me on the way out.

Something I had at the ball must have sat with me wrong. Ordering from the kitchens to my rooms seemed the only safe option. Besides, it gave me an excuse to have dinner with Tristan.

On my way out, I passed the snake.

The hate pouring off her was palpable, but when I raised an

eyebrow at her and set my jaw, she turned around to her Ladies in Waiting.

Coward.

No matter what happened, I was going to make sure she never became Queen of Onyx.

CHAPTER 29

EMPTY

I reached my room and opened the door, but a hand caught it as I stepped inside.

Looking up, Tristan was so close his eyes were all I could see.

"You were fast," I said, stepping into my parlor.

He smiled and followed me in, closing the door behind him.

"Well, I have something very important to do."

"Very important?" I tried not to let the disappointment show on my face, but his smile was soft as he walked across the room to the small player piano and wound the dial.

"Yes. I need to dance with you."

I sucked in a breath and my heart battered the inside of my ribs like all the birds in Onyx took off at once.

Tristan came to me on the first notes of the song, wrapping me up in his arms to hold me close like he did the night before.

We swayed side to side, but there was no attempt at real dancing, just moving as one with the music in the background.

He sighed.

"Now this is what I was missing," he whispered, his heart pounding faster than it should be under the circumstances.

Part of me wanted to ask him why his heart was galloping along in his chest under my hand. But I liked the idea that it was for the same reason mine was too much to break the illusion.

One day soon I would never be able to dance with him like this again, but for now he was with me.

"Did I see you talking to the Marquessa at the ball?" he asked after a time.

"Sort of," I said with a huff of a laugh.

"Cinder." There were equal parts warning and amusement in his voice.

But I couldn't tell him about what she accused me of. If I did, he would probably limit his time with me to avoid a scandal.

"It's fine. She's just a slave trader who disrespected you and I don't like her." There. I didn't need to elaborate from that.

"What? When did she disrespect me?" He pulled back to look me in the eye and seemed genuine in his confusion.

"You didn't notice the little stunt at the Corvid funeral?" Was he not paying attention at all?

He furrowed his brow, looked into the middle distance, and shook his head.

"No, I don't remember her at all that day. I was paying too much attention to the Corvids to even notice her,"

"I noticed for you. And she was disrespectful. So we had words." I nodded once. It was understandable he paid more attention to the threat he saw at the time, but that didn't mean she was going to get away with it as long as I was around.

Tristan turned and studied me, not hiding his assessment.

For a moment I wanted to hide my face, but in this there was no point. He needed to see that I meant it. I wouldn't put up with people treating him as Ziya had.

He ran his hand up my back until he cupped my cheek, running a thumb along my cheekbone.

"No matter how much I want to protect you from my problems," he said, "you're just going to keep taking them on as if they're your own."

"Because they are." He was my King. Yes, it took me a while to understand what that meant. But I knew now, the only reason my country and my people were protected at all was because of his lineage. Because of the fear it inspired. I would stand in front of him to protect my people every single day as long as I needed to.

Tristan's eyes melted into mine, eyes that turned dark with gold and green flashing in the low light of the room.

Bending toward me, his eyes slipping shut, I panicked and rested my forehead against his as we continued to sway back and forth.

I wanted to enjoy our time together, but if he kissed me…I didn't trust my ability to let him go when it was time.

His sigh was heavy as the last refrain from the song poured into the room, the final note drowned out by my growling stomach.

"Do we need to order food now?" he asked, laughter in his voice.

"Yes, please." I grinned and he let me go to grab the notepad.

Picking out what food to order with him sent an ache through my heart. It was something I watched my parents do together a thousand times. One day, Tristan would do this with someone else.

He turned to put our finished order into the messenger tube, and I turned away, taking deep breaths to get myself back on track.

Running a hand up my arm, he came up behind me.

I leaned back into him, and he slipped his arms around me.

"Cinder." His voice was soft, and he fit his head into my neck, kissing me on the tender skin there.

My heart ratcheted up the pace, and panic followed on the

frantic heels of the blood in my veins. It was too much. He was too much. I was going to forget myself.

"Did you erect a canopy over an area of the training grounds?" I asked, my voice hurried and too loud in the quiet of the room.

But he only breathed out a laugh, just a burst of hot air on my neck and said, "Of course. Your suggestion was a good one. In fact, I think you'll like what we did with it."

I turned around and grinned at him, getting out of his embrace to hang onto only his hand as I sat at the table.

Distance. Distance was good.

"Really? Are you saying there's a surprise for me tomorrow when we get there?"

"Actually," he said, sitting across from me, taking my hand in both of his, "I think there will be a few while we're there. Or I hope so anyway."

"That sounds like you've been plotting." I grinned and laughed when he put a hand to his cheek in mock surprise.

"No, not plotting." The smile on his face changed from mischievous to thoughtful and he pulled my hand to him to kiss my palm, keeping his eyes on me. "Just dreaming."

"Dreaming," I mumbled, my voice like a sigh.

I understood what that was like, I was doing far too much dreaming lately.

Before I could respond, shake my head, and ask something else that would get us away from the topics that seemed to be dangerous, a knock came at the door.

Tristan smiled and got up, letting go of my hands.

All I had to do was make it through tonight, and then we would both be so busy with the preparations for war that we wouldn't have time to get too close and ruin my mission. But watching as he led the server in and started to unload the plates, I couldn't help wishing it were different.

Even though I knew I was supposed to let go, I grasped at the air while I waited for him to come back to me.

CHAPTER 30

VENOM

Dinner was over, and I needed to make him go so he could sleep, but I couldn't do it.

"It is tents, though, right?" I asked with a small laugh, leaning on my hand with my elbow on the table and my other hand in Tristan's, our fingers threaded together. Long ago, I shoved the straps of my gown that trapped my arms up onto my shoulders so I could move and be comfortable.

"Yes," he said, shaking his head with a smile. "Unfortunately, we will all be staying in tents."

My grin masked the mad laughter I wanted to break out in.

"Tristan, I don't care about a tent."

He pulled his fingers from mine and ran them down my hand instead, nodding as he looked down at the small scars still left on the knuckles he played with.

"Gus and Jacquetta might hate it," I said, and it was his turn to squeeze his mouth tight so he didn't laugh too hard.

Our voices were low, the hellfire lights turned to a glow, and it seemed like magic, this quiet. So much so I was loathe to break the spell with an outburst, and by some unvoiced agreement, Tristan seemed to do the same.

We existed in a bubble that didn't stretch beyond this room. One in which I could pretend that I would always be as happy as I was while he played with my hand.

"Cinder," he said, his voice so low and rich it hummed within me, "can I ask a favor of you?"

"Of course." What part of all the promises I made to him did he question?

"There will be times, while we're at the training ground, that things are going to go bad—"

"No." I grabbed his hand, holding it tight.

"No?" He snapped his eyes to mine, worry etching a line between his brows.

"Tristan, whatever you need of me, it's yours. But we aren't going to talk about what could go wrong tonight. I want to have tonight with you to pretend that nothing will go wrong ever again."

His eyes, the hazel that took on different colors in different light and seemed to hold every possible color within their depths, changed in front of my eyes from deep, rich brown to a vibrant green. It was as if the fertile soil within him sprouted life and grew as I watched.

"Come on," he said, pulling me to my feet and folding me into his arms.

"Are we dancing without music?" I asked, my voice barely a whisper.

"No—Yes—I—"

"It's okay. You can just hold me." I moved my hands up his chest to play with his hair at the nape of his neck.

He closed his eyes and hummed the contented sound of a well-loved cat.

"One day," he said, kissing me on the forehead and then the cheek. "Every day..." he fluttered soft kisses along my neck while my heart stuttered, and the air after a thousand arrows parted it whirled in my stomach.

"Why didn't you tell us—" Gus' voice sliced through our bubble and stopped just as fast as it came.

I looked up toward the door along with Tristan, but I didn't let go of him.

Gus and Jacquetta stood there, mouths agape. But they existed in a different reality than the bubble of Tristan and I, and my mind couldn't put the two together.

Tristan sighed and pulled back until my hands fell to rest on his chest.

"Pardon the intrusion," Jacquetta said, recovering first and dropping into a curtsy as she tugged Gus down with her.

"You're fine," I said. "Come on. Shut the door."

I shook my head and Tristan grinned, turning to bury his face in my hair as he chuckled silently.

My friends did as I asked, but their shock morphed into sly grins and sideways glances.

"We were worried when we realized you were gone," Jacquetta said.

"Everyone else is still dancing and acting like this is the biggest party of the year," Gus said, shaking her head.

Tristan and I looked at each other, both of us knowing it was possible this was the *last* party of the year. At least at the palace. And any other party that happened in Onyx while we were under the threat of war breaking out all over the country, or while we were fighting the war itself, would be shadowed by the long pall of death as it stalked the battlefield.

"Cinder didn't feel well for a moment, but she's fine now." Tristan smiled at me, as if they were going to believe that was the reason why we came up here. "I got her to sit and eat with me."

Gus nudged Jacquetta, her face falling into hard lines and pursed lips.

"I told you that's what she said."

"That's what who said?" I asked, adjusting my position so

Tristan and I stood side by side, linked by his hand at the small of my back and mine on his chest, not willing to let go of him completely yet.

"Gus heard a couple Ladies whispering that one of the potentials was angry and put something poisonous in your drink," Jacquetta said, her face in a grimace.

"What?" I asked, my voice hard. Which one of them tried to make me sick?

"But," Tristan said, narrowing his eyes under a furrowed brow and looking at me, "you got better so fast. What kind of poison does that?"

"One that didn't work," I said and turned back to Gus. "Which one?" They needed a visit from my knife before I left for the training grounds.

"I don't know," Gus said, her voice as sharp as mine and her eyes sharper. "They whispered it on the other side of one of those pillars, by the time I shoved my way around it to see who was there, they were in the crowd."

Even though I asked, it didn't matter that she wasn't sure. As far as I was concerned, there was only one of the potentials who was likely to try and poison me.

Poison was the weapon of a snake.

Tristan's arm came around me and held me close to his side as he turned, his eyes squeezed shut and his breaths deep through his nose.

"I'm okay." I took his free hand, unfurled his fist and threaded my fingers with his. "It's okay because I'm fine. And I'll be going to the training grounds tomorrow where none of them will be."

He opened his eyes and nodded, looking down at me as a muscle in his jaw jumped.

"And we won't let any of them get anywhere near your food or drinks again," Jacquetta said, crossing her arms to hide the shaking in her hands.

Judging by the fury in her eyes, I assumed she wasn't shaking in fear.

"No, but some of them will get a little pep talk about what happened at the Battle," Gus said, turning around and calling over her shoulder, "I'll be right back."

"So will I," Jacquetta said, following after Gus.

The second the door shut behind them, Tristan wrapped me up, lifting me from the floor and carrying me to the sofa.

He sat down and folded me onto his lap, holding me as if he could cover me completely.

"It will never happen again," he said, his voice low but as dark as the obsidian walls. "As soon as we return from the training grounds, I will see to it."

A promise he couldn't keep, but something cracked in me as I tightened my hold on him because I knew he would try.

CHAPTER 31

PROMISES

When Gus and Jacquetta returned, it was to Tristan and me in the same position, wrapped up in each other and holding on like if we didn't the other would be snatched away.

Jacquetta brought out a blanket, dragged from my bed, and draped it over us.

Gus sighed and they retreated to their rooms.

Tristan shifted so his legs were on the sofa and swept mine over to lay alongside his.

"Everything in me says not to put you at risk," he said, his voice a hushed croak. "I want you there with me. You're more than capable, but if something happens to you...and now, if I leave you here, it might be just as bad."

"I'm going with you," I ran a hand along his cheek, the muscles in his jaw relaxing as I did. "Whoever did this won't get another chance."

"No, they won't." He tucked the blanket in tighter around us and kissed my forehead. "And I'm going to put someone in charge of finding out who did this."

"You can't." He stiffened, but I kept on. "No one should be distracted from the real threat. And I'm going to be fine. I am fine. We both are."

"We will be." He kissed my head again and ran his hand up my back.

I fell asleep to his heartbeat, and wondering how long we would have to wait until the snake left the country. Because she did this. And Tristan couldn't know. If he did, we might end up at war with Corvid and Amethyst at the same time.

Before I even opened my eyes in the morning, I knew he was already gone from my apartment. It was cold. And when he was with me, that was impossible.

Gus and Jacquetta were pensive and jittery while we made the final preparations to leave the palace, but they would be more comfortable once we were all at the training grounds. They had to be, because we had a lot of work to do.

"Do we have everything ready?" I asked, stepping out of my room and looking at the collected trunks.

"Yes, we're ready," Gus said, throwing the lock on one of the trunks.

"Let's go. I want to get there before lunch," Jacquetta said and refastened her cloak for the third time.

They were both in their training clothes and I was in mine. There was no point in bringing most of our trunks. Madam was going to send more training clothes for us, and we all had some things we didn't want to leave behind.

At least the rest of our trunks were being put in storage. I didn't trust the snake not to destroy everything if she could.

I opened the door to the hallway and almost ran into a guard who marched back and forth in front of it.

"Hello," I said, Gus and Jacquetta leaning around me so they could see who I was talking to.

"My Lady," the guard said, saluting and bowing. "I will escort you to your carriage."

Looking back at Gus and Jacquetta, I nodded.

All of us trailed the guard, except for the servants carrying our trunks to all the places they needed to go.

Part of me chafed at having this guard, no matter how good she was at her job, and no matter how loyal she might be. But I tried not to be irritated knowing it was something Tristan did so *he* felt better about being away from me.

If he continued trying to look out for me, chances were it was going to get him hurt.

He would get less protective at the training grounds…I told myself that anyway.

Out front, the carriage waited, and the rest of the traffic in the courtyard was all made up of guards.

Gus and Jacquetta probably felt even more out of place as they fidgeted.

But this made more sense to me.

Every section of road we passed closer to the training grounds was one step closer to being safe from poison, being useful, and doing what was needed for Tristan and Onyx.

I kept my focus on that, the promise of where we were headed, and not on the thick air in the carriage. So much so that by the time we rolled to a stop, my leg was bouncing up and down, and I almost leapt out the door as soon as the footman opened it.

Making my way out, my hands in fists, I finally understood what Tristan meant.

Overhead was no longer a wide-open sky.

The entire training grounds were covered in a massive dome supported by sweeping arches of what looked like metal or smooth stone. Through the dome, the sky was visible, but only to a certain extent.

It was muted and turned into a play of light and shadow instead of sun and clouds.

Whatever it was made of, it wasn't glass. It was in panels that spanned from one arch to another, and there were varying levels of opacity and clarity, almost clear and tinted white.

"Beautiful, isn't it?" Tristan asked.

I whirled around to find him staring at me, his smile soft.

"Amazing," I said, my heart speeding up. "We made it."

"Yes." He grinned, stepping closer to me and threading our fingers together. "Now no one can hurt you."

My stomach dropped. He had to know it was a lie even as he said it.

He may have wanted to believe it, but he had to know, none of us were safe.

"Tristan," I said, shaking my head.

"No, Cinder, listen." He came closer and put his other hand to my cheek. "As long as we're together, I won't let anyone hurt you."

"You will."

"Stop—"

"Listen. I know you want that. I know you believe it. But I want you to promise me. This is a war. We're not playing a game here, under this dome. I want you to promise me that you won't try and protect me and hurt yourself in the process. The country needs the Dragon King."

He let out a long rasping breath that sounded as if he wanted to growl instead, but his hand was still gentle as he moved it from my face to trail down my back and pull me into his arms.

"It won't come to that," he said, as if it was a vow.

"Promise me."

"Wow," Gus said, staring up and turning slowly in a circle.

"So, which tent is ours?" Jacquetta asked. Her voice in the curl of her lip made it seem as if forcing her to spend time in a tent was a personal insult to her.

Tristan let me go and turned toward my friends, swallowing and shaking his head before he plastered on a good-natured grin.

"I'll show you to your tent, Ladies."

As they walked away, leaving me to follow after them, all I could think about was that he didn't promise.

CHAPTER 32

ALL OF THEM

Our tent was larger than I was expecting.

Standing in the middle of it, I couldn't help but smile.

"Are the barracks tents this nice?" I asked and Tristan slipped his arms around me, his chest to my back and his palms on my stomach.

"Unfortunately, General Pace thinks tents like this are too extravagant." He kissed my neck, and I could feel his grin.

My tent was shaped like an x. Three of the offshoots held beds almost as large and opulent as our beds at the palace, filling those sections of the tent from one wall to the other.

Gus and Jacquetta directed the guards carrying in our trunks to the beds that the trunks belonged at the foot of.

If I had my way, I would have put them somewhere I didn't have to climb over them to get into bed, but I let Gus and Jacquetta set everything up as they chose. Which included moving the round dining table and all four chairs around it to the front of the tent and putting the two desks together with their chairs side by side in the space closest to the beds.

Narrowing my eyes as they unloaded some things from the trunks onto the desks, I shook my head.

They were turning the desks into vanities.

Here.

It didn't matter, we had a lot of work to do.

"What about your tent?" I whispered, turning my head to kiss Tristan's cheek.

"Do you want to see it?" His voice was even lower than mine, right into my ear, his lips brushing the earlobe.

A pounding coursed through my veins. I knew I needed to move soon, or I was likely to break my own rule and kiss him even if it was in front of all the people around us who were so far dutifully ignoring us.

"Of course."

He grinned and broke away, taking my hand to turn us toward the door.

We made our way through the guards moving at steady clips all over the training grounds as all the last things to get this whole process started were put into place.

Two tents and a main thoroughfare sat between Tristan's and mine, which was fine with me. It would look good for those people who cared, and work well for him coming to spend his nights with me.

But before we reached it, I knew it was his.

Larger than mine, yet still dwarfed by the barracks tents and some of the others the guard were using for I didn't know what, it was as black as the Obsidian Palace with small flags of the Dragon King sigil flying from the center post and all the corners.

"Subtle," I muttered, and he grinned.

"For some reason, General Pace said this would be good for morale." He tugged me in the canvas door, and I had to think about that later.

Inside the tent, it was much larger than I assumed from outside.

Right inside the doorway were two guards, just past them were dummies with different suits of light and heavy armor hanging on them.

I paused, wondering if I was supposed to go any further. This seemed set aside as a kind of foyer, but Tristan pulled me after him past the figures and into a space with a giant metal table with maps of Onyx laid out across it.

Maps of every duchy seemed to be there, in haphazard stacks with small rocks holding down the corners where they wanted to curl.

Beyond the large main space were two open offshoots, one packed with trunks, the other with shelves full of books and parchment. One more offshoot had a panel of canvas covering the entryway, blocking it off.

"This reminds me of your public office at the palace," I said, looking around at what was a great war room, but seemed like a shitty place to sleep.

"You're right," he said, walking backward and pulling on my hand so I followed him to the canvas flap.

He pushed it aside and gestured with his head for me to look inside.

But when I did, I didn't find a bed like I expected.

There was nothing in there but a cot, more trunks, and the outline of a door on the other side leading to the outside.

"Where is your bed?" I whispered. The King should have had at least one as nice as mine.

"You already saw it," he whispered back, squeezing my hand and making me bite my lip. "That is, if that's okay with you."

"I'm pretty sure I already said it was." My voice was more playful than the fear doing sword fighting maneuvers through my body made me think it would be.The sweat popping up along the small of my back also didn't make me trust saying anything else or I might betray myself.

Tristan lifted his other hand, and brushed the hair away from my cheek.

"Cinder." His voice was like a hand running along my skin. All at once, the fear changed, morphing into heat that settled in my stomach and went lower. I wanted to drag him back to my bed right away, to have him wrap me in his arms and whisper in that same voice while he ki— No. I couldn't kiss him.

Smiling, I tugged on his hand, pulling him after me back into the main room.

"But first," I said, "I don't know what you need to do today. I need to eat and then I want to tour this entire place."

He laughed, but stopped following after me.

I turned back to him, taking a step so we were close again, so I could feel the warmth radiating off him and bask in it.

"Trust me when I say that I want to go with you," he said, "eat with you, take you on that tour, all of it."

"But you're busy. And probably will be every day, all day." I nodded. I didn't expect anything else.

He sighed and touched his forehead to mine.

"Nights, though…" he whispered.

"Yes." I reached up a hand and put it against his cheek. He leaned into it before turning his head and kissing my palm. "Those are mine."

"All of them." His eyes, flashing green, bored into mine and my heartbeat skipped, losing all rhythm.

Those words required a response, but I couldn't form one. I didn't know how. Did he mean it? Or was he just saying them now, while we were here? What would happen after the war when we were all back at the palace with the other potentials? With Ziya? I wasn't the right one. No amount of wanting to be would change that.

I nodded anyway, hoping he took it to mean whatever he

wanted. Because I didn't know what I did. And one of us should have felt secure in that moment.

He smiled and let out a shaky breath before he picked me up, lifting me above him so I could look down onto his shining, beautiful face full of joy.

"King Tristan," General Pace said from the space by the armor and Tristan put me down, kissing me on the forehead before he turned to look her way.

"Yes, General?"

"The others will be here any minute to start their reports," she said, her eyes darting back and forth between us with a twitch of her brow.

"Don't worry, I need to go," I said, pulling away from him and heading toward the door.

For a minute, I thought he would let me leave without anything else to confuse me. But he ran his hand down my arm as I walked away, and squeezed my fingers before he let me go.

Why did I agree to let him come to my tent?

Making my way past the General, avoiding her searching eyes, I pushed aside the tent flap and stepped into the light of the chilled winter day.

The air set my body back to its baseline, and I breathed in greedy gasps.

All around me people prepared for war.

I was supposed to help keep them alive, to help all of Onyx survive this. But how was I supposed to survive all the nights with Tristan in my bed without shattering into a thousand pieces when it was all over?

CHAPTER 33

LEGEND

"This is really how we're going to eat every single meal?" Jacquetta asked, sitting next to me, and looking down at the plates in front of her, despondent.

"Probably not every meal," I said, taking a big bite of my roll. I was more at home in this giant mess hall tent surrounded by guards than I ever was at the quartz table with the other potentials.

"Come on, Jacquetta," Gus said, patting her hand, "it isn't so bad."

"Listen," I said, pushing my little ramekin of berries her way as a peace offering, "the cooks here are very busy, and I know you don't want to add to their workload."

Sure, this was strange for Jacquetta, but she was too good a person not to see that a bunch of demands from us for private dining arrangements would a be a shit thing to do under the circumstances.

"Maybe we can make friends with some of the guards," Gus said, smiling and looking around like she would be able to find one right then and there with just a glance to be fast friends with.

Maybe she could. Gus and Jacquetta were both better people than me, and far better *at* people than me. Just because I didn't know how to walk up to someone and be friendly, didn't mean that everyone had the same challenge.

I preferred to hide and then stab. Not conducive to making friends.

Being forced to not stab anyone for a while did mean I was amassing quite the collection of them, though.

"Do you think you'll be part of the war councils the King is having?" Jacquetta asked, finally breaking off her funk, and snapping me away from my thoughts.

"Maybe. I don't know." I popped another bite into my mouth and thought about it. "To be honest, I'm helping in the way I know how to. All I know of trying to manage troops and coming up with an actual battle plan is from far too long ago, and I was only marginally successful."

And that success came because of the explosion that tore apart my parents. It had nothing to do with me, so I didn't count it.

"So," Gus said, playing with her food and drawing out the word, which concerned me, "are you going to keep training us, too?"

"Oh," for some reason I wasn't expecting her to ask that, and I didn't really have an answer. "If you want me to. I spent all day running through how I thought I would train the guards and what equipment we have. I'm sorry, I didn't think of how I would train you at all today."

"Which is fine," Jacquetta said, shooting a look Gus' way that I didn't understand. "Maybe in the morning just give us a task to work on together, and then check back every once in a while?"

"You still want to learn, too?" I asked, expecting it from Gus, but not from Jacquetta.

"Everyone needs to be ready," Jacquetta said, and Gus nodded.

I smiled. They would be better off the next time they were in danger. I had no doubt about that.

"Then, no problem. I'll come up with something for you every day, too."

Gus did a little dance in her seat, and Jacquetta grinned.

But I was far away in my mind, running through the ways in which I would form a training plan for the guard, and the way I would work with Gus and Jacquetta, too.

"Lady Cinder," someone said over my shoulder, and I turned around.

The young man from the Shield House stood near my chair.

"Hello," I said, my voice bright, but a second later the smile on my face dropped. Was something wrong? "What are you doing here?"

"Do you mind if I sit?" he asked, and I nodded, holding out a hand for him to sit next to me.

"Augustina, Jacquetta, my Ladies in Waiting," I said, introducing them and waiting for him to say his own name because I didn't catch it while we were there.

They all nodded to one another, hellos muttered all around.

"I am Layton, one of King Tristan's wards." He grinned at them, and they smiled back.

"My Lady," he said, "the Shield House is fine, all the children were well when I left, if that is what you mean."

It was my turn to nod while I took another bite.

"But I needed to move on. I have been working there for three years. It is wonderful but exhausting, and I wanted to try and make it on my own."

"So you joined the guard?"

"Only just. I want to be of service to the country and the King after so much was done for me when I really needed it."

"Well, Layton," I said, "I think you'll find this is a bit different than working with the kids at the Shield House."

He laughed and nodded.

"I hope so. Although I can't imagine it will be tougher."

"Probably not." I shook my head, laughing with him. "I know I couldn't take care of all those children. But this, this I can do."

"You did well with them," he said, taking a bite.

Jacquetta and Gus followed every word of our conversation, but seemed confused about what to add. And I couldn't blame them. This was foreign to them in every way.

"Are you really our trainer?" he asked finally.

"She's the best trainer the guard could ask for," Gus said.

"If she can help a bunch of Ladies in Waiting," Jacquetta said, "she can help the guard."

"They're just proud of me," I said, trying to wave off their praise.

"But I heard you're the hero of the Battle of Obsidian Wings," Layton said.

I sighed. That title was going too far. I wished I knew who came up with the whole melodramatic thing. But instead, I just got to walk around carrying it. Like the title of Lady, it chafed.

"Lady Cinder was so good at the battle," Gus said, as if she was there for all of it and not just the first tiny part, "you wouldn't believe it."

"She rode a Corvid," said a guard sitting down the table from us, turning toward the conversation.

It was as if the damn was broken.

From all over the dining tent, guards came to tell the stories they heard of the battle. Most of them were true, but a few times I had to interject with a correction. The problem was that as they told the story, as more and more 'I heard this' and 'I heard that' pieces of it came out, the awe on the faces around me grew.

No matter how much I wanted just to be another trainer,

just to lead them through the skills and the drills I thought they would need, as they all talked about me and the things I had done, my stomach sank more. Because they were building me up to be so much more than an assassin.

An assassin wasn't a hero of anything. An assassin was supposed to be a shadow, coming and going with barely anyone registering their presence or the lack of it. The most important ability any assassin could develop was the ability to be invisible.

But now, as they bandied about the tales of what I did, the light shining on me grew brighter by the second.

I clenched my fists in my lap, my appetite disappearing as they talked and rallied around the myth of me as hero.

With every new set of ears listening, and with every new mouth singing my praises, the reality of what it meant settled further into my veins.

My days as an assassin were over. Whether I wanted them to be or not.

CHAPTER 34

HIGH

I stood in the middle of the open space where we would be training the guard, my hands on my hips and my head tilted back while people went in all directions around me as if I was a boulder in the middle of a meeting of more rivers than there were in Thirteen Rivers Valley.

But Gus and Jacquetta were on either side of me, watching out for anyone who might not see me here while I tried to figure out if my plan would work.

I had one day, less than that now, until I needed to have a plan in place to train these guards. The guards who were already trained up in the traditional manner, and the ones who I needed to start from scratch with. And my plan had to take them both into account if this was going to be a success.

This had to be a success.

War was an unforgiving mistress.

And I needed to be an even bigger bitch than she was.

"Okay, I think I know what I need to do." I turned to Gus and Jacquetta and took a deep breath. This idea was more than a little nuts.

"So, what do we need to do to help?" Gus asked, without

even trying to ask what it was she was signing up to help with.

"I need a bunch of ropes tied together. A bunch."

"You know what?" Jacquetta said after a moment while she shook her head. "I'm not going to ask why."

"Good," I said. It was better if they didn't try to talk me out of it. "Meet me over at the edge."

Pointing to the base of one of the stone support pillars, I waited until Gus and Jacquetta both nodded and headed off to find ropes. Then I made my way to the pillar at the edge of the training grounds.

It didn't take them as long as I expected to collect the ropes.

They found me, carrying some ropes in their arms, with a few guards following after them hauling even more.

"Perfect," I said, tying a couple ends together to start right away. "But I will probably need even more than this."

Gus and Jacquetta sighed in unison, and Gus nodded to the guards who shrugged and ran off.

"More coming up," Gus said, and started tying the lengths together herself while Jacquetta made a line out of the piles of each length of rope, so we knew what was tied to what. And I hoped, so they were less likely to end up in a giant mess of knot.

I took the first coil of rope and draped it over my shoulder, across my body.

The pillar of stone was smooth on the sides, but I ran my hands over it to see if I could find a place where there was something I could grab onto. No luck.

So, the only option left for me was the rampart wall.

Here, a mere step or two away from the pillars holding up the dome, the stone was so old that there was more than enough room in the mortared joints to scale the wall.

Once I was up high enough, the connected lengths of rope trailing after me, I looked back toward the pillar that I really needed to get to. Just to be sure, it was better to go a little higher still.

Someone didn't make the pillars as tall as the ramparts, and I wasn't sure if that was smart or not. The whole place was teeming with guards, so taking away the easy shot at us with the dome seemed like it would make any attack foolish.

At regular intervals along the wall, guards were staring up into the sky. None of them noticed a Lady of the court climbing the wall beneath them on the inside of the training grounds.

Being invisible to them, if only for a moment, somehow gave me the confidence to stop worrying if this would work and know that it would.

Turning to check again, I was high enough over the top lip of the pillar that I trusted I could make it.

So, I brought my feet up another notch in the mortar, gave myself some more push and spring, and leapt, twisting in the air, to grab onto the edge of the pillar's top stone. Jumping with the rope dragging at me left me frozen for a moment on the pillar, wondering if I would fall after all. It was a strange and unnatural feeling to be tied to the ground.

"Cinder," Gus yelled below me, panic in her voice.

"Have you dropped your brain?" Jacquetta screeched.

"You both watched me climb the wall, what did you think I was going to do?" I shook my head and made my way around to the other side of the pillar, inching my hands along the edge because I couldn't rely on my feet at all.

"Not that," Gus said.

"You're not a squirrel," Jacquetta yelled.

Laughing, I got to the giant metal arches that held up the massive panels of the dome. They were almost a solid beam of thick metal, but someone put circular holes in them at regular intervals as if they wanted to make the beams lighter. Or maybe they just wanted to make sure I could climb them.

I moved my way onto the beam, using the holes for hand and foot holds. Once I was in a more secure position, hanging with my back to the ground below me, I shook out my hands one at a time and adjusted the rope where it hung across my chest.

Murmurs floated up to me, but I didn't bother to check what Gus and Jacquetta were talking about. The sooner I finished this, the better.

Climbing up the curved beam, hand over hand and foot after foot tucked into the holes, I made it far enough to check where I was in the arch and where I was in relationship to the ground.

Almost halfway up the curved dome, I shook out one hand after another and then took the time to shake out my feet, allowing all the blood to flow back into them before putting them back. Then I turned, letting go with one hand, to dangle and look down below me.

Gus and Jacquetta, surrounded by a massive mob of guards, all with their faces turned up to stare at me, were almost in the middle of the space I wanted the rope to dangle down to.

But the rope hanging off me, tied length after length together, stopped before it reached the group.

"Tie on more ropes," I yelled down at them.

Jacquetta shook her head.

Shit. I was too high for them to hear me clearly.

I tugged on the rope dangling from me until I pulled up the spot where the first two were connected. I held it up then pointed down to the dangling end before dropping the rope to display my hand to them with four fingers held up and point at the end again.

Gus nodded and started pointing at guards around her who ran off.

The bigger problem was that for them to reach the dangling end of the rope, I needed to climb back down part way again.

I sighed and moved back the way I came, checking below me more regularly than when I came up. I didn't want to do more of this damn climbing than I had to.

Finally, I got to the point that the end of the rope, far below, was in one of the guard's hands and they were attaching more lengths to the end.

While they did that, I rested my limbs, one at a time.

After spending so much time at the palace, my first thought about the body aches I would get when this was done and what I would do about them, was that a bath would help. But here, I didn't have a bath. I had the massive shower tent like everyone else. And that didn't sound relaxing at all.

One of the guards below me held out a thumbs up, which looked a little wavery from up here, but I was relatively sure that's what they did.

So, I was off again, climbing back to the place I reached before, not quite the middle and height of the giant arch.

Getting there seemed to be faster this time. Once I was there, tying off the rope that was wrapped around my chest was more complicated.

The hole in the beam was perfect, wrapping it through two holes gave me plenty of strength, but holding onto the whole thing as it dragged at me while I unwound it from my body was a pain in the ass.

Finally, I got it done, tied tight, and unwrapped from me.

I took hold of the rope and swung my legs off the beam, wrapping the rope between my feet.

But looking down at the crowd below me as the rope stilled, I realized that it wasn't just the guard and Gus and Jacquetta gathered around to watch now.

Tristan held the end of the rope in his hands, his head tipped back to stare up at me, and I didn't think it was a trick of the distance that his face was all angles and pissed off lines.

"Shit," I muttered. He said he would trust me to train the guard the way I saw fit, but he was going to be livid that it included me taking a risk he would probably see as unnecessary. Just wait until he saw why I needed to do this.

As much as I was looking forward to training the guard, I

assumed this was going to be an ongoing problem.

I climbed down the rope using my legs. Squeezing the rope with my feet gave my arms more of a break on the way.

Every time I came to one of the knots in the rope, I pulled it up to me and checked the connection before I put my weight on the next section.

Finally, I got close enough to the crowd to be sure that what I heard was real. None of them were talking now.

Maybe they were when I heard them earlier, but with the King in their midst, none of them were making a sound.

The silence was unnerving as I got even closer.

But before my feet hit the ground, Tristan, finally letting go of the rope entirely and not just letting out slack so I could do with it what I needed, grabbed me off the rope and held me tight to him instead of putting me down.

"I'm fine," I said.

His heart hammered away in his chest, and he still didn't put me down, just shook his head.

"King Tristan," Jacquetta said, putting the lightest touch on his arm.

Finally, a deep breath, and he put me down.

"Please don't ever do that again," he said into my ear.

"You know I can't promise that." I hugged him and pulled his hands from me to hold them between us, forcing him to look at me. His eyes darted back and forth on my face, then up and down my body in frantic sweeps as if he didn't believe I was whole. "But this needed to be done. And I'm fine."

He nodded and swallowed.

"Alright, the show is done," General Pace yelled from so close she made me jump, "get back to your duties."

The crowd around us dissipated, but Gus, Jacquetta, General Pace, Tristan, and I remained.

"I need to talk to you," he said.

Shit again, but bigger. I probably needed to yell at the King.

CHAPTER 35
TONIGHT

"Cinder, what were you thinking?" Tristan yelled, grabbing me by the arms the second the door flap to my tent closed.

"Don't you yell at me," I said, finger pointed at him and growl in my voice.

"I will do whatever I want when you act insane. You're supposed to be done with this." He let me go to wave his hands in the air toward the door behind me, but at least he wasn't yelling anymore.

"Get out," I said, pointing at the door behind me.

"What?" he asked, pulling his head back like I slapped him, which was exactly what I wanted to do. "Why would I leave?"

"Because," I shoved past him, knocking into his shoulder with mine as I stomped to the trunk at the end of my bed and sat on it, crossing my arms. "No man gets to yell at me, and question my sanity, in my own damn room...tent. Whatever."

He ran his hands through his hair in a rough, swift motion, leaving it sticking up in all directions as he slapped them back at his sides.

"You can't do this anymore." He waved at the door behind him, and I rolled my eyes.

"Tristan, you're not my dad, and you're not my brother." My voice cracked on 'brother,' and I ground my teeth together. Ash questioned everything I did. He didn't do shit, but everything I did was suspect every step of the way. This was supposed to be different.

Dropping his head back, he stared at the ceiling of the tent, and I clenched my hands into fists.

Finally, he brought his face back to look at me, and kneeled on the floor in front of me, putting his hands on my knees in a gentle touch.

"Listen, I'm sorry," he said, and it was my turn to snap my head back like he slapped me.

"Excuse me?" My voice was as devoid of inflection as my mind was empty of understanding. What was he talking about? If I questioned Ash the way I just did Tristan, he would not have apologized.

"I can't yell at you and tell you what to do," he said.

Although he could have, really. He was the King. I was his subject. He technically had more right to order me around than Ash did, no matter how much I hated it. But I wasn't going to point that out. He told me to train the guard. I was training the guard. He needed to get over his issues with the way I did it.

"But, please," he said, putting his face in my lap, a shudder running through him, "please be more careful."

"Tristan," I said, the ice that had formed around my heart thawing until my fists unfurled and I put my hands on the back of his head, brushing out the wild parts of his hair with my fingers. "Nothing I did was dangerous."

"Liar," he said, lifting his head to look at me as I froze again, ice enclosing my entire body. "No matter how good you are, that was dangerous. There had to be another way to do that without risking your life."

I took in a shuddering breath and had to focus on his words, running them through my mind multiple times before I could exhale again. Even then, I couldn't speak. All I could do was shake my head.

He squeezed his eyes shut and sighed before looking back at me and running a hand along my cheek.

"My beautiful flame, I'm afraid you'll burn so bright you'll burn out. And I need your light."

Thaw. The rest of the ice encasing me, trapping me, keeping me from moving, disappeared. It was replaced by the kind of heat he always had, but it flared up within me instead. I slid down off the trunk to sit in his lap, my legs straddling him.

"Please believe me. I know it looks scary. I know that you worry, and I'm sorry it upsets you, but this is what I do. This is what I need to keep doing to train them, to protect you, and to protect Onyx."

"But I don't want you to have to protect me or the country. I should be protecting you and Onyx. I'm the King. It's my job."

I cupped his face, my palms on his cheeks.

"Your job is to live. And this is war. If only one person survives this war, it has to be you."

His face crumpled, his entire body wilting in front of me as he leaned forward, pulling me to him so he could bury his face in my neck.

"Cinder," he said, my name a lament, like he was mourning me already.

"Shh. I'm here."

"Cinder." This time it was like a ballad, haunting but less mournful.

"We're okay."

"Cinder." Now it was like a love song.

I sucked in a breath as he kissed my neck, suddenly more than aware of how we were tangled up together.

"Tristan," I said, trying to imbue my voice with warning and landing somewhere closer to a plea.

But he stopped, just running his hands up and down my back.

"No matter what," he said, "no matter how much I try and make it okay in my head, I can't stop seeing you up on that beam, and wanting to keep you hidden away in here, with me." He sighed at the same time I did.

"And no matter what you say, you know this is part of who I am." I moved slightly, making him lift his head so we were staring into each other's eyes. I wanted to kiss him, to lose myself to this, to throw all my caution into the hellfire source. But there was no better time to make my point. "It will always be a part of me."

A line appeared between his brows, and the corners of his mouth turned down. Still, I waited.

This was it. I gave him the best reason to get rid of me, to relegate me to just a trainer and a fighter, not the one he slept next to. And not the one he was going to make Queen.

My lungs screamed for me to breathe, but I couldn't. All I could do was wait.

For the moment he realized what I meant.

And left me there on the floor.

He took a hand from my back and my heart stuttered. But he brought it to my face and ran a tender finger along my jaw.

"Do you really think that I don't want you because you make me worry?" he asked, and I took a shaking breath.

"It would be better for you if you didn't want me." My voice was thin, but I managed to say it.

Tristan shook his head and smiled a soft smile.

"Easier, maybe." His smile grew into a grin, but flattened out a moment later to that same look he got every time my traitorous heart said to kiss him. "But, Cinder, there was little better for me before you."

I opened my mouth to answer. What I was planning to say, I didn't know. Maybe I was planning on giving in and kissing him, no matter how much it would hurt later.

But the flap of the tent flung back and General Pace, her eyes squeezed shut, said, "King Tristan, there's been an attack."

He leaned forward to stand and picked me up, setting me on my feet all in one fluid motion.

"I'll see you tonight," he said, with a perfunctory kiss on the forehead, and he was gone.

Tonight…my legs gave out and I plopped down onto the trunk again.

After all of that, I still had to face him tonight. In my bed.

CHAPTER 36

SO THIS IS

"Cinder," Gus said, "you have to stop."

But I couldn't stop pacing back and forth across the tent. Not until Tristan was here. Not until I knew.

"Please, come eat something," Jacquetta said, gesturing to the spread they brought back from the dining tent.

"You weren't here," I said. "You don't know."

My throat was dry, and my voice sounded like rocks tumbling along cobblestones. But the idea of stopping my movement made all the muscles in my legs shake even as I kept pacing.

"Then tell us what happened." Gus dropped her head back on her chair and addressed the ceiling like she couldn't believe she had to say it again.

How was I supposed to explain?

I gave him a reason. I told him to send me away.

But he didn't.

Not yet.

And it didn't feel like a reprieve. It felt like a blade hanging over my head.

It wasn't as if he was going to walk in after spending all day with the General and all the other commanders of the war effort, and decide that I was still worth additional stress.

"Just…a lot." It was the same non-explanation I gave them an hour ago, and a half hour ago, and every other time they asked me since they found me sitting on the trunk staring at the place on the floor where we were together. Where he said he wanted me.

"Any word on what the attack was?" I asked, continuing to pace, and finally remembering that maybe Gus and Jacquetta knew more than I did. They always seemed to know more than I did.

"No. Not anything I would say was valuable information," Jacquetta said, taking the last bite of her meal.

"The guards are all speculating, and trading concerned whispers about where it was and how bad." Gus said, taking another roll from the ones in the middle of the table even though she had been done with her food for a while, she kept getting more.

It was for the best. I didn't think I was going to be able to sit still long enough to eat while my stomach continuously flopped around inside me, twisting itself into intricate sailing knots.

Once I knew for sure if he was going to send me home—

Movement at the door stopped me mid-step, my weight balanced halfway between one foot and the other made my feet feel as likely to topple over as my heart.

The tent door moved again, but I remained still.

Finally, Tristan swept aside the door, his face haggard, his shoulders slumped.

Just beyond him, the General was walking away.

"Cinder," he said. His voice was low and barely there, but it still sounded like a love song. I could move again.

I went to him, and he wrapped his arms around me, burying his face in my neck. I held onto him like he would fly away at any moment.

"Are you okay?" I asked, my voice still rough and raw.

"Yes, but a lot of people aren't." He pulled back to let out a shaking breath, rubbing his eyes with the heel of a hand. "I'm going to be late. But I wanted to tell you that I will be back later. Please, go to sleep."

Nodding, I couldn't find the words to explain or to question him. I wanted to know where the attack was, who was hurt, what techniques the attackers used, if birds were involved. And I wanted to tell him, to blurt out everything I was obsessing about while he was gone.

He lifted a hand to my cheek.

I leaned into it.

"Tonight," he whispered, putting his forehead to mine and looking into my eyes, "I will be back tonight. But please don't worry."

"You need to eat something, too," I said, taking a deep breath. Finally, my stomach settled, and I knew I would be able to finish my meal after all.

"The General will make sure I do." He kissed me on the cheek and looked past me to Gus and Jacquetta at the table. "Please make sure she doesn't do anything to try and save the world by herself while I'm gone. I need her when I get back."

He smiled at them, squeezed my hand, and left again, with me standing in the middle of the entryway replaying his words.

"Did..." I asked, my grating voice trailing off. I whirled around and looked at Gus and Jacquetta, their mouths hanging open. "Did the King just say he needed me? Me?"

"What did you two talk about earlier?" Gus asked, eyes wide.

"Cinder, did he propose?" Jacquetta asked, bouncing up and down in her seat.

"No, stop." I shook my head and made my way to them, taking a seat of my own and piling a plate high with food.

But, first, I drained an entire glass of water and refilled it.

"Seriously, I'm starting to feel dizzy," Gus said, putting both her hands flat on the table and leaning forward.

"A minute ago, you were a wreck," Jacquetta said, "and you were acting like a tragedy happened that was even worse than the attack. Now you're just fine."

"I…" I looked off to the side of the tent, to where my bed and my trunk were, to where Tristan and I…what? What *did* happen? "Something changed. And I don't even know how to explain it."

"Oh, oh, oh," Gus said, pawing frantically at Jacquetta's arm, her face in a grin so wide it looked like it hurt.

"Cinder?" Jacquetta said, making my name a long, leading question. But where she thought it was leading to, I had no idea.

"What?" I asked, shoving another giant bite in my mouth. They were starting to send all my suspicions into overdrive. It didn't make the food taste better.

"She does." Gus hugged Jacquetta's arm, her face going all mooney like she was looking at a basket full of puppies.

"I'm so happy," Jacquetta said, leaning her head on Gus' and matching her look of sappy sentimentality, as if I was a particularly gushing love letter from the person of her dreams.

Taking another bite and looking around me, I couldn't figure out what was so different that made them act this way.

"Okay, fine. I'll ask the stupid thing even though I know you're both going to make me regret this. I do, what?" I twisted my face up and squinted at them, trying to prepare myself for whatever they were about to say.

"No, we shouldn't say anything," Gus said, sitting up and taking another roll from the table, smiling around the bite she took.

"You'll figure it out. That comes next," Jacquetta said, standing and taking her plate and Gus', puttering around to clean up everything.

"I'm not done with that," I said, snagging a plate of some

kind of yummy meat on a stick that we never got in Lehar, and that I had never tried at any of the little roadside Inns I visited throughout Onyx.

"Okay, you're allowed to eat anything you want," Jacquetta said, that ridiculous grin plastered on her face.

Gus stood up with her as they wandered around the tent picking up, but was she…humming?

What was wrong with them?

I continued to shovel food in my mouth, and paid no attention to their muttered conversation until one word popped out to me, louder than all the others even though it was said at the same volume.

"Marriage."

Slowing down my chewing, trying to listen as hard as I could, the hairs on my arms rose.

"They'll figure it out," Gus said.

"I just wish they would hurry up. I mean, have you ever seen two people more in love?" Jacquetta asked, and my hearing disappeared.

While they continued to talk, all the sound was sucked out of the room and left me in a vortex full of the remembered sound of his heart, and the answering sound of my own.

No.

Tristan couldn't love me.

I couldn't love him.

All of it was exactly the opposite of what the country needed to happen.

But…my heart thudded in my chest as I swallowed the over-chewed bite in my mouth, the flavor long since wrung out of it, and all I could think about was that he would be here tonight. In my bed.

CHAPTER 37

NOT WINNING

I tossed and turned, rolling from one side to the other in the comfortable bed, wholly uncomfortable.

Gus and Jacquetta had long since gone to sleep. But I…couldn't.

All I could do was lay in the bed, turn back and forth, and try to find the peace I had in my mind before Gus and Jacquetta put the 'L' word in my head.

Why couldn't they just keep their thoughts to themselves? Why did they have to infect me with their lunacy?

I rolled again, and let out a heavy breath, but cut it off and eked out the remainder of my air as the tent door moved.

The low light of a light stone shone along the floor, and I squeezed my eyes shut while I tried to even out my breathing.

Beneath me, the bed moved, and the light that filtered through my eyelids went out.

Where he put the light stone, I didn't know, but I hoped he hid it somewhere so we would be in the full dark when I opened my eyes. Although I kept them shut until he was laying at my back with an arm on my waist.

Finally, I opened my eyes again, and it was as black as the Obsidian Palace in here.

He was on top of the bedclothes, I was tucked well into them, but the heat of his body laying along mine still reached me.

I rolled over, and he held me tighter.

"You're awake," he said, his voice low and muffled as if he was partially pressing his face into the pillows.

"Are you okay?" I asked, trying to be as quiet as he was.

"Now I am. Just…" he yawned, his jaw popping, "exhausted."

"Then go to sleep. You can tell me all about it in the morning."

"In a few hours." His words were even more garbled. A second after he spoke his breathing was even, and the weight of his arm draped across my waist was heavier.

Lifting a hand from underneath the blanket, I ran it along the side of his face.

He didn't stir.

But that was what I wanted, for him to stay asleep, and for me to be able to grapple with this in the dark, yet not alone.

No, the worst part of thinking about what Gus and Jacquetta said, was that it made it more difficult to realize how little I wanted to be alone again.

"Good night, Tristan," I whispered, and kissed his face, right next to his mouth.

In the morning, I woke to heat tracing my hairline.

"Wake up, sleepyhead," he whispered.

"Do I have to?" I whispered back, not yet opening my eyes.

"Yes, you do," Jacquetta said, her voice sounding like she was in the bed with us.

That made me open my eyes.

She stood over us at the end of the bed, her hands on her hips and one eyebrow raised high.

"Why?" I asked, shoving myself up to sitting, while Tristan stayed where he was and just propped himself up on one elbow.

"Today is the first training day," she said.

I flopped back onto the bed and sighed.

"So tired," I whined.

"Can you wake her up?" Gus asked, looking at Tristan from over Jacquetta's shoulder.

"Yes, I need to get up, too," he said, leaning down to kiss me on the neck.

"As much as I want to lay here with you all day," he whispered into my skin between feather light kisses, "we both need to go to work."

"How did the planning go?" I asked, turning toward him and ruining his tender moment, but needing answers about the attack.

Tristan sat up then and rubbed his fingers over his face.

"It was a bad one," he said.

Now I leaned forward and ran a hand along his back.

Gus and Jacquetta paused as they pulled another training outfit for me from the trunk at the foot of the bed.

"What happened?" I asked, quiet and pressing against his shoulder.

"They attacked Breakwater again. This time with birds, too."

"Fucking crows," I said, "Duchess Inara?"

"She lost a leg, but she'll survive. There were a lot of losses, but she gave them the worse end of the fight, and they didn't manage to land like they wanted to."

"Fuck those flying Corvid rats."

I took a deep breath and wanted to run to her so bad, even though I knew it was already too late. I ground my teeth together.

Tristan turned toward me and took my free hand.

"Cinder, the best thing you can do for her now is get these

guards trained up, so when the Corvids attack next, we're more than ready."

"Right," I said, forcing my jaw to loosen and breathing through my open mouth. "But, Tristan, we need to help Breakwater."

"And we will. It was part of our planning session last night. Trust me."

I nodded and kissed his cheek, shoving myself up and out of the bed, crawling over the trunk at the end of it.

"Cinder," Jacquetta said, throwing a bath sheet around me.

"What?" I looked down at my nightgown. This covered more than some of the gowns they put me in.

"No, that's okay. I need to go back and get ready myself." Tristan shoved himself up from the bed, and it was his turn to kiss me on the cheek. Although he had to do it around a stern-faced Jacquetta with her hands on her hips.

He gave her and Gus each a nod, and he was gone.

"I wasn't going to strip down in front of him," I said, throwing off the bath sheet and pulling off my nightgown. Well, I sure wasn't going to do it when they were watching.

"Aren't you going to take a trip to the shower tent?" Gus asked as I pulled on my new training clothes.

"No, why would I do that?" I hopped around, pulling on the tight pants.

"Because you climbed the dome yesterday," Jacquetta said, waving her hands in the general direction of up.

"And?" I shoved a foot into one of the tall, supple boots, and rolled my ankle around to make sure I had full movement in it and my foot was in a good position.

"She's worried you're probably sweaty and smelly," Gus said, biting her lips like she was holding off laughter.

"Jacquetta, I'm only going to get a lot grosser today. I can shower later." I held the stomach bracer up to me and raised my brows in a look to her and Gus. "This is a bit much for a training outfit."

"Mother had an armorer make it," Jacquetta said, her nose in the air, but she pulled on the strings in the bracer and started to tighten the leather panel that went above my waist and formed cups over my breasts.

"An armorer?" I asked, looking again at the whole outfit. The tight pants had thicker areas over all the major arteries in the legs, although how they managed not to bunch up where they covered my femoral artery was some kind of fabric manipulation magic. Other than the leather bracer protecting my breasts and not my heart, it made sense.

"You didn't think that Madam would try and get dressmakers well-versed in lace to make your training clothes, did you?" Gus asked, laughing as she handed one of the arm braces to Jacquetta to put on me.

"I kind of did, actually."

They both laughed at that, and Jacquetta shook her head.

"No, the lace she saved for your new nightgowns," Jacquetta said.

"My new what?" I had plenty of pretty little nightgowns that Madam had made for me that I wore at the palace. Why would she order more when my brother was definitely not paying for them?

"She said you would need a different kind of nightgown if the King was spending the night with you," Jacquetta said, and Gus wrinkled her nose on a silent giggle while she bit her bottom lip, failing to hide her wicked grin.

"It's not like that." Oh, Gods and Goddesses, what did they tell her?

"We know," Gus said. "And Madam knows, but she insisted this would help."

Snatching a small piece of cloth that I was now afraid was larger than the new nightgowns from the table, I asked, "Do I want to see them?" My voice was flat, because it was the only way to ask the question without showing exactly how fucking terrifying the prospect was.

"Not until after you take a shower tonight," Jacquetta said with a nod and then she walked out of the tent, Gus in tow, leaving me to trail after them.

CHAPTER 38

FIGHTER

We walked across the training grounds at a clip that bordered on jogging. It surprised me that Gus and Jacquetta moved so fast, although it shouldn't have. They did all kinds of things that I didn't know how to do, it made sense they could do things I could just as well.

On our way, the steady stream of guards heading in the same direction let me know that at least we weren't late to breakfast.

I tied a leather thong around my hair, pulling it back into a ponytail as I followed after my friends, and started to form my plan for the first training day in my mind.

At the tent, the sheer number of people lined up for their food, already sitting, leaving, or just arriving like us, forced me to make a conscious effort not to roll my shoulders like I used to. Especially when far too many sets of eyes turned to watch us.

"Let's...get in line," I said and swallowed. This was even more different from yesterday than I imagined it would be.

"General Pace is waving us over," Jacquetta said and walked between rows of tables toward the General, who wasn't waving us anywhere.

She sat with plates in front of her and a bite already on her fork heading into her mouth while a guard next to her was half out of his seat and doing the waving.

"But we need to get food," I said. Looking at the number of people there, I was seriously concerned there wouldn't be any left by the time we got done with whatever was happening at the General's table.

Jacquetta ignored me and Gus just shrugged.

I sighed. Even here, where we were far more in my element than theirs, I was at their mercy.

At the table, General Pace gestured for us to sit down.

We had to wedge ourselves into the tightly packed people, but they moved as much as they could to accommodate us, with nods of recognition all around. According to their uniforms we were in a mixed group of lower-level guard and higher ups like the General.

Interesting.

"Lady Cinder," the guard who waved us over said, taking the last bite from his plate, "I would be happy to get breakfast for you and your Ladies in Waiting."

Jacquetta and Gus brightened, but I shook my head.

"No, that's unnecessary, we can get it. And please, don't call me that here."

General Pace raised her eyebrows, and the guard turned to her along with most of the others around us.

I wasn't sure I wanted to try and explain that I never liked the title of Lady, and here, where being a Duke's sister had nothing to do with my position or my job, was the last place I wanted to use it. I wasn't born to this position. I earned this with blood and pain.

"You can address Lady Cinder as..." the General said, pausing with her face in that still mask long enough for my hands to itch for a blade to fidget with, "Fighter Cinder. And, yes, please get some help, and bring them breakfast."

Fighter.

Handler wasn't right. I didn't earn that formal position. And Trainer wasn't right either. There was a formal position called Trainer, too.

No, I was an anomaly here. So, an odd title for me, one made up on the spot by the General, made sense.

The problem was that now, every single time someone called me Fighter Cinder, Jocelyn would flash through my mind. Her cryptic mentions of the prophecy she claimed brought her to us. And the last time I asked for her help. And her refusal.

But I couldn't tell General Pace. I couldn't stop it from happening.

All I could do was nod, and accept the ache that would follow my name now.

Pain was a great tutor. Ash was right about that. What was this new hurt supposed to teach me?

Jacquetta and Gus spoke to the people around us about the schedule, about the best time for the shower tent, about nothing, everything, and all the little things.

I pressed my hands together under the table, and focused on what I knew to do: plan how to train these guards. How I would give them even a fraction of the techniques that Jocelyn gave me over years.

The answer was obvious, I wouldn't be able to teach them much in the way of special techniques when we needed to focus on basic skills with the weapons they needed to use.

Maybe, though, just maybe, I might be able to teach them the one important point that all the other things Jocelyn taught me were built on.

Even with the war falling from the sky all around us, we might have time for that.

Good. Because that's what the rope was for.

"Do you think, General," I said, interrupting an entirely

different conversation happening around me, "that I could train the guard in two different groups? Or maybe even three?"

That would make it much easier for what I had in mind, and get them some more guards to deploy right away.

"Of course," she said. "What did you have in mind?"

"First, delineate between those having some training, and no training from the guard."

"Done," she said, nodding. "That makes sense."

"Second, among those who have trained, who has reached the point where they worked on long-range and close, light infantry fighting."

"Not as easy. Just because they reached, or even completed that portion of the training with their Handler, it doesn't mean they're good at it."

"Right." I chewed on the inside of my cheek and cocked my head to the side. "Don't you all do some kind of ranking or grading on their proficiency in certain disciplines so you know which position they will fill in which regiment?"

"Yes. Normally that isn't common knowledge." Her eyes narrowed, like I shouldn't press that hard.

But Onyx didn't have time to tiptoe around a bunch of the guards' egos.

"Okay, then it still doesn't have to be. If you can get a list together of the guard who passed those disciplines with developed skills, and the ones who didn't, then add the people who didn't reach that part of their training yet to that second list, no one will know. Our other list will be all the brand-new people."

The General looked around, making eye contact with every single guard who was near her until they all looked away nodding. I didn't know what it all meant, but when she turned back to me, she nodded.

"Done. We'll get you a list, and no one will find out what it means."

How she could assure me of that I didn't understand, not when there were so many people who heard it.

The guard came back with my food, and two more guards came behind him with more plates for Jacquetta and Gus.

I looked around me at the number of people who did know because of my big mouth, and took a bite too big to eat comfortably, just to have some reason to stop talking.

CHAPTER 39

BEGINNING

After breakfast we gathered by the wall in the open section of the arena.

Guards lined up in front of us, arranged by some method clear to them but that remained a mystery to me.

The truth was, as much as I once wanted to lead a force like this, I didn't bother to learn anything about the intricacies of the way the guard was run after Mother and Father died. I didn't have the time or the heart to continue to learn about anything I once wanted. And before they died, I didn't have the time yet to focus on it.

I always thought there would be more time for my goals and dreams. Just like I always thought there would be more time for my parents.

Until there wasn't time for anything.

Finally, General Pace, standing next to me and watching them line up, nodded.

"Good morning," I called out, trying to project my voice, but not yell at the same time. "Before we get started, we are going to break you up into three groups to make this more manageable as different groups work on different aspects of the training we will be doing."

I stepped back and gestured to General Pace.

She stepped forward and called out entire regiments who went to stand at one end of the large open space. Then she called two lists of specific names. These lists amounted to a lot fewer people than the crowd from the regiments.

Part of me wondered how I was actually going to train the largest group once we got to the more advanced things, but that was a problem for a different time. By then, I expected to leave this place, and other people would pick up where I left off.

Once she was done, I stepped forward again.

"This group," I said, gesturing to the largest one, "will be working with their officers on the weapons we know will be most useful against the crows."

Mumbling went up from the gathered guards as they shuffled in their groups.

"What you heard was true. The Corvids have magic that turns them into massive crows with talons and beaks they use like weapons."

I started to walk back and forth, continuing to address them all as they fell silent and listened intently.

"So, we will be working with that knowledge to prepare to drive those damn birds out of Onyx skies."

Cheers. They erupted into cheers and yells that verged on delirious excitement.

"Listen," I bellowed, and they stopped.

The training grounds around us were so still and silent I thought I heard the susurrations of the river on the other side of the wall.

"Your cheers remind me that none of you know what is coming."

I scanned the guards, all of whom weren't part of the force

that fought in the last war, or they would already be out defending Onyx. All of them were new, and some of them signed up for this because they were inspired. But inspired to what?

Swallowing, I took a moment. To close my eyes, to take a deep breath, and prepare myself.

They needed to know something real.

"Who am I?" I asked, my voice low, but loud enough for them all to hear me in this stillness.

"Fighter Cinder," someone yelled, brave at the back of the group.

"The Lady Hero of the Battle of Obsidian Wings," someone else called from the back on the other side.

"I am a killer."

General Pace turned toward me, a line between her brows.

Jacquetta and Gus froze, the looks of pride they had all day turning to strange masks, tight with tension.

All across the grounds, silence reigned, and the gathered guards seemed to be made out of it, a part of the hush, so complete in their waiting.

"Even though I am what I am—and I am damn good at it— the birds even threw me. More than once, if something went differently, I would have died."

They couldn't know exactly how good I was, or that I enjoyed it. But they could handle this. They needed to handle this.

I let it sink in. Let them come to understand that while their exuberance was good, confidence was good, underestimating their opponent, and being too excited was a disaster.

"What I am going to try and teach you will help give you and Onyx a better chance at winning this war. But you need to understand. War changes you. War will change us all. And war, no matter how much we all want to defeat the opponent, is never something to cheer about."

They looked to the ground or the sky, or each other. But none of them kept looking at me. Except General Pace.

She blinked and the line between her brows was gone. Then she nodded.

"Right." Now that I told them all of that, I wasn't sure what to do next.

"First, you'll work on the distance weapons," General Pace said to the large group, gesturing for them to head toward the range.

I nodded to her and took over from there.

"Now, to start us off, I need one volunteer who thinks they can stand a version of sparring with me." I rubbed my hands together and grinned, unable to keep the glee from my face.

At first, some of them stepped forward like they were going to volunteer, but one after another looked at me and suspicion formed on their features.

"Cinder, you look deranged," Jacquetta whispered.

"Seriously, 'I'm a killer now fight me,' isn't exactly a thrilling prospect," Gus muttered.

"Fight me," Tristan called, stepping through a parting line of guards who looked at him with awe.

I dropped my hands to my side and sighed.

"No, my King." This was a terrible idea. I shouldn't beat their king in front of them on the first day. How demoralizing would that be?

"Yes, I think it is a fine idea." He walked across the grounds to stand directly in front of me.

"Tristan, they need to fight me eventually," I whispered.

"Are you really going to make a liar out of me in front of them?" he smiled.

"Liar? How would I make you a liar?"

"I said it was a good idea."

"Which may as well have been a command." My voice was as weak as the last gasp of dying lungs.

"Fine," I said. "But this won't be like last time." I stepped past him to address the guards again. "This sparring session will be different. What I want you all to learn how to do is trust your instincts."

Some of them relaxed, one even grinned. They had no idea.

"Okay, after I show you this little thing, I want this group," I said, gesturing to the more advanced of the two, "to stay here, and we will work on the same thing with you in your regiments."

The guards started to move amongst themselves, grouping up.

"For this group," I gestured to the less advanced of the two, "you're going to head to the other side of the grounds, and train in the disciplines we suggest, with the weapons we suggest, using the things you come to understand today."

Most of them nodded and those in the back leaned around others to see what I was about to do.

"Gus, Jacquetta, help me tie this around Tristan's eyes," I said, turning back to them, and pulling out the piece of cloth I grabbed from our tent.

"What?" he asked, his eyebrows shooting up. "How are we supposed to do any kind of sparring when you cover my eyes?"

"You'll see," I said, and grinned as they covered those color-shifting eyes.

It made it a lot easier for me to attack him with his eyes covered, but that wasn't the goal behind this.

No, this was an old trick of Jocelyn's. And all I could do was hope it worked as well on all of them as it did when she trained me.

"Alright," I waved to General Pace, who stepped forward and took Tristan's arm while I went to the rope hanging down from the arch and took hold of it.

"If everyone can form a wide circle around this space." I moved a hand, and they all did as I commanded, even Gus and

Jacquetta who both had wide eyes, and stared at me as if I was actually going to kill Tristan.

Looking at him, for a moment I thought about the time when I wanted to—when I planned on it, and fury flared in my veins.

The rope hung down far enough for a small length of it to pool on the ground. There was more than enough room in the rope to wrap it around my hand and pull myself up.

I pushed off the ground, running across the open space until my feet left the dirt, and I hung from the arm I wrapped the rope around as I swung out.

Coming back toward the ground, I dropped down far enough to run along the dirt again, to push off on the other side, gaining height and speed.

But it wasn't fast enough.

Making eye contact with Gus and Jacquetta, I motioned with my free arm for what I wanted them to do. When they moved into position, I wrapped the rope around my legs and freed my arm.

On the swing back, Gus and Jacquetta grabbed the rope, now about their chest level, and ran with it, flinging me faster the other way.

Another pass, and I was ready.

To attack the King.

CHAPTER 40

TAKING TURNS

General Pace saw as I leaned and changed the trajectory of my swing.

Jacquetta and Gus saw it, too, and stepped back into the crowd, breathing heavily.

Tristan didn't see anything. Standing close to the middle of the open circle, he held his face at an angle as if he was trying to listen to what was happening around him while his eyes were covered.

I bent forward, holding myself out like an arrow, relying on the way the rope was wrapped around my legs to hold me up, and tapped Tristan on the shoulder as I flew by.

"One death to me," I called as I passed him. "Now throw me a short sword. And arm the King."

Holding out my hand for one of the blunted blades, I grabbed the first one thrust into the air as I sailed past.

"So," Tristan yelled, taking a blade from the General before she darted back to the edge of the group, "trust my instincts."

Exactly.

But I couldn't say it out loud as I leaned and changed course again. I couldn't give him any more hint at my location, or, more importantly, my direction.

He crouched, pulling his sword in, setting himself in a guarding stance as he bent his head toward the ground and listened.

I leaned and turned into the position I wanted, heading his way, but held my arm and sword back.

Not yet…

Flying through the air, I waited for the perfect time.

He turned and faced more my direction.

Good.

But not good enough.

On my way past him, he swung and missed, but I darted out with my sword at the last second, when I was almost past him, and tapped his shoulder.

"Another death to you," he yelled, turning to face where I would have been if I kept on the same trajectory.

Part of me wondered how many passes I would have to make before he caught me. Would Gus and Jacquetta need to run along with the rope again and get me back up to speed?

For now, the leaning and changing course kept me going fast enough.

I shifted again, this time making my body a smaller target, and lashing out just as he started to respond to me getting nearer.

"Death again," he called.

This time, he crouched down and held his sword in front of his face as he took a deep breath while I allowed myself to turn and head back toward him on almost the same line as before.

Adding another death to my tally wasn't what surprised me on that pass, it was that Tristan didn't move and didn't call out.

He stayed in the same position, and I twisted and reeled to come at him almost head on.

Closer…

Moving too soon would give me away…

Almost there…

Tristan drove up with his sword and it clashed against my own.

In the circle around us a cheer went up while I dropped, allowing the rope to unwrap from around my legs until I was on the furthest point of my swing, holding on with only my hand.

Around us, the guards went quiet as I rolled down the rope and caught myself before I fell to the ground.

I lifted my legs so they didn't touch the ground on my way by him again, and this time when he lifted his sword to meet mine, I let go of the rope.

Barreling into him, we both went flying backward, our swords out to our sides. But I was expecting it.

When we came to a rest, I straddled his waist, my sword at his throat, and his flung out to the side, dust settling around us.

He whipped his blindfold off and stared up at me, breathing hard.

My mouth turned up in a soft smile as I looked down on his wide eyes flashing green.

"You're dead again," I said and pulled the sword away from him. "Did I hurt you?"

"No, only my pride," he said and finally smiled back. "So, is this how you got so fast?"

"There was no rope, but basically." I left out the speed drills, how long it all took, and how the ashes at home were sometimes so thick footsteps didn't make any noise at all when we were outside.

"Can I get up now?" he asked, his smile turning into a leering grin.

I rolled my eyes and stood up, looking down at him as he propped himself up on his elbows.

"Everyone," I yelled, holding out a hand for him to pull

himself up by, "what did the King finally do that allowed him to block me?"

"He trusted his instincts," several people yelled at once.

Conversations, all volume levels, rattled around us, but I didn't look to see what the reaction was to my little demonstration.

All I could do was stare at Tristan as he stared back at me, the green in his eyes still bright in the light pouring through the dome overhead.

"You really aren't," he said, taking a hand and tucking a fly away bit of hair behind my ear.

I waited for him to continue, but he didn't.

"What do you mean?" I asked, my voice low.

"But Fighter Cinder, how do we know what it would look like if someone did trust their instincts completely? Would that really help?" someone in crowd yelled, finally pulling my attention back to my work.

"Tristan?" I whispered, raising my brows to him in question.

"How about," he yelled, not looking away from me, "I get tied up in that rope and swung around?"

More cheering. This time it bordered on wildly out of control. But I couldn't blame them now.

Not when I wanted to see it as bad as they did.

"What we're going to do is this," I yelled, keeping my gaze locked with his, "I will help the King into the rope, and step out of the circle. You all will help him to get up to speed and change direction in the air to come at me. And I am going to be blindfolded and brought back in once he's already flying."

He nodded and I walked past him, bending down to snatch up the blindfold from the ground.

Getting him into the ropes, showing him how he was locked in there until he chose to stop and get out of it, left him just as agape as before.

On my way out of the circle, I put the blindfold on and tightened it.

The crowd shuffling around me invaded my senses, but I closed my eyes behind the piece of cloth and took a deep breath.

I found the place in my mind where Lehar was always present. The place where ashes coated the ground, where gray silence permeated every second of the world as I moved through it.

A gust of wind moved the small hairs along my forehead where they escaped from my ponytail.

People around me shuffled their feet, whispering to each other.

On the other side of the wall, the river sent a constant, cool rumbling through the air.

Beyond all the sounds, and all the movements around me, thudding of feet and grunting alerted me to the group flinging Tristan though the air in preparation of his own flight.

Now I knew where he was.

The cleared circle in the middle formed in my mind along with the conjured vision of him, wrapped in the rope, still holding on with one hand because he didn't trust the wrap entirely, swinging by.

I waited until the sound of the crowd hushed, and General Pace touched my elbow, her scent of shoe polish and starch a clear difference from the general scent of soap and breakfast all around me.

My turn toward the circle was slow, and I used the time to find the sound of the rope's hushed creak far overhead where it moved against the hole in the beam.

When it made the distinct low noise of the apex of the swing, I lifted my sword and crouched.

Everyone around me tensed, and I held myself still until I knew it was time.

I darted out from the crowd and turned, clanging my sword against Tristan's on his way by me.

Whirling around, I stood low with my knees bent and my sword in guard.

He came again, and this time I dropped to the ground and struck up, scoring a light tap on some part of him as he went by.

Jumping back up, I faced the way the rope brought him and turned with him as he changed positions, sending himself in another direction.

More passes, and more wins for me.

Either blocks or strikes, he only got past me twice.

"Alright," he called, and I lowered my sword. "My legs hurt."

The crowd around us didn't cheer this time. They barely breathed.

I pulled up my blindfold, not sure what I was going to find when I did.

CHAPTER 41

BEST OF INTENTIONS

All around me, the guard stood frozen and staring.

There were no cheers now.

When I finished my flying, they seemed eager to start, eager to have a turn in the middle, eager to learn how to trust themselves and their senses to protect themselves better.

Now, though, they didn't even shuffle their feet, they didn't seem to breathe. They all looked at me with fear in their eyes.

"Lady Cinder," Tristan called from where he was pulling himself up on the rope while others held it steady so he could unwrap himself.

"Fighter Cinder," the General corrected, and I nodded to her.

Between her, Gus, Jacquetta, and Tristan, at least some of the people around us didn't look fazed by what just happened.

"Fighter Cinder," Tristan said, lowering himself to the ground with a wry smile at the new title, "how long have you been training?"

Ah, so the guard watched me react with the blindfold on, and were doubting themselves. That inclination I understood.

"Every single day, at least twelve hours a day, for seven years." Tristan knew the answer, but the guards around us didn't, and the wide eyes and intakes of breath reminded me how abnormal my life was. How abnormal I made it in the wake of the death of my parents.

"Do you expect the guards here to be able to do all the things and use all the moves you do?" he asked, walking closer to me, and still projecting his voice to the crowd.

"No," I said, and more than one of them scowled, "and they don't need to."

Mumbling started up among them, along with a lot of shaking heads.

"What you are trained to do, the moves and maneuvers you have been perfecting through your training, will serve you well." I turned to them, making sure to rotate slowly to look upon them all.

Tristan came to my side, a smile tugging at his lips.

"But what we learned at the battle with the Corvids was that they use our training against us. They used simultaneous attacks from ground and sky, and we would have been faster at driving them off if we trusted our instincts as the threat dive-bombed."

Foreheads smoothed out, and shaking of heads turned into nods.

Good. Now we were ready to teach them how to do that.

"Everyone," General Pace said, stepping forward, "it's time for lunch, and afterward we will get started on your direct training."

The guards around us headed in the direction of the dining tent, but almost every head turned back to look at me more than once on their way.

"Why do I get the feeling that didn't go well?" I asked, leaning closer to Tristan, and keeping my voice down so the last of the guards didn't hear me.

"You really have no idea, do you?" Tristan said, the smile on his face burning bright now.

"No idea about what?" I turned to him. His grin softened, and the green in his eyes flared up.

He turned toward me, lifting a hand toward my face.

"Cinder," Gus yelled, her hands on her hips as she came up to us.

She seemed angry, but there was no reason for her to be. Nothing made sense right now.

"Are you going to explain why you've been holding out on us?" Jacquetta asked, coming up beside Gus with her mouth in a line and one eyebrow raised high.

"One of you needs to start making a lot more sense," I said, shaking my head and addressing all of them.

"Even I have never seen anything like that," General Pace said, joining the others, but she didn't seem angry. Her face was open, and her mouth hung slightly agape.

"Fine," I said, throwing my hands in the air, "no one wants to explain to me what has you all acting strange. I'm going to eat."

I stomped past them, and they trailed after me, muttering more half sentences and non-sensical things to each other as we went. I tried to shove my stomach back into place as it crept its way into my throat.

"Cinder," Tristan caught up to me, and threaded his fingers through mine. "Are you upset?"

"No, I'm fine." It was a huge lie, but I didn't feel like hearing more things that left me feeling stupid. I had more work to do today, and this wasn't helping me to focus.

"Okay." He didn't look convinced when I peeked over at him, but he did look distracted. "I need to get back to work, but can we spend some time together later?"

Taking a deep breath, I turned my head to face him and even though my stomach still felt too high in my chest, I nodded. I did want to spend time with him. And maybe he would explain everything to me.

"Good." He grinned, and it was as if the stars shone on me on a clear night before he leaned down and kissed my cheek then turned and went toward his tent.

"I must also go with the King," the General said behind me, and followed after him without another word.

"Do you think she approves of the way I plan to train the guard?" I asked, my voice low, and a quaver sneaking past my efforts to hold it back on the word 'approve.'

"Cinder," Gus said, passing me with a pat on my shoulder, "I don't think you have her approval to worry about."

Again, I had no idea what that meant. Not really.

Should I not have worried because she clearly did approve, and it was a silly question? Or should I not have been focused on her approval because what I did was so bad I needed to worry about coming up with an entirely new plan?

Understanding people when it was a life and death situation was easy. Assessing threats was easy. Every other possible inter-action with people was so much more difficult, and made so much less sense than anything done with a blade.

Now behind Gus and Jacquetta on our way to the dining tent, I shook my head, once again one of the last to get in line for food.

Everyone around me talked and chatted, laughed and enjoyed their little break in the middle of the day to only think about food instead of the war in our country, and the real, heavy reason we were all here.

But I couldn't stop thinking about it.

I couldn't rid my mind of the doubts that what I was doing was going to end this war faster, that I wasn't helping to stop more kids from losing their parents. I struggled to ease the ache in my chest every time the doubt got too loud.

My intentions didn't matter. What mattered were the actions they caused.

CHAPTER 42

REAL

"Are you sure you don't want to stay and eat with us?" Gus asked, a line between her brows like she didn't believe my excuse for leaving.

"Yeah, I'm still full from lunch," I said, "I need to walk and think through tomorrow's plans, and then I'm sure I'll be hungry enough when I get back."

Jacquetta made a 'hmph' sound through her nose, but I had to get out of this tent and away from them. Their silent looks back and forth, full of meaning that were beyond my comprehension at the moment, were my constant companion all day, and I just couldn't think about what they meant anymore.

Walking out of the tent, I took a deep breath of the chilled air as night fell, and the busy movements of the camp faded into the subdued steps of preparing for bed all around me. My stomach finally found its way back into place.

It only lasted a minute.

Shaking my head and chewing on my lip, I ran through it all again. For the thousandth time, I thought about all I had done since we got here, and how everyone reacted to it all.

Getting to the spot in the open where the rope dragged on

the ground, I grabbed it and lowered myself down to lay in the dirt, looking up at the massive dome above us all.

The light of the moon was a fuzzy, pale glow through the strange ceiling, but the stars weren't visible at all.

I sighed.

When Tristan brought me here the first time, the best part was the view of the sky.

Fucking birds stole the sky from me.

Maybe this was a terrible mistake, this attempt to help others fight more like me. Maybe it was best that no one ever developed the kind of skills I had.

Tristan would be safer that way.

Rubbing my hands over my face, I let myself fade from the world around me, and go deep inside my mind.

I tried to go back to the place in my head where I was still a child, and my parents were still alive.

But I missed it.

My traitorous thoughts brought me instead to the first time my brother beat me when I made a mistake.

No.

It didn't matter how much I struggled to do what I wanted to here, I was not going to become my brother. I wouldn't let Ash's lessons in pain become my blueprint for how to train the guards.

The only real options for me were to succeed, or to admit defeat and leave to fight by myself, following after the groups of guards all over the country until I found the one that the Corvids attacked next.

Just, please, I prayed to Mother and Father, don't let them attack Breakwater again.

Duchess Inara and Breakwater had already been through enough.

But this was war, and hoping for any kind of fairness was a fool's folly. I knew that better than most.

So did my parents, and praying to them to make it otherwise wasn't kind to their memories.

"I'm sorry," I whispered out loud, hoping they knew what I meant. Everything. I meant I was sorry about everything.

"What do you have to be sorry about?" Tristan asked, taking a seat next to me and touching my hand.

"Just thinking out loud." I sat up and found he brought me a container of food along with one for himself.

"You brought me dinner?" I smiled, leaning forward to grab the container.

"No, these are both mine," he said, snatching it from me, but he had a wicked grin on his face.

"Really, a terrible liar," I said, shaking my head.

"Maybe you should pay me for it." His grin softened, and he looked at my mouth. "By telling me what's upset you," he said, handing the container to me.

"And not a great negotiator." I took a bite, and looked down at the food, the flavors melting away in a river of my uncertainty.

"Cinder," he said, touching my chin to point my face toward his, "please. What's wrong?"

"Do you ever wonder if you're making a mistake? If what you're doing isn't going to help? And then wonder how many people it will hurt if you get it wrong?"

He squeezed his eyes shut and took my hand, threading our fingers together and rubbing his thumb over the back of mine. When he opened his eyes again, there was a weight in his gaze.

"I'm King. Every minute of every day I feel that."

"You're a good King." As the words left my mouth, I realized how much I believed it. Beyond all the ways that killing him would have endangered my friends, and my kingdom with the loss of the Dragon King threat, it was him. Tristan himself made me believe that he was a good king, and loved and tried his best for the people. That mattered.

"And you're a gifted fighter who can teach these guards more than anyone I've ever known."

I cringed.

"But they seem so wary of me, like they don't trust me." I shook my head, trying to find the words to explain the feeling I got when I took off my blindfold was close to impossible. Even after we ran regular drills and I helped each of them with their grips and their techniques, the way they acted toward me was as if there was an invisible bubble around me that they couldn't cross.

"Cinder," he smiled and shook his head, tucking me under his arm and pulling me into his side.

"Do you remember what I said after the battle with the Corvids?" He picked at the edge of his container of food, directing his words to it instead of me.

"Of course."

"Right now," he turned his gaze to meet mine, "they're trying to figure out if you're real, too, and they can't touch you like this to help them understand."

"Why would they wonder?" I still didn't fully grasp why he ever questioned.

"Because no one has ever seen someone do what you do, let alone a member of nobility who they normally see in limited circumstances anyway. Plus…" He took a deep breath and lifted his free hand to my cheek, staring into my eyes, while his turned green around the edges.

He looked down at my mouth again, and my breath hitched in my chest.

I shouldn't say anything. I shouldn't do anything. I should pull away.

"Plus what?" I asked, my voice a whisper and every nerve in my body on alert.

Leaning toward me, he touched his forehead to mine, his

breath uneven and his eyes still locked on mine, growing greener by the second.

"They can all tell how I feel," he said, his voice barely there even though he was so close to me.

How he felt?

Oh, gods and goddesses and all the hellfire in Onyx.

If he kissed me, I would be lost. But if he said what I thought he might, I would never be found.

There weren't words in my head, not ones to make him let me go when I didn't want him to. And not any to explain the ricocheting feelings flaring to life in me that were so foreign. Nothing, no words, no actions came to me.

Looking into his green eyes as they shifted made it worse, so I closed my own.

And he lowered his mouth to mine.

CHAPTER 43

LOST

I was right.

The minute he kissed me, with lips soft, full, and gentle on mine, I was lost.

Any semblance of distance I managed to keep from him, from myself, dissolved in the sweet, tender flame that flared between us.

He pulled away a fraction and a sound escaped my lips.

I grabbed onto his jacket and climbed onto his lap, my legs on either side of him and my mouth claiming his again.

Deepening the kiss, his mouth yielded to mine and the heat of him, that shocking, hot touch, was a higher temperature than ever before, pouring into me.

The hand on my cheek tangled in my hair, and the one around my back held me tight against him where I could feel that he wanted me as much as I wanted him.

If I was lost, he found me, and I took him for my own all in that kiss.

But the sound of wings flapping, the feathery light sound of a bird in flight, made its way past the walls of the all-consuming blaze inside me.

Shoving Tristan flat to his back on the ground, I broke the kiss and looked up, laying across him to shield him until I found the source of the sound.

A pigeon, white with a gray, speckled head, landed not far from us and pecked at the ground.

Climbing off Tristan and into a crouch, I scanned the rest of the training grounds, even with the dark that limited how far I could see, trying to find anything else with wings waiting to get at my King.

"It's just a pigeon," he said, touching my hand.

Looking back at him, his eyes bright green with no other colors mixed in now, I took a deep breath,

"But it could have been something else." I shook my head and grabbed his hand, tugging him to his feet. "We shouldn't be out here. Especially not..."

He grinned and stepped closer.

"Distracted," I said, bending to pick up the containers. Mine tipped over and all the food scattered on the ground.

"Maybe you're right," he said, taking the containers from me, with the grin still in place, "but I liked that distraction."

Falling. I felt like I was falling, my legs losing their ability to stay upright even while I stood still.

"I did, too." Too much. I liked it far too much.

"Will..." he bit his bottom lip and looked down at the containers in his hands before he swallowed and went on, "tonight I should probably sleep in my own tent."

"No." My voice was too sharp, and I smiled to soften it. "Why would you?"

His smile was radiant, and he nodded before kissing me on the cheek and walking backward toward his tent.

"Then I'll see you tonight," he said, turning and continuing on his way.

Every step he took away from me tore something from me that left my hands shaking.

Maybe sleeping next to him would be more challenging now, but every minute he was too far away for me to know that he was safe, for me to protect him, would be my biggest challenge.

How he walked away, seeming to have no trouble at all with the distance, made the shaking in my hands worse.

I knotted them together in front of me, and watched until he was inside his tent, the door flap opening and closing on the lights inside, and General Pace waiting with others for more news on the war.

Nodding, I made my way to my own tent. He would be okay. She would make sure he was safe.

But the fear—the kind that hadn't plagued me to the point of physical limitation since just after my parents died and I worried for Ash's safety every minute of the day—raced through my body.

My muscles bunched and tugged, leaving my gait awkward and jumpy, and my breath didn't come easy.

Getting to my tent and opening the door, all I wanted was to sit down, to try and find a place in my mind where I could be okay again.

Jacquetta and Gus stopped mid-sentence, eyeing me as I stumbled to the table and took a seat, barely registering the food in front of me and the fact I still had not eaten.

"Cinder?" Gus asked, her voice careful as if she were addressing a wild animal that she thought might rip her face off.

I looked up and tried to find the words to explain how much I needed Tristan to be okay now. How, even when he was with the General, it was all I could think about. How was I going to save the King?

"He can't marry me," I stammered, panic replaced all the fear with a sudden whoosh of every nightmare I could think of.

Onyx would suffer, the people would be left without a real queen, and my brother would be too close to Tristan.

The thought of Ash getting so close to him chased off every bit of Tristan's warmth still on my skin.

My brother would use my place as Queen, and the silence I would be forced to keep, to get close to and kill Tristan himself.

"Did the King propose?" Jacquetta asked, her voice too high-pitched and too loud.

"No. Shhh." I waved my shaking hands in her direction.

"Then why do you look like you were just attacked by ghosts?" Gus asked, the same note of caution in her.

"We…I…oh, no." I put my face in my hands, and leaned down to rest my head on the table.

"Cinder," Gus said, her voice all honey now.

"You just figured it out, didn't you?" Jacquetta asked, patting me on the shoulder.

"Figured what out?" I didn't sound like me to my own ears, didn't sound like any version of myself I knew.

"That you love him, and he loves you." Gus' words were blunt, and there was a note of truth in them, even if it was terrible.

"But he can't." There it was again, that strange version of me, plaintive and full of terror.

"He does," Jacquetta said, "and you do, too. Anyone paying attention could see it. But why does it scare you so much?"

Even though her question was gentle, the words carried blades that stabbed into every part of me at once.

Gus and Jacquetta were the only people outside of home who came close to knowing what I was, how ill-suited I was for the monarchy, and I couldn't explain it any more clearly. I couldn't expose them any further to my secrets, and risk Ash finding out and thinking them a threat.

My secrets would be buried with me as I ensured my targets were buried with theirs.

Tonight, though, wasn't yet my time.

And until then, I had to keep those tales deep inside me, and let no one else know.

Not Gus. Not Jacquetta. Not Tristan. No one could know.

Somehow, I had to put it all away, close my worry and my fears in a pocket in my mind with the blood on my hands, and never let anyone see me break again.

I took one more deep breath and raised my head, staring at the food in front of me.

More breaths while Gus and Jacquetta talked of weddings and proposals after the war was over.

All of my words were pushed into the pocket of my mind with my secrets as I shoved food in my mouth, my hand no longer shaking.

"That's why he hasn't asked yet," Gus said.

"Of course it is," Jacquetta said, "he can't ask Cinder and risk the Marquessa turning Amethyst against Onyx while we fight Corvid. As long as the crown is a possibility for her, we have a better chance at winning this war."

Moments of Tristan, with half sentences and cryptic words ran through my mind.

She was right.

If I survived this war, he was going to make me Queen.

The thought probably should have made me hide my face again. Instead, it brought the flavor back to the food, and let me breathe easier.

Now, all I had to do to save Onyx was find someone who wasn't the Marquessa to marry Tristan, and then I needed to die in this war.

CHAPTER 44

CLAIM

Fresh from the shower tent, wearing a ridiculous lace nightgown that covered nothing, my hair still wet where it laid brushed out on the pillow next to me, I stared into the darkness above my head.

Gus and Jacquetta's steady breathing told me they were already asleep, but I needed to wait for Tristan.

I wasn't going to survive this war. And that meant I had time.

The tent door moved. The unique sound of the extra thick, coated canvas moving out of the way as he came inside, then let it fall again, sent my heart pounding.

He didn't bring a light with him this time, but came unerringly to my bed anyway.

Under me, the mattress moved as he climbed onto it and laid his head on the pillow.

Last night his hand came to rest on my waist. But I was on my back tonight, and he put his hand on mine.

Biting my lip, I turned my hand to thread my fingers with his.

"You don't have to wait up for me," he whispered, his voice barely there in the night although it sang through me as if it contained a whole choir.

"No," I whispered, turning toward him, "I wanted to."

His intake of breath was hitching and uneven. He let go of my hand and wrapped his arm around my back, his fingers touching my wet hair.

"Did you take a shower before bed?" He sounded like he was smiling.

"To get the training dust off." I ran my hand up his chest, but his jacket felt strange.

"What are you wearing?" There was no collar when I got to the neckline.

"My pajamas. I took a shower, too."

"In the same giant shower tent I was in?" The idea made me picture him finding me there...of seeing him there, and my throat closed.

"General Pace made a small tent in one corner of it that's private for me. She says it's safer that way. Although, how I could be any safer than I am when I'm surrounded by the guard, under a dome, I don't know." He shook his head, the movement making my fingers move.

"I do." I tangled my fingers into his hair and pulled his lips to mine.

He made a low noise that was close to a growl and pulled me in tighter as he opened his mouth and deepened the kiss.

Again, I was falling into him and his heat, and the dream of the time I was allowed to have this.

The taste of him was clean and fresh, still with that hint of the sweet tanginess that reminded me of the treats everyone made that smelled so much like hellfire water, the treats we never ate in Lehar.

But I wanted my fill of him. I never wanted to taste anything else.

Just like last night, he was on top of the blankets, and I was under them. But I wanted him with me, close to me.

I broke the kiss and tugged the blanket down from under him.

"Come here," I whispered.

"No, Cinder, wait." He sat up and pulled me up with him. "I don't want your Ladies to wake up and think less of me."

"Because you're under my covers?" That didn't make any sense.

"They'll think I took advantage of my position as King. I don't want that." He ran his fingers along my hairline and down through my hair, pulling me close and kissing my neck.

From my neck through every other part of my body his fire flowed, and I melted against him.

"After I tell everyone," he whispered into my skin, "after the whole world knows, then I never want to sleep anywhere else but under the covers with you."

He was going to ask me to be Queen. Any doubt I had before tonight was gone. But it didn't scare me anymore. It was never going to happen, and when I went to my grave, I got to do it knowing he wanted me.

"Tristan, I don't care what anyone thinks. I know," I whispered, pulling his face from my neck so I could kiss him again.

Moments later, as my hands roamed over the strength of his chest, he broke the kiss, and adjusted the covers before he laid me back down, leaning over me in the dark.

"Cinder, when we're finally together, no one else will be in the room," he whispered. "I want to be able to hear you."

His mouth crashed into mine and I pulled him to me. I couldn't get him close enough. All that fire, from him, in me, collected in my stomach and moved lower until I was aching for him.

"I didn't expect you," he whispered into my mouth.

"Expect me?" I pulled back, even as I wanted to have no

more space between us, those words sent my heart hurtling toward the heat at my center. Expect me of what? Was this a ploy? Did he know?

"When we started this stupid potential search, I never expected to find you. I want you to know that. How much you surprise me." He leaned over to my hand on his shoulder and kissed the back of it.

I sighed.

"That makes two of us."

He smiled against my hand, and laid down next to me pulling me close.

"You said you could think of a way to be safer. If there's something I could do to keep you safer, tell me."

"No. I meant as long as you're with me, you're safer than anywhere else."

"Promise me you won't put yourself at greater risk for me."

"Tristan, I can't do that." Even the idea of putting my own survival above his made me recoil, trying to pull back from him.

But his arms kept me in place, tight against him.

"More than anything else," he said, "I want you safe. Please. Promise me."

"Onyx needs the Dragon King, and I need you to trust me." It was a risk, to turn it back on him. When all I wanted was to spend our limited time together as happy as possible when I knew the way it would end. And that when it ended, he would be hurt.

He put his forehead to mine, and took a deep shuddering breath.

"I do trust you. But this is war. And even though I know what you can do, the thought of losing you…"

Even under normal circumstances, the heat of his skin could be intense, but now it blazed up to almost scalding.

"You have me." And he did.

Tristan kissed me, his mouth hard on mine and claiming my breath as he already claimed my heart.

We kissed and held each other late into the night, in the middle of the preparations for war.

CHAPTER 45

AWAY

"We will make you proud, Fighter Cinder," the regiment captain said as all the guards filed past while we saluted them.

"I'm already proud of all of you," I said, loud enough that some of the guards walking past grinned and one blushed.

And they did make me proud. What they managed to learn and develop in the skills they would need for this particular enemy in the month of non-stop training was impressive.

Still. I knew many of them would not survive their deployments, and the weight of that, wondering if I prepared them enough to give them a chance, was heavier than I ever imagined.

The years I spent carrying out my brother's missions, the blood that stained my soul as it spilled over my hands, was nothing compared to this. Those deaths were justified. They were men like Lord Fall. Men who didn't deserve the life they were given, and the world was better for their absence.

But this? This was senseless slaughter because my brother caught the wrong bird out of her quarters when he was sending a message to me.

No matter that it was Ash, and not me, who made the choice to attack the palace, it wouldn't have happened but for me.

And now, some of the guards I trained, who I could name along with their faces and picture as they worked hard to learn a new skill, some of them were going to die.

War was never fair.

But this one seemed petty.

Until I looked at the faces of the people who were fighting in it.

There was only a week left to ensure that my replacement trainers were up to the task before we left to Breakwater and wherever else the battles led us.

So far, the vast majority of the fighting was focused on Breakwater, which made no sense to me. There had to be a better way for them to get into the country.

It also enraged me.

Duchess Inara and her people had been through enough.

As the regiment leader turned and saluted me in a farewell that I returned, I spotted Tristan nodding to the guards he passed, his face in grim lines.

He reached me and sighed.

"This is the hardest part," he said.

"King Tristan, you're doing the right thing," General Pace said, leaving us behind to go off to whatever was next on her list of unending work and plans.

"You're doubting yourself again?" I asked, wanting to reach out to him, to pull him close, and remind him how good a King he was.

"No. Even when I know that this needs to happen, the fact I'm not there at the front with them yet is grating at me."

"It was different with your parents. They had an heir. Onyx wouldn't be without a Dragon King."

He laughed, a low, humorless sound.

"Do you really think anyone believes the old tales anymore? It's been generations," he said, shaking his head.

"People do believe. More since the Corvids exposed their power." I grinned and stepped closer to him. "Now, some people think you must turn into a dragon."

"Turn into a…" His laugh this time was quiet and subdued, but it was real.

I smiled and took his hand.

He squeezed my hand, and I bit my lip.

"Cinder, don't do that when we're out here in front of everyone and I can't do anything about it." His eyes softened, and his smile was real too.

"Don't do what?" And I did it again, my smile growing wider as he growled low in his throat.

"You're going to make me cut our trip short tonight."

"What trip?" All the playfulness jumped out of my mind. Any trip outside the dome, unless we were going back to the palace, wasn't something to play about.

"Before we go to Breakwater, I want to take you back to the Shield House for a visit." He smiled, and I had to force myself not to grab his hand and run with him there right now.

"Really? Oh, Tristan, I'm so glad we get to see the kids again. Will Layton come with us?"

"Do you realize that since that first visit," he reached out and tucked a strand of hair that had escaped my ponytail back behind my ear, letting his fingers linger on my cheek, "you light up every time you talk about the kids at the Shield House."

I shook my head and looked down at my hand in his.

"What you're doing there," I looked back at him, his eyes a warm brown now, "it's a good thing. Being there…"

How was I supposed to explain what that place meant, what seeing those kids meant?

Yes, meeting them, knowing what he was doing there, giving

to them, had saved his life that night. But it also gave me something.

"Seeing them being saved, and being even a tiny part of their story when I met them, it felt like I did something good, too."

"Cinder," he said, his voice thick. He gripped my hands like he was holding himself back.

If I had to wager a guess, it was as if he was fighting the urge to pull me into him and wrap his arms around me. But that was probably just me assuming he was struggling with the same thing I was.

"We're going in a carriage?" I asked, letting go of his hands and stepping back, making his decision for him.

He gave a me a wry smile and a heavy breath, but he nodded.

"Good. When do we leave?"

"Right before dinner if that works for you."

I turned and surveyed everything I needed to accomplish today with the other guards before I turned back to Tristan.

"That works. Are you sure you'll be able to get away?"

"Do you doubt me?" He raised a brow at me, and one corner of his mouth turned up along with it.

"Never."

He smiled and kissed me on the cheek before he headed back to his never-ending meetings, and he didn't see the lie in my answer.

Of course, when I had doubted him, I didn't know him. And the majority of my doubt was now directed at myself.

That, and how he would react when I died in this war.

But I shook my head and went to the newer guards to work with them on their technique, knowing that no matter the things I doubted and the things I worried about, my death was the right choice.

My visit with Tristan to the Shield House would probably be the last time I saw the kids.

At least we all got to say goodbye.

Not only would that help me, but it would help them, too.

Well, I told myself that anyway.

I wasn't very good at watching the clock, but an hour before dinner was supposed to start, Gus and Jacquetta came and got me like we arranged.

The guards kept working on their maneuvers, my replacement trainers doing good work with them, and I was hustled toward the shower tent.

"Are you sure we have time?" I asked Gus and Jacquetta. "I should probably just go change and wait for Tristan in our tent."

"Cinder," Gus said, rolling her eyes.

"You always do this," Jacquetta said, pushing me in the middle of my back like I was really going to make a break for it. "I don't know why you don't know better by now."

"What do I always do?" This was not an argument about spending ten hours getting ready for some event at the palace. We were just going to see some kids.

"Every time we have a chance to prepare you for something with the King," Gus said.

"You act like it makes no sense to try and look like you care," Jacquetta said.

"Alright," I said, "I'll stop complaining."

They looked at each other and had a whole conversation with their eyes.

Normally, I didn't have a clue what they said when they did that, but right then, I knew.

We got to the shower tent, and I turned back to them before I went inside.

"Both of you have done so much for me, including making me more beautiful than I ever would be otherwise. Thank you." I smiled while their mouths fell open and their faces went blank, and went inside to get ready for a night with Tristan away from work.

CHAPTER 46

TELL OURSELVES

"How did you do this?" I asked, looking in the large mirror at myself.

I looked like we were still in the palace, and they had hours to get me ready. Even though I was in a day dress and not one of the elaborate evening gowns I had worn so many other times. My makeup was done, and my hair was in long curls with a small braid framing my face.

"We are very good," Gus said, smiling and handing me my cloak.

"And we decided that because you were nice, maybe we should be, too," Jacquetta said, her nose in the air, and I couldn't help laughing.

"Hello," Tristan called from the other side of the tent door.

"She's ready," Gus called back, grinning with her shoulders hitched up like she was more excited than I was for him to come inside.

Opening the tent door, Tristan stepped inside, wearing a suit almost designed for court, but lacking all the ostentatious details court truly required of the men.

When I first met him and thought he was just a guard, I

thought he was good looking. Now…now he was beautiful. A storm churned in my stomach just looking at him.

"Cinder," he said, my name like a poem, "you look amazing."

He pulled roses from behind his back. They were the exact shade of the ones that used to grow up the walls of our manor in Lehar.

I sucked in a shaking breath, forcing the pressure at the backs of my eyes not to turn into tears.

But he didn't hand them to me. The massive bouquet was split into three parts. Two of them were still large bouquets, and the last was a single rose.

Gus and Jacquetta got the bouquets, and I got the single rose.

They were so thrilled that they almost swooned to the floor, but I just kissed his cheek and whispered in his ear, "You are sometimes too good."

"So you're happy?" he asked, his brows up in the center and his eyes soft.

"You make me very happy."

He took a deep breath and took my cloak, slipping it on me before he wrapped an arm around my back to hold onto my waist.

"We won't be too late," he said over his shoulder at Gus and Jacquetta as we headed outside.

"Don't worry about the time," Gus said.

I grinned and managed to keep my laugh small.

"Maybe I should have given them flowers a long time ago," Tristan said.

"They're having a good day." I didn't bother to explain what all that meant, and I didn't think he would understand it all anyway.

Frigid air made its way under the hem of my dress and all the way up my legs, but I wasn't cold. Even as the chill iced its way across my skin, it didn't penetrate through me. It couldn't while Tristan had me tucked against his side, and the Dragon heat of him ran through my body.

We got to the carriage waiting at the edge of the tents, and Tristan helped me inside.

He wrapped his arm around me again once we were in the seat and ran his hand up and down my arm.

The footman finally closed the door, and I took his face in my hands, pulling his lips to mine.

A low noise came from his throat, and I was lost all over again.

I did want to go to the Shield House, but as the carriage started moving, I just wanted to stay with him inside it and revel in our privacy, too.

Breaking the kiss, he held me tight, and leaned his forehead against mine.

"Part of me wants to cancel going to the Shield House," he said, "and stay in here with you."

Deep inside me, a sinking sensation dropped me further into this version of magic, the one where I was allowed to have this.

"Me, too," I said, which wasn't a lie, and yet felt like I was betraying him. For the first time since I made my decision, it hurt to love him knowing I would leave him.

"We're running out of time, and it makes me want to hold you too tight," he said, shaking his head as he sat back a fraction.

"Running out of time?" My heart raced. Did he figure out my plan somehow?

"In Breakwater, and maybe other places we go for this fight, we won't be able to be together at night as we have been."

He ran a thumb along my cheek, and I smiled.

"Tristan, walls don't usually stop me."

Laughing, he pulled me in and kissed me, a soft caress of lips.

"Now why didn't I think of that?" he asked, and I laughed.

The carriage slowed, and we pulled apart.

"We still have the rest of the night," he said, kissing my cheek and preparing to get out.

Although he was right, and although I wasn't joking about making my way to him no matter the walls between us, it wasn't enough.

In my plans for dying, I managed to skip the part that meant with every day, every kiss, and every time his warmth spread across my skin, I wanted more time.

The footman opened the door, his head tilted back as he scanned the darkening sky.

Climbing out after him, I followed the footman's lead and looked up as Tristan pulled me along to the front door of the Shield House.

Last time we were here, there were toys in the yard, and the clear indication of children who spent a great deal of time playing outside.

Now, there were almost no toys left in the yard, and I got the feeling it had more to do with the sky than the winter weather.

The door swung open, and a young woman, probably eighteen, smiled and stepped back, ushering us in.

"We've been waiting for you," she said, while kids of all ages poured out of the parlor, and wrapped their arms around Tristan and I, half of them talking at once.

"How did you know we were coming?" Tristan asked, ruffling one boy's hair.

"General Pace gave me leave to come a little early so I could help them get ready for dinner," Layton said, coming around the corner.

"So you're the spy," I said, grinning.

Layton's eyes popped open, but he laughed, loud and long a second later.

"Fighter Cinder, for some reason when we're training, I keep forgetting that you're funny," he said.

"That is *Lady* Cinder," Angeline, the young girl I met before, her hair in a braid again, said and I hid my smile.

"Apologies," Layton said with an exaggerated bow, "Lady Cinder."

"How about just Cinder?" I asked, crouched down with a child under each arm. "We're all friends here, right?"

Cheers erupted and I laughed while Tristan nodded.

"We're friends with the King and Queen of Onyx?" one of the little twins asked, and the children all broke out in small groups of conversation at how great that was while I tried not to fall down.

"Oh, no," I said, "I'm not the Queen."

"But you will be," Angeline said and turned back to her friends.

No, I wouldn't be.

I couldn't look at Tristan. I did everything I could to avoid it, including swinging one of the children telling me a story about a game they played to the other side of me.

But when Layton announced dinner was ready and they all started to dart toward the dining room, Tristan and I trailing behind them, he ran a searing hand down my arm to thread his fingers with mine.

Looking at him, I saw it. The yearning for that future was in his flashing green eyes.

The shape of his want fit like a sword in a sheath into the empty and hollow hole left by my own.

"Have dinner with me?" he asked, the words meaning so much more.

It wasn't the words that sent tingles running down my legs, it was the question mark at the end, the fact that I knew he wanted to ask me something else.

"Yes," I said.

And while he swept me into a hug and buried his face in my neck, holding on like he never wanted to let go and like I was as fragile as glass at the same time, I tried to pretend it wasn't a lie.

CHAPTER 47

NEED

"Can't we stay up just a little longer?" Angeline begged, giving Layton the biggest wide-eyed pout I had ever seen.

I bit my lip and tried to suppress the laugh that bubbled up in me watching her.

Tristan turned around and shook his head while he looked steadfastly at the wall just to avoid answering—which in his case would have been giving in to her wishes.

"No, sorry," Layton said, "The King and Lady Cinder need to get back. They have a lot of important work to do."

A round of tight hugs and soft good nights, and the kids were all headed upstairs to their beds. While Tristan and I watched them go, he slipped his hand into mine.

"Hopefully," he whispered, laying my cloak around my shoulders, "this work will mean there are not as many kids joining them as I think there might be."

"Even if there are," I said, putting my hand on his cheek, "at least they have this place and each other."

With a kiss on the palm of my hand and one last heavy-lidded look up the stairs, Tristan led me out the front door of the Shield House.

Someday, when this was done and I was gone, these kids would be able to tell any of the others who joined them about me. About the best of me.

I didn't deserve mourning. And I didn't expect a gravestone. But they would be a living epitaph, and all I could hope was that it would help me reach peace at the end.

We climbed into the carriage, and Tristan still had a cloud over his features, the worries all coming down to rest on his face at once.

But I needed this to remain the positive goodbye I held onto when we left, and I was quickly running out of time to be with him.

Maybe it was selfish. Maybe it was because I didn't have the words to help him lift the darkness, but a fire started in my heart. A burning need to take this time for my own. This time with him.

Flinging my leg over his lap, I climbed on top of him as the carriage started to move, and pulled his lips to mine.

He gripped my waist with hands that grew greedy, and it made the fire in my heart spread through my body.

Pressing myself against him, with the rocking of the carriage, I felt as he grew hard, and the length of him made all the heat in my body focus on where we were connected.

The ride was too short, but by the time we reached the training grounds and the carriage rolled to a stop, I couldn't tell anymore where the heat of him stopped and the fire within me started.

We pulled apart, my breath coming in gasps, and he didn't say a word as he opened the carriage door and pulled me out after him.

Hands locked together, he made a direct line for his tent, which surprised me, I would have thought we would be heading to mine. But there were still people milling about after dinner and Gus and Jacquetta were probably still awake.

Not for the first time, I wanted to be able to steal away with him somewhere away from everyone.

Part of me expected to see General Pace and the others of the war council on the other side of the tent flap as he swung it open.

But we were alone.

Tristan reached for me, and I wrapped my arms around his neck, our mouths crashing together with a hunger that wasn't there in so many of the sweet and gentle kisses of before.

While not sweet or gentle, I couldn't make the kiss deep enough, I couldn't press myself tight enough to him.

My tongue and his explored each other while my fingers dug into his shoulders.

He bent and took hold of my thighs, lifting me up so I wrapped my legs around his waist, and his hands gripped tight into the skin of my thighs through the day dress.

Somehow, he walked with me around the suits of armor and to the large table in the middle of the room.

With one hand, he swept away the maps and whatever else littered the table that they used to plan the war, and sat me on the edge of it, leaning into me.

The full strength of his want for me pressed into me and left my breathing ragged.

I pulled and grabbed at the buttons on his coat, not caring when I heard one pop off and tang against some other metal thing in the room.

The noise he made, low in his throat, sent another surge through me, and I tore the rest of his buttons apart, putting my palms against his chest, which was as hot as touching the hell-fire source.

Lean and hard, his skin was silken fire, and I wanted to be burned.

He slipped his hands under the skirts of my dress, that same searing heat tracing up my legs.

"Tristan," I moaned as his hands explored my thighs and I wanted him to keep going.

My heart thudded faster in my chest, my breathing staccato and frantic as my fingers tried to find purchase on the muscles of his chest and moved to grip his shoulders

Not sharp or long, my fingernails dug into his skin, that heat reaching further inside me.

It wasn't words, but he made a noise in my mouth that sent an echo through every muscle in my body. My legs tightened around him.

A sound escaped me, one I didn't even recognize, but it may as well have called for more.

"Cinder," he said against my mouth, pulling back enough that I could see the glowing green of his eyes, "I love—"

Screams, shouts, and alarms went up outside.

I shoved him back from me and jumped off the table, grabbing one of the swords from a suit of armor on my way by.

"Tristan, stay in the arena," I screamed as I ran out of the tent with all the heat and want pouring through my body turning into adrenaline and the need for a fight.

Dark shapes darted toward the main gates of the arena, and there didn't seem to be any birds flying up by the dome as the full moon illuminated all of it, providing a weak, diffuse light to see by.

Running toward the same place everyone else was seemed to be my only option as I couldn't tell what the hell was going on.

Guards swarmed through the main gates, most not properly armed, and running off in all directions.

"What's happening?" I screamed, not caring who was going to answer me, as long as someone did.

"Bridgeton is under attack," someone yelled back.

"Where?" Was it the whole city? One area? Where did I need to go to stop this?

"Riverun Lane is the worst," someone else screamed.

The last of the heat left in my blood poured out of me as I exhaled in a whoosh of air as if I was just punched in the stomach.

Shield House.

All the kids at Shield House were on Riverun Lane.

<h1 style="text-align:center">CHAPTER 48</h1>

<h1 style="text-align:center">CENTER</h1>

There wasn't time.

No time to get different weapons. I wasn't even wearing my spike. All I had was the sword I grabbed, and the throwing knives sewn into the lining of my cloak.

No time to change into something that would meld into the dark better than a red dress and a red cloak.

No time to check on Jacquetta and Gus, to make sure they stayed with Tristan inside the arena, surrounded by guards and as safe as possible.

And no time to find a way to Riverun Lane that didn't involve sprinting there as fast as I could, which left me more open to air attack than I ever wanted to be, and far more than I knew was smart.

But the kids...

I ran faster.

My legs went from weak, not wanting to do anything but wrap around Tristan, to working harder than they ever had before to run as fast as he always said I moved.

The kids needed me to be more than real now. They needed

me to be the hero they believed me to be, and the fact that I wasn't made my lungs ache as I pushed beyond my own limits.

Familiar sounds of clanging steel and screams found me as I rounded the corner onto the road of Shield House.

Bodies littered the street.

Some doors to homes hung open with blood on the stoops and lifeless forms on the stairs.

At the other end of the street, a giant crow grabbed someone and lifted them into the air.

"Fucking pigeons," I breathed as I pulled a throwing knife out of my cloak and readied it in my free hand without missing a step.

Between me and Shield House, fights happened everywhere. But I didn't see any other crows, and I didn't feel any bearing down on me.

A woman, in a very fine dress, slammed what looked like a carver from her kitchen into the eye of a man in front of her.

He fell in a heap, and she sunk to the ground with a wail, grasping onto the bloody mess nearby of what was left of someone she must have loved.

Just past her, a man waved a shovel and tried to defend himself from two attackers.

One attacker made a move to get past the shovel, and I threw my knife, burying it in the attacker's throat.

Dropping the blade in their hand, the attacker scrambled at the knife in their neck, then did the worst thing they could— they wrenched it out sending a spray of blood flowing between their fingers as they toppled over.

I ran up, shoved the shovel man away and cut the other attacker almost in half.

Wrenching the sword free, I took the short sword the attacker had, picked up my throwing knife, and grabbed the other attacker's short sword, too, before I kept going.

Other fights around me were more even or over before I got close enough to help.

More bodies and more screams clogged the night all around me as the air itself grew thick with the metallic tang of blood.

The attackers were all making their way down toward the other end of the street, but they were met with people coming from their homes wielding whatever they thought would make a decent weapon.

What were they doing?

No shovel or kitchen knife was going to be enough against real weapons. Not in the long run of a fight.

But they delayed them enough for me to finally catch up to the crowd and step over bodies of guards.

The distinct sound of steel against steel rang out again. I spotted another guard, his sword locked in battle with one of the attackers.

He stepped back into the light from a gate and my heart stuttered.

"Layton," I screamed, "get inside."

"No," he grunted, shoving the attacker off his sword and hacking at them again, "I can't."

"Yes," I yelled, stabbing my sword into his attacker's back, spraying him with the blood shooting out of their chest. "You can."

Layton sucked down ragged breaths, leaning down, as I darted past him to cut down another attacker.

In the middle of the street, directly in front of Shield House, another skirmish unfolded. But it looked wrong.

While I grabbed another opponent near me, slit their throat, and sliced through another one's abdomen, their intestines falling to the ground before they did, the group in the middle of the street moved slowly down the road.

But the only fighting was on the outside edge of the mob, like the people in the middle were being protected.

"Attack the center," I screamed.

Who I was screaming at, I didn't know. I didn't want any of the random citizens to try and break through that blockade.

But someone had to.

The only reason for a formation like that was to protect someone on the inside. If there was someone important enough to the other side for them to be in the middle, I wanted them dead.

I ran as fast I could, grinding my teeth on the feral scream that wanted to rip from me every time I had to pass someone I should have killed to get to the middle of that group.

A bird dove from the sky and I threw a knife, lodging it in the bird's neck, sending it toppling the other direction.

Right behind it, another dove, snatching a tiny, flailing body from the crowd.

"No," I screamed, throwing a whole sword like a spear, only managing to catch some feathers as the bird lifted off from the group.

A cry went up as the sword found a home in someone's body. The tight formation shattered.

Running faster, tears from the chill air stinging my eyes and streaming down my face, I hacked my way through the necks of three of the attackers before I thought I saw a face that shouldn't be anywhere near Bridgeton. Let alone the Shield House.

Pawing at my face, I tried to clear my eyes. But it wasn't necessary.

My vision didn't lie to me.

Brix grinned as he stepped into the light from the gate of one of the houses, and lifted his hands in the air as another bird dropped from the sky, gripped him by the shoulders, and lifted off with him.

I screamed and struck down every last one of the attackers I could find, not stopping until I got to one that landed right next to Layton's attacker.

Looking around me, I didn't see Layton. He wasn't on the street, and he wasn't among the bodies.

Staring into the night sky, my stomach dropped into my toes when I thought I knew where he was.

Brix, Layton, and little Angeline were all wherever the Corvids took them.

And the only one even a little safe there, was the one I usually wanted to violently separate from his grin.

CHAPTER 49

LAST PLACE

The door to Shield House hung off the hinges in pieces. Rage made my breathing hitch in my chest. My knuckles popped as my grip tightened on my blades.

I stepped over the threshold into the house, the floor creaking beneath my foot.

From somewhere, a tiny, distorted whimper made me close my eyes and quiet my breathing to listen closer.

But I couldn't get a good read on where the kids were hiding.

Puffing out my cheeks as I blew out the air in my lungs, I turned and checked outside before I decided to risk it. I didn't want to find whatever was hidden in the rooms of the house.

"Everyone," I yelled, "It's Cinder. Please come on out."

Cries and pounding feet came from all over the house as the kids streamed from their hiding places and ran to me, crowding around my legs.

I held the blades tight against me, the point straight up, and hugged as many of them as I could reach with one hand.

"Okay. Is there anyone hurt?"

"Yes."

"Angeline is gone."

"Layton went after them."

"They killed us."

I found one of the twins, at the edge of the group, shaking, his eyes far away.

Wading through the kids with careful steps, I reached him and crouched in front of him, trying to get him to look at me.

But wherever he was, he couldn't see me from there. Not really.

"Killed us?" I asked, my voice a hushed croak.

"His brother is hurt," another little voice offered.

Swallowing, I looked around me and wanted to run away.

These were children. Babies. Not only had they all lost their parents, but war came to their door. Again.

I needed someone to show me where the injured and killed were so I could check them and get them to help. But it would be monstrous to ask them to go back to those spaces.

What the fuck was I supposed to do?

All of them needed to get somewhere safe, but where was that? How in the world was I supposed to lead them through the streets when we might get attacked again, and they would see carnage all the way to the training grounds?

Pounding footsteps rang against the cobblestones of the street outside, and I jumped up, motioning for all the kids to get behind me.

They did it so fast and with so little sound they reminded me of me. The hairs on my arms stood on end as I lifted my blades again.

Seconds later, Tristan and a line of guards filed in the front door.

"Cinder," he said, his face going from panic to exhaustion in a second, and his whole body slumped.

"Some of the kids are hurt in other rooms of the house," I said, focusing on what was the most important thing for right now.

"The rest of the attackers have been driven off," he said, touching my arm, but directing his words to the kids as they hugged him, too. "But no one should go anywhere yet. When we get carriages here for you, I'm going to have them take you to the palace, and someone will come get your things."

"But…" one of them mumbled and others hung their heads.

"King Tristan, this is our home."

Most of the others chimed in with agreement, and a crack formed in my heart so sharp I had to close my eyes.

We couldn't take this place from them, too, but what about the ones who looked at this place and saw ghosts now?

I looked to the little boy who still stared into the middle distance and swallowed, tapping Tristan's arm before I went to the little boy again, trying to get him to look at me.

"Do you want to stay here?" I asked, "Or would you rather go to the palace?"

"This was the place he was alive," he said.

Pressure built behind my eyes and my stomach flipped over.

I nodded and stood up on shaking legs, not capable of saying goodbye as I walked out the front door, and stumbled down the steps toward the road.

Before I got very far, Tristan grabbed my shoulder and pulled me into his arms.

"Are you okay?" he asked. "Stay here. I'll take you back soon."

"They killed his twin. This is the last place his twin was alive next to him. He never wants to leave. And they took Layton and Angeline."

I rambled on while I clung to him, a litany of offenses, and proof our attackers didn't have souls anymore. How could they do this to children on purpose?

But...was Brix with them? Why was Brix in the city? And if Brix was with them, did that mean Ash was?

That didn't make any sense.

Ash wouldn't join the Corvids.

Right?

"Come inside with me," Tristan said, pulling back and looking toward the house.

"No, I can't. I can't be in there when..." I couldn't even say it.

"Okay. Keep your eyes up, and I'll get someone to take you back." He held me tight, his skin colder than he had ever been, and went back inside.

Part of me wanted to snatch him back and kiss him, to hold as tight to him as I could, but he wouldn't want the guards all around us to see. And I had other things to worry about.

I looked up at the deep black of the sky, the color indistinguishable from the sleek feathers of the crows.

A chill ran over my body, and I dropped my gaze back to the street.

Everyone was too busy.

Waiting here for Tristan to finish, for the guards to help the kids, and do everything else that needed to be done, wasn't going to help.

Grabbing a passing guard by the shoulder and turning him toward me, the weight of what I was about to do settled into my bones.

"Please tell the King that I have returned to the training grounds," I said, my voice as hard as the steel that was flowing through my veins.

"Yes, Fighter Cinder," he said, and I released him and took off, running down the street toward the end where the first person I saw get lifted off the ground had been.

The street where Brix was taken, and where the first person was grabbed, didn't yield anything to help me tell which direction the airborne attackers came from.

But it was clear the ones who remained on the ground turned at the end of Riverun Lane.

All I had to do was follow the blood and bodies.

First, though, I had a stop to make.

CHAPTER 50

FACE OF DEATH

Making my way back to the training grounds took almost no time, but navigating my way through the mad scramble under the dome to my tent was much more difficult.

Guards streamed in all directions.

Some carried people to lines forming in the middle of the flying space where medics and physicks tended to the wounds.

Others moved more slowly and more somberly, carrying their charges to the long-distance range where they laid the bodies of the dead out in rows.

And still more ran with papers or weapons in hand, doing some other business that we all needed to be done on our behalf.

Because we did.

Every Onyxian—especially the citizens of Bridgeton— needed us all to do what we did best and handle this.

Which was exactly my plan.

I finally flung back the tent door to find Jacquetta curled up on the floor, sobbing silent tears, and clutching a torn chunk of green fabric.

"Jacquetta?" I asked, my voice weak while all the strength that flowed through me only moments before turned into the puddle she was crying.

"Cinder," she yelled, flinging herself over to me and wrapping her arms around me, her sobs not even slowing down.

"Where's—" I couldn't do it. My throat closed, and I choked on the question. I licked my lips and took in a shaking breath before I tried again, holding her tight, "Where's Gus?"

"No one knows," she wailed, the sound of her voice like the fall of a mountain as it rang through my body.

I squeezed her tighter and gritted my teeth before I shoved her away from me, holding her by the shoulders, staring into her eyes while the vision of her swam in my held-back tears.

"Help me," I said, "I'm getting her back."

She held the scrap of fabric to her face, covering her mouth, and nodded.

Nodding back to her, I let her go, and peeled off my blood-smeared clothes.

Jacquetta handed me a washcloth and the basin for washing our hands.

I scrubbed off some of the blood that had soaked through, printing itself onto my skin.

Training clothes were better than a dress.

Black training clothes were better yet.

But I didn't know how long I was going to be gone, or for how long I needed to be the hunter.

My only option now was to change into the right attire for a long trip, and going after them, ripping the heart out of every person who got in my way.

With Jacquetta's help, I was in the only set of new, all black training clothes Madam sent for me.

And I finally had my spikes.

"You should have someone get your mother. You and

Madam could be helpful for the wounded," I said, and she finally focused on my face before she nodded.

I hugged Jacquetta and darted to the tent door, but a commotion on the other side of it made me peek out of the flap before I flung it back.

Shit.

"Tristan's coming," I said, turning around and running for the back wall of the tent behind Gus' bed. "Tell him I left a while ago to find them all and bring them back, but don't tell him where I left from."

Talking as fast as I could, making quick work of slicing a knife along the bottom edge of the tent, and squeezing myself between it and Gus' bed, I rolled out from under the wall of the tent mere seconds before Tristan's voice carried through from inside.

"Where are Lady Cinder and Augustina?" he asked.

I squeezed my eyes shut on the tears that threatened, and shoved myself up from the ground, darting through the shadows to the stone wall of the arena.

Scaling it was as easy as it had been before, but I almost lost my grip when I looked back and spotted Tristan sprinting from my tent toward the main gates of the training grounds.

Once I reached the top of the wall, I took a moment to spot where the guards were along the ramparts.

But there weren't any.

I shook my head as I pulled myself onto the top, and darted across to begin descending the other side.

Everyone must have been called off the watch on the walls to respond to the city. Which made sense, except that Gus and whoever else became targets inside the training grounds when they were gone were left unprotected.

There was nothing I could do about that right now. I had to focus.

Fixing what went wrong during the attack was General Pace and Tristan's job.

Mine was to kill.

And as I made my way through the dark shadows between lights shining on the blood-splattered streets of Bridgeton, I reminded myself of what that meant.

It meant that even the guards passing me while they collected the bodies, got living victims medical aid, and patrolled for continued threats, didn't see me. And if they did, they didn't recognize me.

Perfect.

Death didn't dance with kings unless it was their time to die.

No matter how well someone knew death, no one knew the face of it.

What death looked like always surprised people when it came for them.

That's what I needed to be again.

The shocking face of death.

I smiled.

Just hold on, Gus.

Stay alive, Angeline.

Keep fighting, Layton.

Death was on the way.

I sped up, knowing that there were two kinds of death heading in the same direction. And I had to be the one who got there first.

CHAPTER 51

MAYBE

They weren't even trying to hide it.

I couldn't think of another explanation.

Just past the edge of town, another home was eerily quiet, and another body was half blocking the threshold into a house.

But I couldn't stop.

There wasn't time to stop and find out if there were any survivors I could help.

Wherever the attackers on foot went, they were my best chance to find the ones the fucking birds took.

And so far, they didn't seem to be trying to hide their movements.

I ran down the road as it narrowed outside of the city, the trees along the side growing thicker, bigger, and closer together, blocking out some of the light of the moon.

Did they really travel down the middle of the most common road from the south into the capitol city?

Even if they were being careless, or even deliberate, by continuing to kill the people they came across, they were giving me clues.

Fools.

Oh, to have been them.

People with mediocre sense were always the ones who thought their ideas were perfect and that they were invincible. The kind of people who thought that they should be in charge, because of course they should. Never mind that they were stupid enough to lead me right to them.

But further along the road and deeper in the tree cover, with the filtered light of the moon showing me the way, I realized that they made at least a small attempt at covering their tracks.

The undergrowth along the edge of the forest, where the road gave way to bracken and tree debris, showed a wide swath trampled flat and ground churned under many heavy feet.

I shook my head and followed their path through the forest, using the edge of what they already tamped down to skirt between the trees, blending into the shadows.

Even with my detour to change and see Jacquetta, I had to be getting closer to them.

I hoped to come upon them when it was still dark.

But whether the sun shone down on us and made my presence impossible to hide in the middle of a field, or they tried to hide in some building somewhere, I would make them all pay.

My black cloak was lined with two dozen throwing knives, two short swords were strapped across my back under my cloak, daggers were in sheaths at my hips, and my spikes were both strapped to my thighs.

Hopefully all my blades would be fed fresh blood soon.

I picked up my pace.

The only thing I worried about was what their captives were put through before I got to them.

But if they kept moving, maybe I could spare them the worst of the possible pain that could be inflicted on them.

Curling my hands into fists, I went even faster, straining to hear any sound in the woods around me.

Animals, most of them small and four-legged, moved through the darkened world around me, not caring about the human drama going on in Onyx.

Even feathered creatures, probably owls, occasionally took off from one tree to fly to another or to some deeper place in the forest.

Maybe I should have been more on edge every time I heard wings, like I had been when I was in the training grounds. But there wasn't room for the giant crows to fly in here.

Not that I needed it, but it offered more proof to me that I wasn't dealing with the best tactical minds on this little trip.

The Corvids managed to accomplish feats of tactics, like their simultaneous attacks, or the way they arrayed themselves among the funeral to do maximum damage.

But this particular retreat seemed…lacking all of the intelligent design of their other attacks.

It also didn't seem to be carried out by slaves of the Corvids.

With all the unnecessary dead left in their wake, it seemed like the people I followed enjoyed this.

Like cruelty was the point. The war was just an excuse to engage in their favorite pastime.

Part of me understood it.

I was good at killing. And I did enjoy sending people like Lord Fall or the Corvids to whatever Gods and Goddesses would mete out justice on the other side.

And I was damn sure going to enjoy sending all these human-shaped pieces of shit to the cold embrace of death.

But that wasn't what they were doing.

The regular people in the streets in Bridgeton, the children at the Shield House, and the random citizens that they left to rot along their path out of town had nothing to do with causing pain.

When I finally caught up to them, they needed to learn the difference.

They should have picked on someone their own size.

Someone like me.

Laughter seemed to ripple through the air, and I paused next to a tree trunk, crouching down and straining to hear it again.

It seemed to take forever, a time I hated holding still and risking falling further behind, but it finally came again.

There.

No question, they were laughing.

Fucking assholes thought this was funny?

Setting off from the tree trunk, I knew where they were now.

After following their tracks so long through the trampled vegetation, I ran into the trees, far enough from their path that there was no way they would see me. And any small sound I made would be chalked up to the same animals I heard earlier.

That assumed they could hear anything over their own stupidity.

Big assumption.

Making my way through the underbrush and between the trees, their voices growing closer and louder, I made note of how many I thought there were.

It was a smaller group than I thought.

And I didn't hear anything that made me think they had any captives with them.

Shit.

Putting on some speed, shaking my head again that they were moving so slow, I got ahead of them and crouched down behind a tree trunk just off the stretch I thought they would walk through.

Jumping up and taking hold of the branch not far above my hands when I was standing up, I pulled myself into the tree and climbed up onto another branch that extended out toward where they would be walking.

There were only twelve or so, all loosely grouped and lazy in their gait.

But in the middle, not tied, but chewing on his bottom lip and looking at the people around him in a wary watch, was Layton.

He had a black eye and one shoulder seemed to bother him, probably from his forced ride via talon.

One of the party trailed behind the others at the back, yawning and rubbing their eyes.

While the others passed below me, I crouched on the branch and waited…

Now.

I dropped down and slit the straggler's throat before they even realized what was happening.

The only warning the rest of the group had was a low gurgling noise as I lowered my kill to the forest floor slowly with a hand over their mouth.

A few seconds later, no longer at risk of them making another sound, I made my way just behind the next one back, and replaced the dagger in my hand with my spike.

Slipping into their shadow, close enough to smell the sweat on their body, I covered their mouth, and drove my spike between their ribs to tear apart their heart in one move.

Now I had two down, only ten to go.

I was leaving my own trail of bodies. Although these deserved worse, I thought as I lowered them down to the forest floor.

The next in the group was in line with one of their comrades, talking back and forth of beer and food when they reached their destination.

Looking behind us, the corpses of their friends weren't immediately obvious in the dark among the trampled detritus along the ground.

Maybe I had enough time to be the presence at their back that wouldn't make them question where their friends went and maybe, if I was lucky, they would give away where they were headed.

A lot of maybes.

CHAPTER 52

HOSTAGE

"I'm hungry," one of them said.

"You should have grabbed something at that last house," another one said, making a show of slipping an apple out of their pack and taking a bite.

"Asshole," the first one said and grinned while the others laughed.

Most of their conversation was just as stupid, and just as unhelpful, and all of it made my hands itch for my spikes and their blood spilling over my fingers.

The minutes ticked by, and we made it almost to the end of the forest without a damn bit of help coming out in their conversation.

Soon the light of sunrise would illuminate us all. Were they just going to keep moving and hope they made it to somewhere before they were stopped by guards?

"We need to take over someone's house for the day," one of them said.

I guess that answered that question at least.

No way was I going to let them kill more innocent people in their need to 'take over' a house.

Listening didn't work, so stabbing was the only way to go.

The two at the back, walking side by side, were close enough together for me to…

After taking out two throwing knives and tucking them into the cuffs of my arm braces, I unsheathed my two short swords.

Before the two directly in front of me could fully turn toward the noise, my blades slammed into them, severing their heads, and sending their bodies crashing into each other.

Four down, eight to go.

The next two, still laughing at a joke from someone else in the group, didn't know it was coming until they joined their friends in a heap in the middle of the forest.

Six down, six to go.

But now, all of them turned toward me.

Either they were alerted by the sounds of death, the dropping of the bodies, or something finally managed to get past their ridiculous levels of stupidity.

Whatever made them turn, their shocked cries swallowed up by the woods around us suggested they didn't have a clue what was really going on.

I grinned and twirled one of my swords.

"Who's next?" I asked.

"Fuck you, bitch," one of them said and darted forward, their sword held high in a sloppy grip.

Slamming one of my swords up to meet theirs, I drove the other home in their chest and kicked them off a second later.

"Get a new insult," I said, "No wonder you all suck at fighting. You're unimaginative fuckwits."

The next two at least tried to get to me at the same time, not that it did them much good.

With a duck, I jabbed into and tore through the abdomen of one while I sliced through the femoral artery running along the interior of the other's thigh.

Bringing my sword from the remnants of the abdomen of

his friend, I stabbed the one working on bleeding out in the sword arm just in case he had it in him to still try and fight.

Jumping over the spilled intestines and wailing body of the one I gutted, I hacked down on the sword arm of the next one to come for me and drove the point of my other sword into their neck.

From behind me, another one ran up, but they yelled while they did it like they thought that would be intimidating.

I whirled and crouched, cutting through their abdomen and sending them toppling to the side as I yanked my sword free.

Turning to focus on the last of the group, I let out a heavy breath.

"You just couldn't do this without pissing me off even more," I said, wiping off one of my short swords on the leg of one of his fallen friends and sliding it into the sheath at my back.

Layton, eyes wide and clawing at the arm across his chest in a desperate scramble while straining to make his neck longer to avoid the blade held to it, stared at me.

His captor, the last one standing, smiled like he thought he had really done something impressive, and this wasn't still going to end up with him dead.

"If you try to kill me, I'll cut his throat first."

"A truly, deeply, stupid thing to say." I shook my head.

"Put down your weapons."

Yeah, that wasn't going to happen.

But of course, it was what he thought was a brilliant plan, and why not let him think it was going to work?

I held up a hand and slowly crouched down, making a show of setting down my sword. With my free hand, I moved so the attacker was watching my sword, and slipped the throwing knife out from my cuff.

Just before I got my sword to the ground, I flung my knife, slamming it right into the attacker's eye.

A noise, like a short shriek cut off by something shoved

down the throat trying to make it, came from the attacker and Layton dropped out of an arm gone slack.

With Layton clear, I surged up and finished the guy off with a jab through his stomach before I shoved him back to fall on the forest floor.

"So fucking stupid," I said, collecting my weapons from the bodies around me, and looking over to Layton as he bent at the waist and took heaving breaths, bracing himself with his hands on his knees.

"How did you find us?" he finally asked, his voice thin and weak.

"Not hard when these dipshits left so many bodies marking their path." I yanked my last throwing knife to collect out of the fallen asshole and ran back to Layton.

"Did they hurt you?" I asked.

Shaking his head, he stood up and took a hitching breath.

"I'm okay," he said, "Mostly. He was going to kill me."

Looking back at the one who held the blade to his neck I shook my head.

"He was never even close to killing you. Hostage situations are stupid. Did they say anything to you about where they were taking you and the others?"

"Angeline? Or were there even more?" he asked.

"There's more." Even though I knew that was true, I had no idea if they were all dead, if Gus was, or if there were more groups like this one with stupid ideas about hostages. But I had to act like there was and hope that I could get them back before they were hurt.

"Why are hostage situations stupid?" he asked, rubbing his hands over his face.

"Because you have to have a specific plan. This dipshit really thought that if he killed you, I wouldn't rip his heart out through his mouth?" I shook my head again and handed Layton one of my short swords.

"Here, take this just in case we run into more Corvids along the way."

"Along the way? Are we going right now to get the others?" He ran along beside me, catching up to me and falling into step as we made our way through the trees.

"We're going to keep heading in this direction unless you know where they were planning on taking you," I said, nodding.

"They didn't say where we were going, but the only place they mentioned by name was Breakwater."

I looked at Layton, at how he was trying to adjust his clothes and his hair, patting himself down as if he was trying to put the skin of the guard trainee back on and prepare to fight again.

Breakwater…

Of course, I was planning on going to Breakwater soon and seeing Inara, but this wasn't how I wanted to or expected it to happen. And it was going to be a long few days.

Layton, though, didn't need to go with me on this.

Stopping in the middle of the forest with no warning meant he took two steps before he halted and turned back toward me.

"What's the plan?" he asked, as if I was just pausing to let him in on it.

"You don't have to come with me on this. You earned more than a return to your training." I put a hand on his arm, and he shuddered beneath my palm.

"I think I do need to come with you on this," he said, his voice wavering and unsure.

"Until we get to Breakwater, we aren't going to stop. We aren't going to rest and sleep at night. We're going until we get there, and then we're going to kill all of them."

He stared at me, his face blank. Looking back the way we came and then in the direction I was headed, the struggle with what to do was all over his face.

"Go back to the training grounds. Give them a report. I can

do this. You don't have to." And I would travel faster on my own, but I wasn't going to tell him that.

"Okay, but only because I'm going to come with backup and meet you there," he said. "Thank you, Fighter Cinder."

"Be careful," I said, and took off through the trees, gaining speed as I left him behind, hoping he would be safe this time.

I needed to get there as fast as possible.

Especially since whatever backup Layton mustered would probably take too damn long to move a whole regiment so far.

Three days. That's how long it would take me to get to the closest edge of Breakwater at a steady clip with no sleep.

All I could do was hope that was fast enough and that the people holding my friends would be close to the spot where I arrived.

CHAPTER 53

SHATTERED

I sent up a silent thank you to my mother and father for the cold weather as I made my way into the small town at the edge of Breakwater.

When summer hung on everything and made the world run at a different speed through the many hours of light, it was much more difficult to stay awake so long, let alone alert.

But here, making my way through the still dark hours of the early morning when frost covered the ground and everything else that didn't move, I still noticed the way the town felt.

The attackers weren't hiding here. No hostages were tucked away in one of the houses sleeping soundly.

How I knew that, I would have never been able to put words to. But my instincts said that no one was more on edge here than people usually were.

None of it had the foreboding of a blade hanging over the head. The waiting for something to happen feeling that I knew from the days in Lehar during the last war was missing here.

It didn't matter that no one was around. Back then, even when I was the only one awake and worrying, I could feel it— the lack of sound sleep happening all around me.

Whatever else was happening in this town, the people slept well.

It took me only a few minutes to go from one end to the other of the tiny town. I stopped by the crossroads of the dirt track heading north to south, and the gravel one I was on that led deeper into Breakwater toward the coast.

After destroying the other group, and getting nothing but the name of the lands they were headed for, I had no leads. Nothing to go on that would indicate where I should head next.

I sat at the crossroads and stretched my legs, bending forward and closing my eyes to listen.

"Mom, Dad," I whispered into the black morning, "I know it's a lot to ask, because this seems like it isn't for me, to protect me. But it is."

Taking a deep breath and shoving the terror coursing through me down into my feet until I finished this and was past all the risk to my friends was harder than any of the rest.

"Of all the things I've mastered, and all the things I've learned, I never figured out how to lose people."

The frigid air as it came into my lungs felt like ice forming around my heart.

"If Gus is…" I couldn't say it out loud. "Or if they hurt little Angeline…"

Blowing the air out through puffed up cheeks, I turned my face to the sky. My hands shook with the effort to keep my tears at bay.

"Just please, Mom, Dad…I don't know how to do this part… please help me find them."

Getting up off the ground, I shook out my legs and my arms.

Maybe stopping was a terrible idea because the ice around my heart didn't thaw, and I wasn't sure I was going to be warm again unless Tristan was around.

But turning back toward the road, the darkness seemed to

coalesce, to grow thicker to the South. So I headed in that direction.

The rest of the world would probably question my decision to head deeper into darkness, but I was going to war whether the light was involved or not. And I knew war well enough to say light was usually a long way away, even if the sun was shining.

After another hour, the sky was just starting to think about lightening. I went through another small town, although this one was a fraction larger than the last.

Again, this somehow didn't feel like the place that people were being held against their will.

People in the town were beginning to stir, and I skirted the edges of their properties, finding the shadows so I didn't set them on edge with my presence.

In the best of times, a stranger coming through a small town dressed all in black with weapons barely concealed or on full display wasn't reassuring to anyone. Now? In the middle of a war?

Not something I wanted to put them through.

By the time I made it back to the road running south, the sky was well on its way to becoming day.

And I was running out of time.

While the ice was still deep inside me, all the small muscles in my hands and feet were zinging with the need to be there, to do, to finish this mission.

Hours later, I followed the road, but did it from the other side of a thick bramble lining the gravel, separating it from fields of tall grass.

Just in case anyone came down the lane, with a cart or not, I could use the bramble to hide myself.

In my mind, I kept the worry for Gus and Angeline at bay by coming up with plans for how I would get them back depending on where they were being held.

Maybe an attic or a tower...no problem. People never seemed to expect me to know how to climb.

Maybe in the open, if they commandeered a whole town... there were ways around that problem.

Finally, a few hours later, with the sun high in the sky, the sound of people, shuffling, and muttering made it to me, carried on the chilled wind.

I stopped and looked through the brambles until I spotted the smallest collection of houses so far, something I wouldn't even classify as a town, up ahead on the other side of the road.

But...the sounds...

One of the noises hidden among the others and not occurring as often, sent my hands reaching for my spikes.

Crouching down and creeping forward, I tried to find a better vantage point without making myself visible at all.

Finally, I found the place where I could see, and I stopped moving, barely letting myself breathe.

The town—more a tight group of five houses—was teeming with people.

On every porch, all through the street, and crowded around one house in particular, people milled about.

And on their hips, slung over their shoulders, and making the occasional clang against things they passed—which was what made me notice in the first place—were weapons.

Fucking hellfire.

In the dark, in the forest, after they just won a lot of battles, and were too stupid to cover their tracks, I took out twelve. And I did that with cunning, taking a couple at a time.

But this?

Counting the people, I tallied thirty-two. And I didn't have a clue how many more were inside the houses.

Where were all the people who lived here?

Scanning the properties, I didn't see any sign of the real occupants.

These fucking Corvids, they just didn't care at all about any of the regular civilians they came across.

I ran a hand over my face and shook my head. I shouldn't have expected anything different from slavers.

Maybe that was where all the Onyxian villagers were, on their way back to Corvid to serve as slaves to their empire.

If they thought that taking Gus and Angeline to Corvid would mean I wouldn't go after them and bring them back, they were wrong.

So, I needed to find a way into the town. There were no other options.

And, if I was reading their formation properly, the house that held the most important things, which would include hostages, was the one with the most people wandering around it.

Watching them closer, trying to map out whatever rounds and assignments they were on in my mind, I stumbled.

They weren't on any clear track of rounds or anything resembling an assignment.

So, they were just as unserious as the last group, but these dipshits had the numbers to be a much bigger problem.

Chewing on my bottom lip, I tried to figure out a way not to delay my fight to get inside until night fell.

I could duck under the edge of the bramble, and sleep until darkness descended. That gave me at least a small advantage from where I was now.

A scream tore through the low hum of the houses, a few of the people milling about laughing in response.

That scream. There was a specific tenor to it that sent the hairs on my entire body standing on end, and shattered my ice-crusted heart like I was made of glass.

Gus was screaming.

Waiting wasn't an option.

Somehow, I was getting in there.

"Right fucking now," I whispered to the bramble in front of me.

Turning around and heading back down the road, away from the little collection of houses, I kept looking back to my ultimate destination, to the place Gus was screaming.

But before I got in, I had to find a way around.

It took longer and I went further than I wanted to finally reach a point where I could cross the road, and remain sure that none of the people at the houses could see me.

Finally, I was across the road and slinking, crouching down, through fields of tall grass, taking a moment to assess every time I got to a bush or a tree.

Nothing about my movements was quick or efficient. It was in fits and starts and checks and rechecks.

And even though I knew I was the only chance Gus had of getting out of there, and I needed to accomplish it fast, I still wanted to run in there headlong and just start stabbing.

Which was stupid. But it didn't matter how much my brain knew that I needed to do this right, my heart, and my hands, itched with the need to act right now.

By the time I got within clear sight of the houses, my hands almost shook, and my legs almost cramped in protest as I knelt down.

I studied the most surrounded house, trying to see inside to any eyes that might be looking out toward me.

Nothing. I saw nothing through the windows, the light of the sun shining on them and creating a glare.

Another reason to wait for nightfall.

Gus screamed again.

This time, I was closer. There was no mistaking her voice now.

She was terrified and in pain, but she was trying to hold back. And I didn't know why.

I was about to find out.

And may all the gods and goddesses help whoever got in my way.

CHAPTER 54

KILL AT EASE

Jumping up from my spot behind the bush, I ran to the wall of the house, grabbing onto the planter box, and using it to climb up and grab the window frame.

No faces looked out at me through the window right in front of me as I climbed. Once I swung one leg up to grip the upper window frame with my toes, I shoved off with my last foot to grab the roof directly above me.

With two hands on the roof, I dropped my legs from the window and swung them to the side as I pulled my body up over the lip of the roof.

Once I was on the roof, I may as well have been walking on the ground.

Especially because this house had dormer windows creating a full second story out of the attic space.

Slipping my thin spike out of its sheath, I slid it into the line between the window and the surrounding frame to lift the latch on the inside. Then I tilted the blade a fraction to pull the window open.

No problem, quick, and no noise.

Before I dropped inside, though, I took a moment to listen.

It was impossible to tell where the sounds I heard were coming from.

Was that laugh from outside, or downstairs?

And the muffled heavy footsteps?

The bedroom I peered into was empty, blankets scattered everywhere, and a funk floated out of the open window smelling of sweat and...beer?

Nothing about the well-loved homemade quilts or the basic furniture made of driftwood that was probably locally sourced and maybe home built made me think that the people who lived here would have been high value targets important to the war. They were just unlucky.

Like most victims of wars.

Shaking my head, I climbed inside, leaving the window open to air it out.

At one point, this was probably an attic, but the floor-boards here were too tight for me to see through the lower level. I only had to crouch down to avoid the ceiling at the edge of the room. The middle by the door was plenty tall enough.

Making my way across the floor, I leaned against the door, listening to whatever was on the other side.

But the noises were everywhere. There were too many people and not enough to block their sounds for me to tell if I was about to open the door to a room full of people to kill, people to protect, or nothing at all.

Slipping throwing knives from my cloak, tucking them in the cuffs of my arm braces, and arming myself with my short sword and my spike, I was as ready as I could be.

Before I could pull the door open, it slammed into me, sending me sprawling back into the tangle of blankets under the sloped part of the ceiling.

A hulking, bearded man with white-blonde hair and black eyes grinned down at me.

"What are you doing in my room?" He glanced back into the hall as I scrambled out of the blankets.

"If you wanted time with me, you should have said so," he said, leering and shutting the door behind him.

Crouching in front of the short wall, it was everything I could do not to tell him exactly what I thought of 'spending time' with him.

But why not let him make stupid assumptions and keep helping me by doing things like shutting the door?

He came toward me, reaching out for me with pan-sized hands like he was going to snatch me from my position.

Instead, I lifted my spike to jab him in the throat.

Jerking away from the end of my spike, he slammed his head into the ceiling, falling at my feet, and passing out.

"To your credit," I whispered, "You trusted your instincts."

Of course, it was five minutes too late, but he managed to avoid my spike the first time. Not the second though as I stabbed it between his ribs and right into his heart.

Well, that was one down.

Part of me felt bad. I didn't earn that kill. He did most of the work for me.

But there were so many more, I would probably appreciate a few easy ones by the time I was done.

Opening the door this time, I didn't wait, just cracked it and peeked to the other side.

Someone was walking past down the hall away from me.

I darted out and slammed a hand over their mouth at the same time my spike slipped between their ribs.

Dragging them back into the little bedroom, I dropped them to the floor and rolled them out of the way.

Now this was a strategy.

Take them all out one at a time in the hall.

But would they all come up here?

Probably not.

And it would take too damn long.

Making my way out of the room, this time I managed to get into the hall completely.

Clearing out all the rooms up here was the only smart thing to do, and there were only two more doors.

The first one opened on a closet, with two small bodies, bloodied and gray, shoved into the bottom of it.

I shut the door and put my hand on the wood, biting my lip on the rage-induced scream that lodged in my throat.

Every single one of the people outside and in, deserved to die.

After I got Gus and Angeline safe, I was coming back to make sure it happened.

Behind me, someone opened the other door.

They stepped out, looking at the buttons they were buttoning on their shirt.

Flying across the hall, I slit their throat before they looked up, the last button still undone.

Dragging them back into the room they left, another one pulled up their pants and turned, smiling.

The smile fell from their face as I dropped their companion's body at their feet and leapt at them, my sword making a satisfying wet crunch sound as it slammed into their face.

Once their body was on the floor, I put a foot on their chest and wrenched my short sword free. Blood, bits of bone, parts of the thin meat of their face, and chunks of brain matter speckled the wall.

"You should have suffered more," I said, looking down at the corpses and wiping my sword off on one of their pant legs before returning it to the sheath on my back.

Leaving the room, I left the door hanging open.

All of them could come at me. I would cut them all down.

Going toward the stairs, two people came up and I grinned.

"So many people are here," one of them said, shaking their head and glancing at me.

There were about to be two less.

CHAPTER 55

TARGET

Before they realized I wasn't on their side, I passed between them and slit both their throats on the way by, letting them fall to the floor behind me, making gurgling, strangled noises.

Going down the stairs, I wiped the knives on my pants and tucked them back into the cuffs of my arm bands.

If those two thought I was one of them, maybe the rest would, too. Maybe this was about to be the easiest infiltration of my career. With the highest body count.

At the bottom of the stairs, I found myself in a cramped hallway with three more people in front of me, leaning against the walls and chatting.

One of them had a large bottle of wine in their hand, drinking from it.

Two of them barely glanced at me, but the third cocked their head to the side and narrowed their eyes, their brow furrowing.

He got a throwing knife right to one of those eyes which I punched further into his skull with the heel of my hand before he could cry out.

279

"What the—" One jumped back, and in the seconds before he realized the knife came from me, I drew one of my daggers.

Then I stabbed him in the throat with my dagger while the drinker choked on his wine.

If the drinker thought I would wait around for them to stop choking, they were very wrong. Instead, I grabbed their wine bottle and shoved it into their mouth.

Flailing, grabbing at my hand while they made a honking noise when they tried to scream around the bottle and the wine flooding into their mouth, wine spilled out either side of their lips and soaked their front.

Another dagger strike, this time right into their ear, and their eyes rolled back in their head before their scrambling fingers lost control and dropped from me.

Letting that one fall to the floor, I stepped over the bodies and kept moving.

So far, not a single one of them lived long enough to put up any kind of alarm.

My grin widened.

How many more could I kill before I finally found Gus? How many more could I leave on the floor before one of them sent up a flag to the others?

"As many as I can," I whispered to the first door in the hall before I opened it.

On the other side, three people were asleep, sprawled around a lounge, on furniture and the floor.

It was almost too easy.

Each of them lay dead before I walked out again, not bothering to shut this door either.

The door across from the last was just a bathroom. Although it smelled like people were already dead inside it, there was no one there.

At the end of the hall, the light told me I was about to walk into the main room of the house, where the kitchen and dining room likely were.

Where more people likely were.

But the real question was, where the fuck was Gus?

I never wanted her to need to scream again, but I wanted her to yell so bad…right now. I wanted to hear her voice yelling right now more than I wanted to breathe.

While I waited to hear her, to know where she was, I adjusted my weapons.

Putting two knives in my cuffs, another two between my fingers so they stuck out when I made a fist, I gripped my spikes, one in each hand.

Crouching down, I peeked around the corner.

There were six people sitting at the table and another few in the kitchen. The front door hung open a bit, the cold winter air coming in. Many people were still outside, visible through the windows and the open section of the door.

Alright, first things first.

Putting my spikes back in place, I pulled all my throwing knives, setting them at the ready between my knuckles and holding one in each hand in place to throw.

With a careful fling, the first knife slammed into the door and shut it, the handle sitting low.

"The damn wind around here is wild," someone said.

"On the coast, wind is always out of control," someone answered.

Breakwater's coast was still a couple hours away, but it was probably the smartest thing any of the attackers I encountered had said so far.

Still, I stepped out from the hall and into the main room, throwing the first two knives into the necks of people sitting at the table.

Toppling backward, their chair upending as they scrambled, I made eye contact with another one while they looked at me upside down from the floor, before I slammed another throwing knife into their eye.

With a cry, the people from the kitchen came at me.

I ducked a blade, turning and throwing to take out another person sitting at the table before lunging up, grabbing my spike on the way, and shoving it home in the spot between the ribs of the person closest to me.

Pulling my spike with me I turned and drove it through another's head as they came at me from behind, up through the soft spot under their chin, and ramming into the top of their skull.

Even as they cried out, yelling incomprehensible outbursts of anger, shock, and pain, I continued to turn and throw, thrust and slice until silence reigned again inside the house.

Looking out the windows, no one yet noticed anything wrong.

Dragging two of the bodies closest to the door over to lean them up against it was the best way I knew to keep all the rest of the threats out.

Noise erupted outside, shouting and feet pounding.

But before I could deal with any of the people who must have finally realized what was going on and would be coming for me, Gus screamed again.

From behind me.

I turned and ran down the hall, following the sound.

Her scream sounded like it was filtered through clenched teeth, like she was trying to hold back still.

"Just hang on," I said to the walls as I darted back into the lounge and frantically searched for why it seemed to be coming from in here.

Shoving furniture aside, sending it crashing to the ground, I couldn't find a door. I couldn't find a line in a wall. I couldn't find anything to tell me how to get to her.

"Fuck," I yelled, and stabbed a knife into the floor causing one of the floorboards to pop up.

Gus screamed again. It was coming from the floor.

Dragging the broken, toppled furniture out of the way and the blankets that were covering the floor, the bodies of the dead just part of the pile of trash now, I uncovered what I was looking for.

A cellar door cut into the floor with a hatch on top made of more floorboards with a handle on one side.

"I'm coming, Gus," I said, pulling up the hatch.

CHAPTER 56

PRICE

A small, cramped, dark, and rickety wooden stairwell led down into what had to be the cellar. I ran down it, adjusting my grip on my spikes, and not giving a damn if the cellar was full of people who were going to try and kill me.

Gus screamed again as I ducked and rolled at the bottom, popping up facing her direction with my heart in my throat at what I would see.

But even as I imagined the worst possibilities on my way down here, what I saw still made me almost drop my spikes.

"Brix?" I asked, as he turned away from Gus and leered at me.

"Well, hello, Cinder. I was wondering when you would arrive," he said, that smarmy tone thick in his voice like he thought he was going to proposition me here.

"Cinder," Gus said, her voice a moan. "Run."

She looked at me through one eye, her other one swollen shut and bleeding.

But even though her face was battered, her dress torn, and

the exposed parts of her torso bruised, that wasn't the worst part.

"Gus," I said, the air leaving my lungs empty as I stared at the arm and leg not chained to a large structural post.

Her free arm bent in two places it shouldn't have, and her free leg was spotted with blackened, oozing wounds.

"What the fuck happened?" Looking back to Brix, I couldn't process what I saw.

He stood next to Gus with a dagger coated in and slowly dripping with something that looked like muddied hellfire water.

This something was thicker than hellfire water, and although bright green, it was darker and swirled with brown and black.

"You've never seen this before?" Brix asked, his eyes widening and a glee shining in them they never contained, like he was a kid with a new pony.

"Angeline," Gus croaked.

Where was Angeline?

Standing up, I scanned the cellar, bile rising in my throat, and all the hairs on my arms standing on end as I turned.

Finally, there was a tiny, crumpled figure with the same blackened spots covering too much skin. It was motionless in a corner, trailing a chain.

"No," I cried, my voice wavering and cracking. "No, no, no."

"Run," Gus said again, as tears streamed down my face.

Collapsing to the dirt-covered stones of the cellar floor, I lowered my head. A dank smell was sent up by the dust I unleashed,.

Mom, Dad, please take care of her. She should have had more time.

"Does her death upset you?" Brix asked from behind me, the tone of his voice genuinely curious.

"Fuck you," I muttered, not bothering to explain to him that of course it fucking did and if it didn't upset him, he was even more of a monster than I thought.

"But this is war." Still the surprised tone coloring his voice.

"And she shouldn't have paid the price for it." Children never should, but always did because people like Brix didn't care.

I choked on the urge to gag and turned away, back to Gus.

"Help me get Gus loose," I said, standing up and looking past Brix to the one person here I still needed to save.

"Why?" he asked, and I froze mid step, looking again at the soaked dagger and the wounds on Gus and Angeline's bodies.

No one else was down here.

"You're not a captive," I said, the words rushing out of me in hushed horror. I knew he was capable of the worst cruelties, but those were focused at me. This was different, this was—

"Is Ash involved on the side of the Corvid kingdom?" I couldn't breathe. My lungs felt like they were full of hellfire water, and no air would ever be able to get in them again.

"Poor, poor, stupid Cinder." Brix came a step closer, looking me up and down with that smirk on his face and a shake of his head. "Duke Ash would never be on the side of Corvid."

Thank all the gods and goddesses. I sucked down as much air as I could, tilting my head back to look at the ceiling.

"He does what is best for him," Brix said, and I snapped my eyes back to him, unsure why him saying what I already knew sent adrenaline flooding through my spine.

"Brix?" I asked, for the first time I could think of, desperate for him to keep talking.

"You really don't know." He tsked at me and lunged.

I raised my spike just in time to block his strike and ducked out of the way.

"What are you doing?" I screamed, but it was drowned out by the hammering of feet above, slamming doors, and shouts of far too many voices.

Even after killing everyone else in the house, now Gus and I were trapped in the fucking cellar with only one way out and the whole of the rest of the attackers seemingly flooding into the building.

"Come on, Cinder. The Dragon Queen of Onyx should be able to fight me off."

"You think you can beat me?"

"Ash does all the time."

He did.

I couldn't argue.

But if Brix thought the same blanket protection existed for him as it did for Ash, that I would just let him beat me when my brother wasn't here, when my brother hadn't ordered it, and after what happened down here, he was about to be disappointed.

"Fuck you," I said, raising my spikes and dropping into fighting stance.

"You can have that anytime you want," he said, grinning and biting his lip, standing again and looking down at my body, talking to my breasts, "with or without the weapons involved.

He was fucking with me. As always, everything with him was a cruel game.

I hated him.

"Asshole," I muttered, turning to Gus and slamming my spikes into the lock closing the chain around her wrist and ankle.

Twisting and wrenching on the locks popped them open. The scream of metal ripping and tearing, reshaping into a broken and jagged mess drowned out whatever else was happening or whatever other nonsense Brix said.

Gus gritted her teeth and cringed. But she didn't cry, and she didn't whimper.

How I was going to get her out of here, I didn't know yet. I wasn't even sure she should be moved, let alone dragged around and left alone in a grass field while I killed more people to make sure she wouldn't be tracked down.

And when I was going to be able to recover Angeline's body to give her a funeral seemed an even bigger question mark.

Right now, I just needed to free Gus from the chains, and the rest I could keep thinking about.

Unhooking her should have been easier than smashing through the lock, but I moved slow, careful not to hurt her more.

Finally, Gus was free from the chains. A shudder went through her, her face contorted, and a low noise escaped her throat.

"It will be okay, Gus." I wanted to wrap her in my arms and hug her, but was too afraid to hurt her, so I just held her good hand. "I'll get you out of here and Tristan will get you to Jacquetta."

"King Tristan…" Brix cooed, and I looked over my shoulder at him wanting to bite through his throat. "You really should have listened to Ash."

"Shut up," I yelled, turning around and glaring at him. I didn't want to talk to this piece of shit anymore, unless he was going to be serious and tell me why he was here, I didn't care what he had to say.

"See? Not listening to the people in charge," he said, and I rolled my eyes.

My brother's fuckwit best friend was a lot of things, but in charge of me outside of Ash's earshot was never one of them.

By the time I was done rolling my eyes, Brix was flying at me, and I was too late.

His dagger sliced into my cheek even as I whirled away from him, pulling out my own dagger and blocking his next attempt.

But the mess on his blade, the black pus-filled sores on Gus and Angeline, Gus' screams—they all made sense now.

I screamed, still fighting. While I blocked and turned and

pulled another blade to fight two-handed against Brix's attacks, the slice to my cheek, one I probably would have barely felt until later, scorched through me.

More than a mere cut, worse than the blows Ash delivered so many times in our past. This was sharp and frantic and continuous.

And in my face.

Never in all the years I saw Brix train did he show more than a basic ability, and Jocelyn never helped him. But fighting him now while agony raged in my face, and all I wanted to do was run away from the pain, was like being brand new at training again.

There were no moves I knew anymore, no noticing his tells, or anticipating his actions. No, now all there was in the world was the torture in my face, and the need to survive one attack after another.

I couldn't think. Could barely keep moving instead of curling up and cradling my cheek.

So, I screamed and hung onto the rage that shot through me that this piece of shit would best me, hurt Gus, and most of all— kill Angeline.

"You killed her," I screamed, the movements of the words in my face making me woozy, but giving me enough to attack instead of just defend.

Finally, Brix started to take steps backward.

And, at last, I stabbed my dagger into him.

It caught him in the shoulder.

He wailed and leapt back while I stopped to grit my teeth and breathe, trying to wait through the last of the pain.

Giving me even a moment to recover was a terrible decision, but I wasn't going to point that out.

Brix stumbled back further, yanked the dagger from his shoulder, and grinned.

Right before he lunged, blade first, at Gus.

"No," I screamed, beyond even feeling the pain in my face as I ran at him.

But Brix was closer to Gus than I was. He was going to reach her first.

And I was going to watch Gus die.

CHAPTER 57

DREAM BEFORE DEATH

An arrow shot from the stairwell and skewered Brix in the back, the head shooting through his gut and spraying blood before Brix fell, sprawling at Gus' feet. Seconds later I reached Gus, whirled, and crouched in front of her, my blade and arm held high and defensive, Tristan stormed into the room with another arrow ready.

"Tristan," I said, sagging to the floor.

"Cinder," he yelled and ran to me, scanning the entire cellar on his way.

He grabbed me and wrapped me in his arms, the shaking and shudders of the poison on my face lessening as the blaze of his skin chased the last of the ice from my heart.

"Someone needs to help Gus," I said, clinging to him while the loud sounds from before continued above us.

"Let me see," he said, pulling back from me and looking at the wound in my cheek. The green of his eyes almost glowed they were so bright and muscles in his jaw jumped.

"No, I'll survive. Please, we need to help Gus."

He tucked me into his side, not letting go, as he leaned toward Gus.

"King Tristan," she croaked with a flicker of a smile, "forgive me…for…not curtseying."

The smile he gave her was soft, and he looked proud of her.

Or maybe that was because I was. Enormously so.

"You're tough," he said, "and we'll get you all the help you need." Leaning further forward, he set a hand on hers, and she snatched it away with a hiss.

"Sorry, um, sorry…your majesty," she stammered, shaking her head, "your hand…too hot."

"Gus has been down here too long," I said. "We need to get her out of here, but I'm afraid to move her."

"No, it's okay," he said, smiling at Gus and curling his fingers back before wrapping my hand in his, "I'll have someone get her to Duchess Inara's castle as fast as we can."

"It's going to be fine, Gus. You'll be out of here soon." I smiled at her, and she nodded. Her eyes slipped shut, but her breathing was still strong.

Her hand though…where Tristan touched it, bright red finger-shaped lines appeared as if she had a sun burn.

What did Brix do to her?

"And you," Tristan said, touching a finger to just under my chin and turning my face so he could see my cheek. "We'll get you help, too."

"Okay, but I have to take care of Gus first." I looked to the corner where the battered body of an innocent little girl laid, "I was too late to help Angeline."

Tristan stiffened and kissed me on the forehead, holding me tighter, before he set me down and stood up.

While he made his way over to Angeline, guards arrived, thundering down the stairs, and began to take over.

For the first time in days, I allowed the exhaustion to seep into my bones, and I allowed the rage to lessen.

In its wake, it left behind an ache, a hollow undoing.

Hate was easy.

Sorrow, on the other hand, was almost impossible.

Guards managed to get Gus on a board without making her scream. Although the number of times Brix must have hurt her with that stuff to make so many spots on her leg, I wondered if she would ever cry out from lesser pain again.

"I'll be with you soon," I said, and she smiled, letting go of my hand as they took her up the stairs.

Right behind her, another board, this one with a sheet over it, carried the tiny body.

As the sounds of the footsteps of those carrying them ended overhead, Tristan came back to me.

"Now you," he said, taking my hand and pulling me to my feet, "you're going to Sandstone, the Duchess's castle, and we'll find some way to heal you, too."

"Jacquetta and Madam Valentin would be best," I said, nodding, the movement making my cheek ache.

"For now, until they get here, we'll have someone come help." He led me up the stairs, not taking his eyes off me for more than a few seconds, the line between his brows deepening as we walked.

"And you should sleep," he said. "Have you slept at all?"

"No, I haven't, and I won't. Not until I know Gus is getting help," I said, a yawn splitting my face, and sending a fresh wave of agony from my cheek that made me whimper.

When my eyes focused again, we stood on the porch of the little house, and bodies were everywhere.

"The family that lived here," I said, whirling on Tristan and grabbing the front of his jacket, "I found children's bodies in the closet upstairs."

"Don't worry, we know what happened to the families. We'll make sure they're taken care of."

He led me down the steps. The guards who swarmed the area stepped out of the way. We picked our way over some of the people dead in the street, toward a waiting line of carriages.

Once I was finally in a carriage, with Tristan's arms around me, the heat of him making sleep a more difficult opponent at the moment than Brix had been, I finally thought about how he came to be there.

"Tristan?" I asked, looking at him.

With a kiss on the palm of my hand, his eyes taking on all the pain that radiated through my cheek with every word, I wondered if I was hallucinating. If this was the dream before dying that people talked about.

"Go ahead, Cinder, I know you're going to ask me a whole bunch of questions. And trust me when I say that I have a lot for you, too."

On 'a lot' his voice was hard, but I wasn't paying attention to the threat in it, not when all the other threats were gone for this second.

"How did you find me?" I asked.

"Layton made it back to us, and we've been scouring Break-water ever since. Duchess Inara and her people have helped."

"So…the entire country, while under threat of a war, was busying the guard with the search for me?" I shook my head, the movement sending jolts through my cheek. "A terrible waste of resources."

Tristan's hand grew even warmer in mine, his grip tighter, but he took a deep breath and touched the top of my head, guiding my good cheek down to rest on his chest.

"Go to sleep, Cinder. We'll talk about it when you wake up, and I know that you won't die from the poison on your face."

"Poison?" I asked in a whisper. I suspected as much, but I didn't know poisons well, and this one, a topical one, wasn't something I had seen before at all.

"Yes, made with hellfire water from Amethyst. We don't know much about it."

"Hellfire water doesn't come from Amethyst."

"The kind that can be used doesn't come from there. But

another kind—one that is only good for destruction—comes from Amethyst."

"Perfect for snakes. And no one should call that hellfire water. It isn't the same." And it seemed they knew at least some things about it.

What I wanted to know was, how the hell did Brix get it? And why was he using it to torture people close to me in the middle of a Corvid camp?

CHAPTER 58

CRASH

Breakwater's capitol extended out over the water of the ocean. The castle looked like worn sandstone, pocked and porous, but in all the years of being attached to the shore by seemingly only thin stalks of stone and bridges, it still stood strong while the waves crashed beneath it.

The crashing of those waves, a lullaby of its own, sent up so much spray that an almost constant rainbow formed over the castle, and turned it into a place not quite of the land and not wholly of the sea.

"Beautiful," I said.

"Yes," Tristan said, helping me down from the carriage and looking at me not at the view.

"Liar. I'm not beautiful now."

"Don't ever say that again." He leaned down and kissed me on the forehead, one of the only places he seemed willing to touch my face, putting the lie to his words even if he wanted to pretend otherwise.

"Get her inside, the physick is waiting," Inara said from the other side of a bridge.

"Thank you, Duchess Inara," Tristan said, holding onto me as we made our way across to her.

She and I met halfway and wrapped our arms around each other.

"Lady Cinder," Inara said, pulling back and looking at me with a shake of her head, "The Dragon Queen usually fights *with* the guard."

"I'm not the Queen," I said, letting go of her, and glancing at Tristan although I was afraid to meet his eye.

"And if you go off on some mission without any backup, you may not survive to become one." She tucked our arms together and walked with me, a slight limp in her step as we made our way across to the door of the castle.

"Speaking of fights, how's your leg?"

"Plenty of sailors have wooden legs. I'm more Duchess now than at any time before this happened." She smiled, and I was confused.

How it made her more Duchess to have a wooden leg didn't make sense to me, but she seemed happy. The tension she used to wear seemed to have been lifted from her shoulders. Even while at war, she was more content here.

My friend, made Duchess so young, had proven herself, in whatever way that mattered to her people, and I was happy for that. But I still wished the war never came to her shores.

"Come, we'll get something for you to eat. You'll see your Lady in Waiting, and see the physick." She leaned closer to me and whispered in my ear, "Then you need to speak to our King before he starts to rage the way he did when he first found out you were gone."

"You were here. How do you know he raged?" I whispered back in her ear.

"The whole country knew. It wasn't a secret. Especially to those of us who get reports from General Pace."

"Does the Chamberlain want me dead, yet?"

"As far as I know, they managed to keep all of it from the Marquessa. The Chamberlain doesn't want to make the war worse."

I nodded, that at least made sense to me.

Finally, we were inside the castle, the walls as thick as Tristan was tall, and the sound of the waves reduced to a low, rhythmic murmur.

She let go of me and held my hand out until Tristan took it in his.

"The physick will be up to your rooms soon," she said, and walked away with a nod to Tristan.

"Can we check on Gus?" I asked him even though I was so tired I wasn't sure I would have the energy to argue if he said no.

"We'll ask the physick."

"Another question?"

"Go ahead," he said, his lips twitching up at the corners in the first smile that wanted to show on his face.

"How did you get to me so fast?" I spent days getting to that place, and a whole additional greater portion of one fighting my way through the people inside.

"Cinder," he shook his head and there was a frustrated growling low in his throat, "you took off on foot and I had all the horses and carriages available to me."

"Oh." I knew that, but the fact he seemed to think it showed I was acting irrationally was probably a bad sign.

"You would have had all that at your disposal, too, if you hadn't run off on your own with no one knowing anything about where you were headed."

"They didn't have time to wait for powerful people to decide they mattered enough to make them a priority." I snatched my hand away from his, and kept walking down the hallway, a lot less tired than I was moments before.

"Why do you assume that I wouldn't think they were important?" He stalked along beside me. His body held too still, too in control.

"Because, you shouldn't have wasted the resources on finding me either. And every single one of your advisors knows that."

He reached for my hand then. I pulled it away from him, but he grabbed my wrist in an iron grip.

"Your rooms are here," he said, gesturing.

"Fine. Let go."

"Why are you angry that I saved your fool life?" he asked, releasing me but staring at me under a lowered brow.

"My *fool* life?" I pulled back and gave him a wide berth as I walked around him into my rooms. "I'm not a fool. And if you think that then kick me out of the potential search, because Onyx doesn't need a fool for a queen."

"Damn it, Cinder." He threw his hands in the air and turned around, standing inside my room but looking out into the hallway.

"No, don't you just turn your back on me. Look at me," I yelled, my cheek screaming louder with every word I said, and sending arcs of pain ricocheting all across my head when I yelled.

"Fine." He turned around, his eyes gone bright green and yet a darkness rose in them. "I'm looking at you while you have your face torn apart from making a rash decision, and risking your life in the process. You can't do that anymore."

"Yes, I can. It's literally my damn job."

"No, it's not." He crossed the room and grabbed me by the shoulders. "Since when is it your job to run right into the mouth of the war, and put yourself at risk every damn time?"

"Since I am a fighter in your army to save this country. I was doing the same thing in the last war." Well, sort of.

"But this isn't the last war. And you know you're more than a fighter." His voice cracked on the word 'fighter.'

"And you know I'm not wrong. I'm not a queen, you can't keep putting other people on the line to save me." Please understand so that when this ended, when this war killed me there could be healing.

"Then I'll—"

He was cut off by guards marching into the room.

"Your Majesty, the prisoner is in the dungeon," one of the guards said.

Tristan's chest heaved in great gulping breaths, his eyes boring into mine, and something running through his head I didn't understand.

Finally, he took a deep breath and slowly let it release, the grip on my arms lessening as it did, and he turned to nod at the guard.

"I will be along soon to begin the interrogations," Tristan said.

"My apologies, sire, but the physick says he won't be available for questioning until at least tomorrow." The guards saluted and turned to walk out.

"What prisoner?" I asked, a chill running up my spine for some reason I didn't understand. But my instincts did.

"The bastard that hurt you, the one with the poison," Tristan said.

Brix.

He was going to question Brix. One of the few people in the world who knew every one of my secrets, including why I was sent to the palace in the first place. Someone who wanted me dead. And Tristan was going to question him.

CHAPTER 59

LEAVE ME

All the blood from my brain fled into my feet and I swayed.

"Woah," Tristan said, releasing one of my arms and scooping me up to carry me across the room to the bed.

He laid me down and started to pull away, but I grabbed onto the front of his shirt and dragged him back.

"Don't leave me," I said, my voice thin and my fingers locked around the fabric of his shirt so tight I thought if he pulled back again it would rip apart.

"I'm not going anywhere." He climbed onto the bed and tucked me into his side so I could rest the uninjured side of my face on his chest. "I can't leave you."

"You can. And you probably should. But I don't want you to." The idea that he would find out what brought me to the palace and hate me made the blood curdle in my veins.

"Cinder, one day you'll believe me when I tell you that I won't leave you. One day, I'll be able to stay with you as long as you want. I just need you to live to see it." His hand, that searing heat and tender trail of touch, ran along my jawline and I slipped into sleep.

When I woke up, the physick had already been by, put some smelly salve on my wound, and a bandage over it. And Tristan was still my royal-shaped pillow.

"You didn't leave," I said, my voice thick with sleep.

"I said I wouldn't. Although it makes for awkward war planning meetings."

"No, you didn't." I sat up and looked down at him while he grinned and slipped one arm behind his head.

"Actually, yeah, I did."

"Tristan, you can't do that. Every one of the people in your war meetings will hate me."

"Cinder, all of them are thinking up new titles for you after the battle in Bridgeton and your ridiculous rescue mission." He shook his head and laughed without humor.

I cringed, which I discovered hurt worse than almost anything else I had done with my face since the injury.

"Don't rush anything. You're still hurt." He touched my jaw again, that flaming heat running a soothing tendril through me that made me close my eyes on the relief.

"Have Jacquetta and Madam Valentin arrived yet?" I sat up the rest of the way and pulled him along with me.

"No, but it shouldn't be long now."

"And how is Gus?"

"The same, but she's been sleeping since we got here, which I think that's a good sign. And the physick says she shouldn't disturb her."

Maybe. It might have been the worst sign possible, but maybe it was good. That was part of why I wanted Jacquetta and Madam to be here. They would know and they would never just tell the King everything was fine. They would tell the truth.

I didn't know if Gus slept at all for those days she was locked down there, but I selfishly wanted her to wake up again soon just so I knew she would.

From my stomach came a growl louder than our voices were, and Tristan laughed.

"Come on, Cinder. We better feed that beast inside you."

After we ate, he kissed my forehead with promises someone would come get me if Gus woke up and apologies that he had to go to a meeting. And I stood in the middle of the parlor wondering if I would have time.

Finding my way through the light stone walls of the castle, weaving through gigantic spaces, some open to the ocean in a way that made me duck behind things and worry about Corvids coming inside, and small cozy ones that I could breathe in better, I finally found stairs that led down behind a driftwood door.

Making my way down the stairs, they curved around in circles, the steps growing darker and the smell growing closer to the surf itself, that strange mixture of seafood and freshness and salt.

At the bottom, I found a cellar with circular windows missing the glass high on the walls, sea spray shooting through whenever the waves crashed under the castle, and iron cages in two long rows in the center.

More than one cage had an occupant, but Brix had to be down here.

Walking along, few of the people in the cages even bothered to look up. And I didn't recognize any of them.

But quite a few had bandages and braces.

These people had fought against Onyx at some point during this war. But why did Tristan let them live?

In my version of war, every person on the other side with a sword in their hand died.

Of course, that was probably one more reason for me not to be Queen.

Queen...I still didn't want to be Queen. But I wanted to be with Tristan, and I didn't want anyone else to be with him.

When Mom and Dad were alive, part of the reason I first thought of being in charge of the guard was so that I wouldn't have to marry. But if I knew about Tristan then, about what it felt like to have someone to love like I did him, I might have changed my mind.

Although, who was I kidding? People like me…nobles, royals, and the wealthy never let their children marry for love.

Even if we had met then, even if he wanted me then and I loved him, his parents would have wanted a stronger alliance or more wealth to come to the crown from any marriage.

Finally, I reached a cage with a person sleeping in it with bandages around his middle and shoulder, and a blanket over his legs.

Brix.

His face was turned away from me and I couldn't see it from this side, but somehow, I knew it was him.

"Why did you do it?" I asked, not bothering with anything other than the important part.

"You should have killed me when you had the chance," he said, not even looking in my direction.

"If I was your mother and knew what you would do one day to a little girl, I would have smothered you in your cradle."

Long before the cellar, I should have killed him years ago, after the first time I saw him for what he was. But back then, and up until today, I made excuses for him. I tried to believe I was wrong, that he couldn't be that because Ash wouldn't be friends with a monster.

"That's where you're wrong, Cinder. My mother was a miserable bitch." He turned his head now, looking at me with eyes empty of any soul. "She would have cheered me on. She taught me everything I know."

His mother taught him…

I was wrong.

All the times I thought I knew the depths of his darkness, all the things I thought he was capable of but didn't want to believe. I was wrong.

Brix was worse than I ever dreamed.

Deep in his eyes, for a moment, just a few short seconds, I saw it. The horror he held inside him, the kinds of things he wanted to do and had done.

"My br—?" I screamed, choking on the word, trying to shake the fucking cage loose and get in there to tear him apart. "Did he know?"

No answer, just a wicked-edged smile.

"Fuck you. You fucking monster. She was a little girl." My voice cracked and my cheek felt like it did when he first stabbed me.

"A beautiful little girl," he said.

I reached through the bars, trying to get to an angle where I could strangle him with my bare hands, while I growled like an animal.

"She loved you. The future queen was her orphan hero."

"Guards," I wailed, wrenching on the cell door and screaming my rage.

One came running.

"Let me in there. Now." My voice was like a lash and for some reason, the guard complied. It was probably shock.

Before the guard was out of the way, I shoved him and lurched across the cage, clawing and punching, while Brix, not fighting back, laughed. I snapped bones in his face and more in his hands.

"Keep laughing, fucker. I will break every bone in your fucking body, and make you snack on your own appendages before I let you die."

Arms wrapped around me, and I flailed, trying to scramble my way back to Brix and complete my threat.

"Cinder, stop," Tristan yelled.

"No. He killed her. He liked it. He needs to fucking die." I didn't want to hurt Tristan, but I pulled on his hands to get them to let go and hooked my feet around the bars as he dragged me past them.

"Stop it. I know. He'll be punished."

Tristan turned, with my back to his chest, his arms wrapped around my front, the twist lost me my grip on the bars, my feet falling to the floor.

Kicking and bucking, squirming and writhing to be let go, he kept dragging me away.

"No. No. No." I sounded like I did in the cellar again, when I first saw her poor crumpled body, and I screamed in fury, "Angeline, I'm sorry."

He dragged me to a room somewhere above the cages, and grabbed me by the arms, turning me to face him.

"Stop. There's nothing more you could have done. Stop it."

"Yes, there was. I should have saved her." My hands grabbed at his shirt and tried to shove him away and shaking started in my legs.

"Cinder, stop."

"I can't. Every time I close my eyes, every time I blink, I see all the ways I fucked it all up, all the ways I could have saved her."

"You couldn't have. No one could. You risked your life, damn it."

"Did I? No. Not really. I took too much time trying to find the sneaky way in. I didn't run the whole way. I should have walked directly into the town and fought my way down there. I should have—"

"Stop. You could have died. And if you did any of that shit, you would have."

I wrenched an arm free of his too tight grip, and growled at him when he clamped the hand down on me again.

"Let go," I said, through my clenched teeth. I had to hold

onto this, keep the anger in a closed fist or the despair would eat me alive.

"No, I won't. The last time I did, you went on a suicide mission," he said, shaking me at the word suicide, but I was pretty sure it was a shudder running through him that transferred to me.

"It was never suicidal."

"Cinder," he said, wrapping me up tight and squeezing me. "I thought I lost you when you ran off."

Shoving him back, I couldn't let him do this to me again, this thing he did that made me forget what was pissing me off.

"You were never going to lose me."

"Really?" He stared at me and there was the bleak truth of my own plan in his eyes that made the words stall in my mouth.

CHAPTER 60

BLACK OF MIDNIGHT

I twisted away and his hands clamped down on my arms again.

"The only way to help was to go," I said.

"Cinder," Tristan yelled, his hold tightening on my arms, eyes bright green and frantic, "never do that again."

"Don't tell me that," I yelled back, pain flaring up from the destroyed side of my face, throwing my arms up to shake off his hands.

He knew better. This was the same damn argument we had before. He knew.

"You almost died. I'll tell you every damn day until you listen."

"No, I didn't. I was never going to die by that fucker's hand." I waved toward the way we came from the cells. I wanted to march down there and kill him now as the move made my cheek hurt.

"If we had been even one minute later..." The green in his eyes flared, and he ducked his head, a low growling sound coming from his throat.

"Then he would be dead." Probably. But my hesitation, the

answers I needed from Brix, the shock of finding him there, my terrible misunderstanding of his presence and the possibilities implied by what happened, weren't things I could explain to Tristan. They would never be available for me to make sense of the way Brix got past my guard, the way I didn't act, the way I stayed my hand and hesitated.

"Damn it, Cinder." He raked a hand over his face and through his hair, his fingers curled like claws, his movements looking like an attack on himself. "You think you're immortal, that nothing can hurt you. But look at your face."

"Yes, Tristan." I said, stepping closer to him and straightening my spine. "Look at my face."

He did, staring into my eyes, his lips in a line. But he finally cut his gaze to my ripped apart cheek, and even though his body grew more rigid, his mouth even tighter, and the green somehow brighter, the corners of his eyes softened, and a line formed between his brows.

"This," I said, gesturing to the wound, "isn't the face of a lady, or a queen."

Pulling his face back like I slapped him, his mouth dropping open, Tristan shook his head.

I said it before, but even now I didn't think he really heard me.

"This is the face of a fighter," I said. "A killer."

"No one is doubting your skill—"

"Just not paying attention to who I am and what the hell we're all doing here." I threw my hands in the air again and the pain shooting through my head only made me angrier.

"Yes, I know who you are." He grabbed me by the shoulders once more, pushed me backward until the backs of my legs hit the chair behind me, and I plopped down into it.

The sting of my torn apart skin turned into an explosion of arcing agony from the impact, and I sucked in a breath.

Following my drop, he lowered himself to kneeling on the floor in front of me, never breaking his grip on my shoulders.

"I know that you *can* be killed, and, if you are, Onyx will never have a queen." He cupped my good cheek and his face crumpled like he could feel my pain.

"Wait…never have a…" What was he saying?

"Cinder." Tristan leaned forward and set his mouth on the good corner of mine, the heat of him pouring into me, and easing the shots ricocheting from my cheek.

"Tristan." His name was like a moan, the relief of his soft caress a balm that eased so many of the aches running through me.

I gripped the front of his shirt, balling the fabric up in my fists, pulling him closer even as I should have been pushing him away.

"You must know," he said, allowing only the amount of distance between us required to speak. "I love you."

Falling. My whole body felt like I wheeled through space as if one of the crows dropped me from the height of the clouds, and that I was going to fall forever and never be found.

"Every part of you," he said. "The part that is a lady, no matter how much you think it doesn't exist. The part that is a fighter and a killer, no matter how much it makes me want to wrap you in forty layers of armor, and set an entire regiment as your personal guard."

A small laugh managed to make it through the shattering of my last hope not to hurt him and past my broken face.

"But my King won't waste the manpower during a war when the whole country needs the protection more than me." He had to agree not to do it again.

"Your King won't, but the man who needs and loves you is willing to let everything else turn to ashes."

"Tristan." If telling me he loved me sent me into a lost,

endless drop, this made me never want to look for a way out of the fall. "I love you, too."

He closed his eyes, his sigh and smile like I gave him water after suffering dehydration before he kissed me again, on the good edge of my mouth.

Pulling back, his hand tangled in my hair and his green gaze on mine, he said, "We will make it out of this. You and I, we will make it through this war. And you will be the fiercest queen Onyx has ever known." He turned his head and kissed my palm.

But I wanted more. It was going to hurt my soul as I died and let him go when I knew he would marry someone else, and people would call her his great love. But that was the King. And I needed the man.

He turned back toward me, and I closed the distance between us, dropping off the end of the chair and onto his lap, closing my eyes a second before our lips met.

Soft, full, sweet, and perfect.

Our kiss managed not to hurt.

But a second later, blood dripped off my chin and hit my hand, fisted in his shirt.

I broke our kiss and looked down at the wet splash on my hand and he followed my gaze.

"Fuck, Cinder, we need to get this seen." He stood me up and followed a second later, leaning down to kiss me again and whisper, "I love you." Before he turned to leave the room and get me help.

The best help would come from Jacquetta or Madam Valentin, but we were a long way from Bridgeton. When they finally got here, Gus needed them a lot more.

And I was a long way from the safety of my friends, and the kinds of things they really could assist me with.

Gus was in no position for me to even try and speak with her about anything, and Jacquetta was going to be the same until Gus was better.

No, I needed to do this on my own.

Even though I had never been more out of my depth to deal with something than I was right now.

But, first, I needed to get back into the cells, this time armed with a blade, and kill Brix before he could tell Tristan about me.

Tristan may have said he loved all of me, but that would cease to be true the minute he knew that all of me included the woman who hated him for so long, and so thoroughly, she was planning on killing him.

No one could really love an assassin. Especially if that assassin had their name on their list while they claimed to love them.

He could never find out.

Or I would lose everything.

AFTERWORD

Thank you for reading!
If you enjoyed this book, please leave a review at your favorite bookseller.
Don't forget to go to jdarleneeverly.com and sign up for the newsletter to be the first to know about all the updates on this series. The third book, Heart of Midnight will be out in Spring of 2022.
As a special exclusive for those who sign up for the newsletter, the author is giving away and exclusive prequel in this series, as well as an exclusive free book in another story world, and more.

ACKNOWLEDGMENTS

A whole hearted thank you to Bean, the Rottens, and all of my friends and family. Again, huge thanks to Jupiter Alley and Krystal for their help in making this happen, Heather Cardona for all she does, Miblart for the gorgeous cover, Lucy at Jupiter Alley for the absolutely brilliant sigil covers for the interior of the hardcovers, as well as the team at Wishing Well.

One more thing, though, to all of the readers who have loved this series so far, especially those wonderful people who have gone out of their way and left me reviews, thank you.

I know it may seem as if the readers and the authors only connect in one direction, from the words in these books to you. But that isn't true. You, the readers, buying our books, reading our books, loving our books, and even those hating them, mean the world to us. Every single person who reads our words feels like a hug from a friend.

We write these stories, sending out these messages into the void, and every now and then one of the readers sends some light back to us.

You, dear reader, are that light.

Thank you.

ABOUT THE AUTHOR

J. Darlene Everly is an author of sci-fi and fantasy stories. Her serial, Crossroad Inn, is available on Vella, her debut trilogy, The Grimm Star Saga: First Light is available everywhere, and two new series will begin in 2o22. Keep an eye out for Major Arcana, and The Grimm Star Saga, and keep reading for all of Cinder's story.

facebook.com/jdarleneeverly
instagram.com/everlystories
patreon.com/Everly

www.ingramcontent.com/pod-product-compliance
Lightning Source LLC
Chambersburg PA
CBHW061055190726
48286CB00006B/1761